TOGETHER WE ROT

TOGETHER WE ROT

SKYLA ARNDT

VIKING

VIKING

An imprint of Penguin Random House LLC, New York

First published in the United States of America by Viking,
an imprint of Penguin Random House LLC, 2023

Library of Congress Cataloging-in-Publication Data is available.

ISBN 9780593526279

4th Printing

Printed in the United States of America

LSCH

Design by Opal Roengchai

Text set in Garamond MT Std

To metamorphosis

And so God damned the garden along with man.

CHAPTER ONE

WIL

"It doesn't count as evidence if you were *stalking* them, Wil."

Sheriff Vrees has been kicking up a storm since I waltzed through the door, but he lets out another groan for good measure. We've got a weekly ritual, the two of us. I've spent the last year digging into his ribs like a thorn, looming over my mother's missing person case, and he's spent the last year looking into early retirement.

"You can't solve crimes by committing your own," he says flatly. Every day, I parade into the Pine Point police station with new clues; he dismisses them, and then we duke it out for fifteen minutes. Today, we've made it to the second minute of our scheduled banter.

I slap my hand on the counter. He's lucky there's a barrier between us. I'd love nothing more than to leap over it some days and throttle him. "So you admit what happened was a crime?"

His co-workers don't bat an eye behind him. They're used to this song and dance. They're also too busy not doing their jobs: chatting among themselves, wadding papers to toss into faraway cans, slurping coffee, and snacking on doughnuts. Overly stereotypical crap. Anything to egg me on, I guess.

One of them is fiddling with the radio and playing tinny Christmas music over the warbled speakers. I don't care how much Michael Bublé plays or how hard the snow falls beyond the glass windows—I'm not in a holly-jolly mood. There's a limit to my patience and we're at the end of it. My mood today is best described as five seconds away from physically assaulting an officer.

"For the last time, Ms. Greene, there is no sign of foul play." His fingers lock together, the way they always do when he's absolutely livid, just barely keeping his shit together. I've done a number on him in a matter of twelve months: Weathered eyes, black hair streaked through with gray, a family of premature wrinkles carved into his skin. "We've looked into your mother's case. Tirelessly. Endlessly. All signs point to your mother leaving town voluntarily."

Behind him, the wall is a boring wash of pale yellow. It bleeds together with the rest of the office. With him. Muted and dull and unremarkable, Sheriff Vrees is about as bland as they come. He's a lukewarm TV dinner or a mindless Saturday afternoon, the kind you spend with your eyes glazed over and the local news playing quietly in the background.

He's shown more emotion in the last couple months than he ever has in his life. He should thank me for that.

I tap a nail-bitten finger on my photo. How I got the evidence shouldn't matter. "*I've also been looking into it, Mark.* Tirelessly. Endlessly. And look what I've found."

The photo I took shows the beloved local preacher—the one seemingly as untouchable as God himself—in the woods beyond his house. Shadows dampen the image, soaking the details of the scene into a blurry haze. Despite this, there's enough moonlight to carve the unmistakable silhouette of him with his hands around a hare's throat. Pastor Clarke had snapped it in two and the blood is staining the ice red.

Sheriff Vrees's eyes glaze over the image for a measly second. "I don't get it."

I scoff. "A man sacrificing an animal out in the woods isn't weird to you?"

"Sacrificing? *Pfft.* With that logic, everyone in the UP is in a cult." To prove his point that ritualistic animal sacrifice is a popular pastime in the Upper Peninsula of Michigan, Vrees nods toward the photos on his desk. Next to a portrait of his pregnant wife is a hunting shot. Vrees with a ruddy red nose, standing in front of a deer stand and grinning proudly beside an animal carcass.

"Twelve-pointer," he says, humming to himself.

"What a beast," Officer Mathers calls from his computer. He's not even looking into anything important on the screen. The bastard's playing a round of solitaire. And losing, at that.

My patience was limited to begin with, but it's long gone now. "Whatever," I gripe, "this is only *one* of the things I've shown you. I was posting again on my forum and—"

"The Nancy Drew gene really runs in your family, huh?" Vrees has a good long laugh at that.

My fists ball tight at my sides. "My mother isn't just some amateur detective, okay? She's a journalist. *Was* a journalist. Had a whole degree before she moved here and became a school counselor—I don't have to explain this shit to you. It's none of your business."

Vrees's scowl disappears under his mustache. "I don't care what you or TrueCrimeLover420 has to say, Wil. We've been through this a million times before. Case closed."

"Yes, we have, and each and every time, you never stop to actually listen to me." I go to snatch my photo back, but Vrees is quicker. He yanks it out of reach and rips my work apart with heartless efficiency.

"What the hell?"

His skin ripples with frustration. "I sympathize with you—believe me, kid, I do—but your mom's case is as good as closed. She skipped town. You and your dad don't deserve that, but life's like that." He sips his coffee like we're talking about the weather, not his own ineptitude and my missing mother. "Now it's time to stop playing Sherlock and leave the Clarke family alone. They're good people. Served this town well."

I'd hardly call them good people. Mom hadn't been missing for more than two days when Mrs. Clarke knocked on our door. "I'm so sorry to hear about your mother, Wilhelmina," she'd crooned, so sickly sweet, it could rot my teeth out. Her eyes were splotches of spilled ink and her smile was full of brilliant white teeth. "Send my regards to your father. Our whole congregation is praying they find her soon." And when she'd reached out to hold my hand, I could've sworn my mother's bracelet jangled from her wrist.

Vrees pinches the bridge of his nose. "For as much as you've been harassing them, they should be the ones filing a complaint. Instead, they're helping free your dad from that money-pit motel."

"Money-pit motel" being code for our family home and the only piece of my mother I have left. "Free my dad" meaning steal the place out from under us and flatten it into a parking lot. Anything to run us out of town. Vrees isn't the only one sick of me at this point. I'll never forget the way Mr. Clarke had stiffened when I'd shouted down the street at his back. The hellfire in his eyes when he turned to face me. *"Watch yourself, Miss Greene."*

There's only so many times you can poke a bear before it finally shows its teeth. But I won't let anyone scare me off. I've got teeth of my own.

My fist slams hard enough on the desk to send every head flying up. "And I've told you a million times too. I'm never giving up on her. Unlike you, I actually care."

"Go home, Wil," he orders.

I huff and shove my phone deep in my pocket before Vrees can confiscate that, too. With a dozen eyes searing into my skin, I storm my way toward the frozen hellscape outside.

"And, Greene," he calls, his voice more grating than usual. "Consider this a warning. Next time I see you bothering anyone in this town, there will be hell to pay."

I freeze with my back to him. My fists clench the door handle and I fear any more pressure will have it ripping right off. Beyond the window, the snow has made the evergreens in the forest twice as vibrant. Just like how your eyes get brighter after you cry. Not in spite of the pain but because of it. I swallow back tears. "Don't worry; I'll do this on my own from now on." The door slams hard behind me.

Naturally, my bike is buried beneath a mound of snow in the parking lot. It takes several minutes of yanking it free before I'm able to mount the slippery seat, but then, with a shaky start, I'm off.

The roads aren't quite treacherous at this hour, but riding in this weather is hardly pleasant.

The storm has bleached the blue right out of the sky. Pine Point is always dreary, but the lack of color makes it worse. It is a ghoulish sort of gray, dismal and infectious; it soaks into my skin, magnifying my bad day until it feels like the entire world has been thrown off-center. Like I might never be happy again.

Get your shit together.

I pedal faster on my bike. I should be going home—warming myself up before my nightly stakeout in front of the Clarke house—but home is the last place I want to be right now. So instead, I veer toward one of the only people in this town I still care about. Ronnie Clearwater is in the middle of her shift at Earl's Diner. I might've been fired from the same place, but Earl has yet to outright ban me, so I loiter there on the regular.

It serves as a neon-red beacon in the distance, EARL'S PASTIES shearing through the soupy stretch of white. I have to hand it to Earl. The rest of his food might be school-cafeteria grade at best, but his signature meat pies are surprisingly good.

The diner is small and severely outdated, but it's got a roof and a heater, so it's fine with me.

It's also got a million of those little scented pine tree air fresheners in the window, so that's an added perk. The real pine trees outside aren't quite as fragrant.

Even in December, the Morguewood forest reeks to high heaven. The stench of decay wafts from the forest's soil, tickling my nose. The nasty, lingering odor lasts all year. The first frost subdues it, but it still looms like bile caught in the back of my throat.

Creatures die in droves out there. Deer stiff with frost. Bears with their eyes trained upward, past the starving flies and swirling maggots, up to the grimy gray sky above. Winter keeps their bodies fresh, and their carcasses thaw in the spring, decomposing with the wet slide of summer.

I rip my eyes away from the trees as I reach Earl's.

I swing the door open after kicking my bike to the curb. I don't bother locking it up. It's a rusted, ancient thing that no one in their right mind would steal. If someone needs it that badly, they're in worse shape than me.

It's important to mention that Earl's isn't one of those cute small-town, fifties-style diners.

There are no trendy black-and-white-tile floors or glossy red chairs, no teens sipping milkshakes at the counter while someone punches in an Elvis song at the jukebox.

Instead, we've got ugly-as-sin wood paneling and an overwhelming number of deer heads and taxidermy fish on the wall staring at you while you eat. A local station plays from the radio. Some twangy country song about a wife who wants to commit a felony on her husband.

I shake the snow off on the grimy mat and step into the sickly white glow of the fluorescents.

There are generations of dead flies trapped in them, and when the lights crackle, it sounds like pattering wings. Typically, this would be the point where I'd slump into one of the worse-for-wear booths and smear the last guy's crumbs off the table. Ronnie would hand me a leftover basket of greasy fries, and we'd gossip back and forth until her shift ends.

Not today. She's busy being held hostage at someone else's table. From the tremble of her fists and the grit of her teeth, I can tell she'd rather run a mile in the cold than talk to this booth right now.

I know who it is before I even look. Ronnie's ex, Lucas Vandenhyde.

There are less than a hundred students in the entire Pine Point school district, but Lucas Vandenhyde has made it his mission to be the most annoying one. He's a walking, talking migraine. Five seconds with him and I need an Excedrin.

Everything about him is too manufactured. Too put in place. His straight white teeth are the product of years of orthodontic work and every word out of his mouth feels like it's been fed to him by a corny eighties high school flick.

"Vee, I only want to talk."

"There's nothing to talk about," Ronnie snips, and I'm proud of her for it. She's taken notes from my daily "How to Be a Bitch" TED Talk.

"Please—"

"Fine, fine. You want to talk?" Ronnie echoes, her voice lowering into a sharp whisper-growl. Not much of a whisper, since I can hear it from across the restaurant. "Okay, let's talk. Let's start with how you've been flirting with Leah Westbrooke all semester. Is that why you're here now? Because she's got a boyfriend? You're wasting your time crawling back to me."

I know she's seething, because she's got a strand of her hair curled around her finger. Some people twirl it like that to flirt, but it's Ronnie's alternative to yanking her hair right out of her scalp. I scowl at its color. Her harpy of a mother was quick to cover the blue. In less than forty-eight hours, she's already driven her daughter an hour away to a salon to fix it. It's no longer virgin blond but a brassy imitation of it.

Lucas's cheeks burn scarlet. "Flirting? She's my lab partner, Vee. What was I supposed to do? Not talk to her on the off chance you decided to stop hating me and make up?"

Lucas's friend Kevin Garcia sits in the middle of their fight like a skittish referee. He looks so thoroughly out of place in their argument that it's almost funny. He's Waldo hidden in the middle of a battlefield, giving a little smile while surrounded by fallen soldiers. Except Kevin's not the red-and-white-striped-T-shirt kind of guy. He's a walking advertisement for the weird and unexplained.

Today he's wearing an extraterrestrial-themed Christmas sweater, I WANT TO BELIEVE (IN SANTA) scrawled on the front, with a UFO led by reindeer. He's "Jack and the Beanstalk" tall, with black hair cropped close to his warm brown skin. He's one of those guys that would have girls lining up for him if he wasn't so obsessed with Bigfoot.

Kevin catches me looking over and gives me a sheepish half smile. We're not friends, but I guess it's one of those "Congrats, you're the only one who found me on this page!" sort of things. I don't return it.

His smile drops and he occupies himself with the syrup container beside him.

Ronnie whips away from Lucas. "Last I checked, making out with your lab partner wasn't on the syllabus . . . and for the love of God, I keep telling you to stop calling me that."

Lucas's earlier bravado is gone completely. He sucks in a sharp breath and guards his heart with two tightly crossed arms. "We were broken up . . . Ronnie. It was one stupid time and it meant nothing and we never—we didn't—it wasn't like that. It was a mistake, and it ended as soon as it began. Please, can we not do this here?" He waves his hand around like *here* speaks for itself.

Ronnie's having none of it.

"If you're not going to order," she snaps, "then leave."

Lucas tuts. "Give me a Sprite, then, and Kevin will have a . . ." He looks over to Kevin and Kevin lurches in his skin. He pushes the syrup dispenser away like he wasn't just playing with it.

"Dr Pepper," Kevin answers. "Please."

Ronnie sneers. "Two lukewarm waters coming right up."

She spins on her heels, but Lucas's hand lurches out to capture her wrist. Kevin sneaks a pleading look my way again, and he gingerly tries to remove Lucas's arm.

No luck.

"Veronica, you know I don't like her, right? It's always been you. I didn't come to fight. I was thinking . . . maybe . . . Well, my dad's in Iron Mountain at the moment, so I'm having a bit of a get-together at my place. I was hoping you'd come and we could talk about us and—"

That does it.

My fury propels me toward them in seconds, and I don't miss Kevin's sigh of relief. He won't be relieved with what comes next.

"Didn't you hear her?" I snarl, slapping his arm back toward the floor. "She doesn't want to talk to you."

"Where the hell did you even come from?" Lucas massages his

temples as though I'm the one giving *him* a headache. "This has nothing to do with you, Wil. Butt out."

"If it's about my best friend, it has everything to do with me." I'm sure I look like one of those dogs with the foaming mouths, peering at him from behind a flimsy fence. My smile is nothing more than clenched teeth and unblinking eyes. A face that says, "Try me; I dare you." My finger juts toward the door and I point a path from here to the parking lot. "Walk away right now."

If someone told me a year ago that I would be standing here defending Veronica Clearwater, I would've thought they were on something. But that was BMD—Before Mom Disappeared. Back when we both still lived in separate worlds and Mom was the glue keeping the universe tethered together. It was back when Ronnie wasn't a social pariah like me but genuinely popular—ponytail bobbing behind her head, soft gold shimmer swept across her lids. When she spent every second slung around Lucas's arm, giggling when he pressed kisses into her cheek.

But neither of us is the same person we were junior year. Fate had Ronnie and I slumping into the bleachers at the same time, worn out and ruddy-eyed and alone. We'd talked about everything and anything. The carton of milk she'd dumped on her stupid ex's head. Elwood's stone-faced silence as he ran away. The night my mother went missing and the night her father took one too many pills. He had slipped into the night with a single note scrawled beside him: *We can't keep doing this.* She'd cried on my shoulder and I'd cried on hers and that one afternoon changed everything.

I'd rubbed off on her like a bad case of poison ivy and she'd kept me from spiraling to the point of no return—and if you asked me now, I'd say I'd do anything for her.

Lucas's cheeks burn scarlet, his teeth grinding together like flint sparking a fire. His eyes whip from mine to hers. "You know she'll turn on you, too, Vee," he spits, "just like she did with Elwood. She doesn't know how to trust people."

Elwood Clarke. The name stokes a flame inside me, rekindling something that never quite died in the first place. He used to sit by my side, his eyes lighting over the tiniest of things, always rambling incessantly about his butterfly collection. We made sense hanging out together. I was the girl that was quick to bite someone's head off and he was the skittish boy who needed me to. Best friends until suddenly we weren't. Before everything in my life went to hell in his family's handbasket.

Now when I think of him, it's like swallowing a lit match. The longer I dwell on what we were, the bigger the hole burns inside me.

Lucas's hands clench at his sides and I know he's on the verge of saying something particularly nasty when he stands. He doesn't disappoint: "Elwood was a mess after you. You know that, right? You ruined a lifelong friendship and you didn't even care. So, what, Wil, did you get tired of ruining your own relationships after your mom left? You had to go and ruin other people's too?"

He's taller than me, but it doesn't stop me from getting close. "Anything else you want to say? You don't know shit, Lucas. You don't have a clue what I've been through."

He didn't spend days sprawled beside Mom on the couch, her nimble fingers twisting intricate braids. He didn't shadow her every summer in the garden with a wicker basket, dutifully collecting fresh herbs and listening to her prattle on about each one. He didn't cry so hard, he threw up when days turned to weeks turned to months of his mother never, ever coming home.

I grind my teeth and hold my ground. Keep talking, Lucas. See what happens.

"Will!"

We've gained an audience, but I'm fine with it. The locals have pulled away from their greasy plates, their eyes shifting from the box TV on the wall to the two high schoolers in the far left booth. WWE has nothing on me.

Lucas breathes in one long, shaky breath through his nose and then out his mouth. "Your mom skipping town on you was some messed-up shit, but, c'mon. You use it as a free hall pass to be an asshole. You need to know your place. You walk around this world like you own it."

Anger twists my ribs into tightly wound knots. I go for the throat. "Then do it. Put me in my place."

My world drips red.

CHAPTER TWO

ELWOOD

I've spent the last sixty minutes praying for a heart attack.

Or a stroke. Or an aneurysm. I'm not picky. All God needs to do is strike me down before my father drags me to the pulpit. The idea of standing in front of anyone—a congregation, a classroom, the mirror, some days—gives me heart palpitations.

But it's official: God's not listening.

"Elwood, won't you come here for a moment?" my father asks, a rare slash of a smile on his face as he beckons me to stand in front of an unblinking crowd. I try to remember how to breathe again, but my lungs have thrown out the owner's manual and left me gasping.

"Don't make him repeat himself," Mom snarls too low for others to hear. I know better than to go against her. Her threats have a way of tallying into scars. She reminds me of a spicebush swallowtail, wings as black as a blooming bruise, edges sharp like a mirror shattered by the weight of a fist.

I grip the back of a pew to steady myself. I've not only forgotten how to breathe; I've forgotten how to walk. It should be easy, but now it feels like flying with tattered wings.

Nothing will pacify her until I'm up on that stage. *"Go."*

And so I do.

The church scrutinizes my every creaking step and tries to fit me into the same cookie-cutter mold as my father—but they fail, no doubt, when they see the two of us side by side. My father, the "Right Hand of God" for seventeen years. Me, the boy who doesn't know what to do with his own hands. Behind my back? Wrung out in front of me? Definitely, a hundred percent, not in my pockets.

"Elwood's big day is coming soon," Father says with a pride I desperately hope is real. I resist the urge to smile. I must look solemn, serious, ready. My father isn't a butterfly. He's a praying mantis. If I'm not careful, I might lose my head.

He clamps a frigid hand on my shoulder and I risk a tiny look his way. From a distance, there are some undeniable similarities between us. I've grown in his image—wild, woodsy hair; eyes more golden than green, amber spilling in the center. Identical right down to the moles marring our skin. But despite it all, we're not the same. He's taller, broader, his personality a knife wrench to the gut. He twists my features in strange ways, making my eyes too harsh, my lips too cruel.

I've always pictured God with his face.

"Soon he will come of age and abandon his worldly studies for a more important mission." He's talking about my eighteenth birthday. The day I graduate early and life as I know it uproots.

I'm not sure where my parents are shipping me away to, but I know what awaits me: intense scripture study, prayers, and painful devotion. I'm to follow in my father's footsteps no matter how large they may be. Maybe when I return, I can finally fill them.

Devotees lift their hands to that, their fingers reaching toward the heavens. There are so many familiar faces in the crowd, people who've spent their whole lives watching mine. They were there when I was born and they'll be here when I come back. Mrs. Wallace, an older woman who has been our school receptionist since the dawn of time; one of the PTO moms, Mrs. Clearwater, who stares at me some days like I'm a specimen under glass; Prudence Vrees, the sheriff's wife, always cradling her blossoming stomach, so large now, she might easily topple over.

The church is the only family I have.

"Our final lesson today revolves around change and the necessary transformations we go through under God's will." Satisfied that everyone has properly acknowledged my fate, my father shifts focus. He splays his hands against the pulpit, and for a fleeting moment, beside him, I spy the key swinging from my father's throat.

I've seen him open the tabernacle door with it a million times, watched each and every twist of the lock. As a child, I used to think he kept his heart locked alongside the chalice. But I've looked within and while there's a torn page squirreled inside and perhaps an old cobweb in the corner, there's no softer part of him he's kept hidden away.

Before Father can catch me staring at the lock, I avert my eyes and gaze beyond the pews. I study the ceiling, my tongue tripping over the Latin as I hum the words to myself.

CRESCIMUS IN HORTO DEI, the script reads. We grow in God's garden. It's a fitting quote for our church's name. It's carved on a wooden slab beyond the doors: THE GARDEN OF ADAM. It's nothing commercially produced, no clean lines for your finger to follow. One of our ancestors had whittled the letters freehand with the edge of a knife and the sign has sat there in front ever since.

When my father turns, his eyes swarm across my skin like flies to fresh roadkill. "Elwood, if you will." With a pointed glance, he beckons for me to retrieve the cage in the corner.

I respond with a shaky nod, and it takes the rest of my body a second longer to catch up. I know exactly where the creature is—Father made me catch it, trap it, sit with it in the back seat the entire ride here. My heart is alive in my chest, no longer trapped within a cocoon but ready to fly away from all the guilt. The creature trusted me. It trusts me now. *Run*, I'd begged. *Run far from here.* It hadn't.

The rabbit shivers inside its cage. It's plump and white like a mound of ice. Silent, save for the occasional twitch. I try not to think about what will happen to it later tonight after the service. It never gets easier to watch. The plunge of the blade spewing through its throat, the blood dripping from the branches. My father's merciless with a knife. *Men have offered sacrifices to the Lord since the dawn of time, Elwood. Who are we to go against His word?* I dread the day my father passes the knife to me. I know I'll hesitate. *Man disobeyed God in the very beginning, son, and we are here to atone for that sin.* You *are here to atone.*

For now, though, the rabbit will serve as a lesson.

"God gave you ribs for a reason, Elwood," my father scolds quietly when I return. I don't need a mirror to know my lower lip is trembling. "Don't wear your heart so openly on your sleeve." I hope while he's at it, he can't read the rest of the lies off my face. He's always been good at picking my brain and locating the most treacherous parts.

If he figures out what I have planned for tonight, he might swap me for the rabbit. With one last pointed look in my direction, he lifts the caged creature onto the pulpit. "What beautiful white fur, unblemished as fresh snow. If we released it outside now, it would blend in easily." He snaps his fingers for emphasis and the noise spooks it. "But that's only because of its winter coat. If it hadn't changed color with the seasons, we probably wouldn't have it here with us. Some larger creature would've snapped it up as prey. Thanks to the Lord, of course, it's got a working advantage. The world changes and we change with it."

The church's silence opens the door for the world outside. Wind howls through the pine and dead branches scrape the glass. Soon the moon will swallow the sun whole. What's left of it spills like yolk over the trees and dies on the horizon.

"Church, you might think you have nothing in common with this rabbit. There are no predators to hide from, your hair doesn't change through the year—well, ignoring the occasional gray hair." That earns a slight chuckle from the crowd, enough to cut through any of the tension. He never jokes like that at home. He saves his smiles for an audience. "But I'm here to tell you today that's simply not true. We are precisely like this rabbit in God's eyes. When we encounter obstacles and opportunities in life, we cannot always face them as we are currently. We must ask the Lord to change us—whether we need to become stronger in the face of adversity or we need to summon the courage to follow the path laid out for us. I want transformation to be our theme this Christmas. Stasis is death."

His words have talons, clutching and digging into my already-tender flesh. "If we do not change to adapt to God's plans, we are no better than a brown hare in the snow, waiting for Satan or a hawk to swoop down and grab us."

His lesson is accompanied by a harsh gust of snow. Like my father's lesson, the storm is changing too. It's becoming something impossible to outrun.

It will do more than bury the cars in the lot. It will smother our homes, our stores, the school . . .

School.

The word rolls into my mind unprompted, punching deep in my chest and leaving me winded. I try to shake it off, but I can't. All of it, gone. The old, creaky desks, the ivy slithering up the alabaster sides. And, of course, I think of my only two friends.

Living things have always been so difficult. I remember all the times butterflies fluttered away from me, never to be seen again. The dead ones didn't. They let me pin them in place, safe behind glass. Beautiful and mine. No work needed.

People aren't like that. They're more like flowers. If you don't tend to them, they'll shrivel and die and leave you with nothing in the end. When I leave, how long will it take for them to forget me?

"Think of it as a going-away party." That's what my friend Lucas said in the hall today, the start of my moral unraveling. I'd been resolved to my fate until those seven words slithered into my ears. "Please tell me you'll go. It might be the last time we see you for years."

I shot him down instantly. "Hell would have to freeze over before my parents agreed to that." But he was just as fast. "Then don't tell them."

"That's a . . ." I didn't finish, and it turned out I didn't need to. My face gave me away.

Lucas filled in the gaps: "Sin, yeah, we know the drill. C'mon, live a little before you go away, Elwood. You really want to go your whole life without ever having fun? Give yourself one night."

"One night," I'd parroted.

"That's all we're asking for, buddy. You can pray about it after. You'll be there and back before anyone notices. What do you say?"

I know what the wind says now. It screams beyond the stained glass. *Sinner, sinner, sinner.*

I shouldn't have entertained Lucas's plan or told him that I'd go if he parked the car far into the trees. One last taste of the outside world—that's how I'd rationalized it to myself. Now I'm wondering if I should've changed like the hare. If clinging to the past really will be the death of me after all.

"A prayer for Elwood's big day," my father finishes, and his palms lift skyward. "That he may continue to change as God commands him to."

The church bows their heads on cue. Their eyes might be closed, but mine are locked on the rabbit's. Its eyes are glossy, black, and unyielding.

"We bring Elwood before you, O Lord, as a testament of our eternal devotion. We ask for his strength and for his transformation. Let him reach manhood in accordance with your word and inherit the heritage he was born to receive. For with life there is death, but with sacrifice, there is eternity." My father's eyes reopen as he calls to the church. "We are seeds in the wind."

That always marks the end of our prayer, a final tribute to the forest around us before we begin the sacrament. Every seed planted in this forest is blessed. Our trees stand like saints, our livelihood, our *Eden*. We whisper our thanks to them when we drive past, when we link hands for dinner, when we gather in church. Father worships each trunk before he cleaves his axe through it.

"And we shall grow in His image," the church returns dutifully, and the sound builds with every voice.

"Amen."

My stomach burns from the sins I've yet to commit.

CHAPTER THREE

WIL

By the way Lucas's cousin is looking at me, you'd think I was a convicted felon. Admittedly, I'm not a saint. Mother Teresa might not be known for shoving people in greasy diners, but I'm certain she would've given me a pass if she'd been there. I'm only standing here now because as much as I hate Vrees, he had the "stalking" part right.

My typical Friday night involves a stakeout in the bushes in front of the Clarke house.

Usually, if I'm lucky, I'll catch a glimpse of Mrs. Clarke fussing with her blinds or Mr. Clarke loudly rehearsing his sermon—or sacrificing rabbits randomly in the snow that one time—but tonight was different. Not once have I seen Elwood—perfect, rule-abiding Elwood—sneak out. Yet here he was acting like a normal human teenager and jumping out his bedroom window. To local law enforcement and God, I'm willing to bet my spying was both a state crime and mortal sin, but I don't care. Sober Elwood might keep his family's secrets under lock and key, but a tipsy tongue will tell me everything I need to know. So to Lucas's party we go.

Still. I could do without Harvey Vandenhyde's stink eye. "You act like I killed Lucas. I lightly tapped him before it got broken up. See? Like this." I demonstrate by giving his flannel chest a shove. I don't think he owns a shirt that *isn't* flannel. His uniform is a long-sleeved shirt tucked into an oversize belt, dark cowboy boots despite the fact we live in northern Michigan, and blond hair hidden beneath a John Deere trucker hat.

He must have lead inserts in his shoes, too, because he doesn't so much as flinch.

"No one wants you here, Wil," he spits, holding his ground. Each word sprays on my cheek, and I make a show of hastily smearing it away.

Damn him and his cowboy boots.

I sneer at Lucas's invite-only house. It's big—not mansion big and not even "my dad works in middle management" big, but bigger than most of the trailers around here. We're not exactly Silicon Valley.

It's big enough for two more people, certainly. Golden light streams through the windows, bright enough to make up for the pitch-black sky. Silhouettes of gyrating bodies are illuminated on the other side of the glass, people dancing and spinning and laughing.

"Does Lucas pay you to bounce for him or do you do it for free?" I gripe. If Harvey doesn't let us in, breaking into the house is plan B and another chip on my unethical bingo card. Not sure if Ronnie will tag along for that, so I plan out a solo mission in my head. Would anyone even hear shattering glass?

Whatever song they're playing is lost out here, but the ground pulses with the bones of it. Surely that would drown out—

"For the love of God, Wil, why are you still standing here? Go be weird somewhere else."

Before I can mindlessly spout any obscenities and make our situation worse, Ronnie steps out from behind me and decides to save the day with the feminine wiles I clearly don't possess.

Harvey drinks in the sight of her shamelessly. As much as I want to slap him for it, I can see why. She might've rushed every part of this look in her mom's car after I called with an emergency party plan, but she looks good. With fishnet sleeves and a bodycon dress, nothing about her screams *I'm borrowing the car to study algebra in the library*. I think if her religious mother saw her, she would keel over on the spot. Ronnie finished her look with dark metallic glitter on her lids and a nearly translucent sheen of blue highlighter swept across her cheekbones.

Meanwhile most of me is covered in crusted dirt. Creeping around in someone's bushes will do that.

"Oh, uh, hey, Vee," Harvey says blankly.

She traces a circle on the cement with the front of her shoe. One idle pattern after the other. "Lucas actually *did* invite me. I said no at the time, but"—she pauses to tuck a strand of hair behind her ear—"the more I thought about it, though, the more I realized I wanted to hear him out."

What Ronnie actually said when I asked her to come was something more along the lines of *You want me to go to that asshole's party? I'd sooner die and go to hell*. Followed by some heavy groveling on my part. With the way she's dressed, though, maybe there's an ounce of truth to her words.

Harvey's having a hard time coming up with something coherent to say. Ronnie speeds the process with a puff of her lip and a genuine shiver.

It works like magic. He steps aside, his meaty hand rubbing sweat from the back of his neck. "Sorry, it's freezing. Go ahead and come in."

Wow.

She shimmies past and before he can fully lift his arm up to bar me, she tacks on a "Where I go, she goes," and that's the end of that.

The warmth hits me first. Body heat has raised the room several degrees and then some. It's more than welcome. I've lost feeling in every part of me.

Once I'm confident my arms haven't succumbed to frostbite, I take the time to assess my surroundings; the decorating style consists almost solely of breakable shit. Very old-lady chic. I'm talking about knickknacks everywhere. Little glass baby cherubs and bizarrely showcased fine china.

Some kid is going to break all of this for the fun of it.

The foyer is already littered with red Solo cups and crushed cans. I'd say this place is going to get trashed, but it's already there.

"Where's Lucas? Does he have this party under control?" Ronnie's words are punctuated by the sound of a bottle breaking against the wall.

"Uh . . . yeah. Don't worry about it." Harvey clears his throat and I get the sense that he's talking more to himself than us. His dad's a former Navy SEAL or something. If he gets caught, he'll probably be sent off to boot camp. His expression shifts and his patchy mustache raises with his grin. Well, it's less of a mustache and more like five stray hairs he refuses to pluck. "Can I get you something to drink? Maybe a little Christmas eggnog to be festive?"

I'm going to barf. "I'll have a beer."

He sneers at me like he forgot I was there already. "Do I look like a bartender, Greene? Go get it yourself." His breath reeks.

I roll my eyes. So much for the party of the century. "Ronnie, you want one?"

"Yeah, get me whatever you're having."

Harvey sidesteps me instantly. "Kidding, kidding." He isn't kidding. "I'll get it."

He squints, rifling around in one of the dozen coolers on the floor. I hear the slosh of half-melted ice and the wet grip of his hand on the can. Harvey pulls back with one for the both of us.

He offers it to me like it's his firstborn son and I'm the devil he was stupid enough to make a deal with.

Ronnie shuts him up before he can say anything else. "I'll see you around, okay?" she lies.

She loops her arm around mine, pulling me out of the kitchen and into the smoke-hazed living room despite Harvey's pathetic mewls for attention. The music is blurred over the sound of tipsy laughter and shouted conversations. Drunk people only shut up when they're passed out or throwing up.

"You owe me for all of this," she whispers once we're out of earshot. We might be surrounded by people (in a county this small, this has got to be the highlight of the year, and that says something), but the music is loud enough to drown us out. "Big-time."

"I am indebted to you forever, my liege," I promise.

Ronnie rolls her eyes and gestures with a nod of her head to the staircase. I take a seat beside her and I'm enormously thankful that no one has sloshed beer on this carpet yet. I highly doubt it will stay that way. The whole place reeks of Budweiser, sweat, and Axe body spray.

"God, everyone and their cousin is here," Ronnie groans. There's a shy edge to her voice; I don't miss the subtle twinge of pink on her cheeks. "Do I look okay? Is this too much?"

Not that long ago Ronnie's perfume of choice was Catholic Guilt. She reeked of it. No wonder her mom despises me. Her daughter, Veronica, is long gone. Ronnie, however, is much more fun.

"Are you kidding? You look amazing!" I flick her shoulder. I pretend I'm injecting her with confidence, a syringe piercing the vein.

She shimmies a little, my words rolling over her. I hope they hit the mark. "Thanks, Wil. You look great too."

I snort, but it's not worth correcting her. Everything about me is messy. I look worse than I did this morning. Black bags have sprung up beneath my eyes, and you can tell my haircut is the lovechild of a rusty pair of scissors and a two a.m. breakdown. I don't make a habit of looking in the mirror. If it's not my own reflection I see, it's my mother's. All the little imprints she left behind.

Don't think about that.

I busy myself with people-watching. Seeing as how Pine Point has the population of another town's food court, I know everyone here.

Brian Schmidt is laughing about something with his posse. He's as big of a delinquent as I am, but popular. He not-so-casually snakes an arm around his girlfriend, pulling her so close that she's practically sitting in his lap. The two of them are shameless with each other when they're sober. Get a bit of alcohol in their system and they're downright disgusting.

Her shrill laughter nearly shatters my eardrums. "*Stooooop*, Brian!" She's got a voice like a wounded hawk, one that needs to be put out of its misery. Her main claim to popularity is being the loudest one in the room. "You're the worst."

That much is true.

"I think I'd have more fun in an intensive care unit," I growl under my breath.

Ronnie rests her cheek in her palm. "Remind me again, whose idea was this?"

Ugh. Okay. She's got a point. "Mine," I drawl, "but I've got a plan."

She cocks her head. "And what was that plan again? Corner Elwood and badger him for information he may or may not have? You never even told me how you *know* he's here."

I bite my tongue. I really don't think she'd approve of me lurking outside of someone else's house with binoculars. "It's a hunch."

She side-eyes me. "I barely know the guy and my hunch is that this is hardly his scene. I don't think he even knows what alcohol is."

"Speaking of that . . ." I pop open my beer and take a quick gulp for confidence.

Unfortunately—due to my missing mom and all—I've grown quite the tolerance for binge drinking. But I'm not the one here who needs to get plastered and spill all their dark secrets. "Okay, Ron, let's go track that loser down."

I offer her a hand and she clutches it, allowing me to guide her through the human sea that used to be Lucas's living room. We don't get very far before the chanting starts. "Drink, drink, drink, drink!"

I look toward Brian Schmidt on instinct. If anyone's getting wasted for attention, it's got to be him, right? But when I track down his drunken face, he's busy sloppily making out with his girlfriend. I wish I could burn that image out of my retinas. I trace the chants to the very corner of the room and find a boy upside down doing a keg stand. His shirt lifts a little and I see the scarred pale skin beneath. I recognize his familiar soft curls, the dark lashes, the little mole resting on his cheek.

"Oh shit, you were right," Ronnie gasps. "That's—"

"*Yeah.*"

Elwood Clarke.

CHAPTER FOUR

ELWOOD

Time twists out of reach, seconds and minutes drifting downstream. My own thoughts are held underwater, drowned by the heavy bass and the veil of gyrating bodies. I'm not sure if I've been standing in the corner for twelve minutes or twelve hours.

I can't believe I'm doing this.

The thought loops in my head, over and over. I heard it first when I was wadding my pillow under my blanket.

Again, when I was fiddling with the latch on the window, desperately trying to gently pry the thing open. Once again when I was darting out into the trees. The car wasn't far from the outskirts of my backyard. Headlights off, nothing but the quiet thrum of the engine.

I can't believe I'm doing this, I'd told them, and they'd laughed.

"Here. Want to try a keg stand?" Lucas breaks away from Kevin and slouches over me.

Lucas is the emperor moth of our group. I've got one pinned above my dresser back home. Its wings are like sunlight melting through the trees. Orange spilling into a woodsy wash of brown. Impressive and confident and totally at odds with me and Kevin. Kevin's an emerald swallowtail. Metallic UFO-green paths streaking across each wing. And then there's me. I'm more like an eastern comma—wings a smoky, burnt brown shriveled like autumn leaves. Something that blends in and hides. Something you miss unless you really stop to look.

Lucas gestures to an enormous-looking barrel on the floor, a funnel, and a long tube interlocking the two. "If you're feeling up to it—"

I hate the way his expression peels back when he talks to me. Each time he forgets who I am—treats me like Kevin or anyone else—but then pulls back. Remembers.

"I want to," I say, even though the guilt has already soured my stomach. All I want is to be tucked back in bed. Warm from the blanket thrown around me, not from the burning flush of my cheeks.

One night before everything changes.

I rip the bottle from his hand. He's already downed a quarter of it and the glass is still warm from his sweaty palms. There's a twisting serpent across the label, a scaly print stretching from one end to the other. In my mind I'm wrapped in foliage, teeth grazing against an already bitten apple. This isn't my first sin of the night, but each one is a shot into the night sky, explosive and heaven bound.

The liquid doesn't burn this time. It rolls down my throat, bitter. A full-bodied mix with the lingering stench of wheat. I want to spit it out, but I know I can't, so I drink and drink and drink.

Done.

I shake the bottle for more, but all I get is the rush of my own sticky, hot breath. Trapped air and the hollow ring of an empty bottle.

I drop it. It shatters. I decide then and there that I love the sound of broken things. The thud of something whole, followed by the splintering crack of it breaking into tiny, impossible pieces. Never to be put back together, but it's okay. Crushed glass looks like stardust.

"You're really going to drink all that and do the keg?"

I nod. Or I think I do. I don't know. All I know is I need to wash this out of my system for good. "Is that really Elwood Clarke getting shit-faced?" Brian Schmidt breaks away from his girlfriend's mouth to sneer my way. He's less of a butterfly and more of a cockroach. His left hand combs through his over-yellow bangs. "I thought his wild Friday nights were him reciting Bible verses for fun."

If he only knew how many lived in my mind. My father made me memorize hundreds, and when my tongue tripped or the words failed me, he'd beat the line into my skin.

My nail carves a crescent into my palm as Brian doubles over in laughter. This will pass soon enough when I'm shipped away. All of it. The stilted day-to-day interactions, the "playful" jabs in my ribs from Brian and his lackeys on my way to class, the constant desire to melt into the floor. My vision blurs and I see Brian molt: hideous expression smeared away, eyes wide and mouth agape, blood dripping, dripping, dripping. The roar of the party fades and my thoughts scream like a biblical swarm of locusts.

Before I can focus, there are arms on my legs. Lifting me up and up until I'm staring down at the floor, suspended in midair over a keg. I hold the tube to my lips.

One gulp. Two. The sound of my name comes from all sides. It doesn't last—the letters dissolve, reshaping in the air to form something else. They chant the new word again and again and I think they're telling me to drink so I do and—

"Way to go, Elwood!" It's Kevin. He's beaming at me like this was some sort of contest, like I won something. Maybe I did. Maybe my reward is the tipsy sensation prickling beneath my skin, the strange buzz of happiness overtaking my fear.

When they lower me back down, my legs feel like jelly and Brian's no longer even a speck on my radar.

I laugh. It's suddenly so easy to laugh. The anchor I've been tethered to forever has been torn loose. Bright lights catch on the broken bottle still on the floor, throwing color like a kaleidoscope. That's what a group of butterflies are called. A kaleidoscope. I've always loved that.

"Hey, look, she came." Kevin paws at Lucas's shoulder and Lucas's jaw hits the ground. "I didn't think Veronica would show up."

Since I've become so enamored with the glittering glass, I almost forgot where I was. With a bit of effort, I manage to lift my head and look out.

The details drift in and out of clarity. One second they're there; the next they're gone. "You think she's actually going to give me the time of day?"

Kevin shrugs. "She's here, isn't she?"

"God, I'm already sweating. I didn't plan this out. I don't know what to say to her."

Laughter bubbles from my chest for no reason, light and airy and soft. I want to tell him to open his heart, to offer her all the tender truths he's kept buried and make amends. But it's too much work to make my lips cooperate. So instead, I focus on finding Veronica in the crowd.

She's certainly pretty—long lashes, clear eyes, rosy cheeks—but . . . I don't know. My heart is calm. I don't look at her and see days stretched out on the grass; I can't imagine counting the freckles on her skin or picking branches out from her messy, tousled hair.

There's only ever been one girl like that for me.

And the very thought of her now washes over my bones like an arctic tide. There's no warmth left. *Your family knows what happened to my mom. I know they do.* Her teeth scraped over the accusation, her eyes were fire-bright and raging. I'd come that day to console her, but the grief wasn't there. Just rage. *You need to choose right now.* Our friendship hung on a single question: *Who do you believe, your family or me?*

"You should talk to her." At least that's what I try to say. The words are sticky in my mouth. Lucas has gone a peculiar shade of pink. It stretches from his ears to his nose to his chin. "I'm not sure if I can. God, I'm such a loser. I fucked things up in the diner."

"Just tell her everything you've told us." I drag him by the sleeve. "That you love her."

I'm a wingman. If I concentrate really hard, I can even feel the wings ripping out from my back. I'll fly him over to her. They'll talk and he'll apologize and everything will be okay. Maybe I won't feel so guilty for leaving tonight and never coming back.

"Every time I try to say something to her, it all goes wrong, man. Things go one way in my head and then I see her and I forget how to speak and suddenly I blink and the whole thing's over and I'm the asshole again."

I want to argue, but I don't know what to say. Spinning back, I look for her again, but the crowd's already begun to disperse. Now that I'm no longer drinking, there's nothing to watch. Perhaps I should grab the drink from Lucas's hand again, if only to bring her back over here.

My eyes catch on a familiar face.

There's nothing soft about this girl. Eyes blacker than dripping ink, her mouth twisted in a permanent sneer. She's the type of pretty that could get you killed; if you stare too long, you'll turn to stone. She has dark roots, hair swinging in jagged strands to her shoulders. All thorn, no flower.

I stare at her and her thirty-two freckles. Wilhelmina Greene.

The sight of her throws the world apart. I see her and the butterflies in my chest drop dead.

The surge of happiness I'm feeling—a grin I couldn't shake, laughter that gushed out of me—ends abruptly.

She stalks my way. Closer and closer until she's got a fistful of my shirt.

It's been one awful, tense year. A whole year trapped in her vicious storm cloud, caught in a hatred so deep and deadly, it's left me permanently winded. She asked me to choose and I did, and I've been living in the aftermath of my decision ever since.

All the pointed looks she gave me when she thought I wasn't looking, the way her smile would shrivel and die when her eyes met mine.

And now her fingers are locked tight.

"W-Wil." The name goes down hard. I have to swallow twice to force it through my throat. I hyperfixate on every little movement—the slosh of my voice rising like bile in my throat, my knees cracking as I shift in place, the sluggish weight of my body.

And she's pulling me, dragging me forward like I weigh nothing. I feel featherlight.

There are catcalls and jeers from all sides. People are looking, but I can't bring myself to look back. The lights morph: The vivid hues from before have vanished. Now it's a steady flash of deep red. The same harsh hue of a trickling cut or a festering, angry wound.

My chest hurts. Really, really bad. Each breath is a rattling hiss in my lungs. Wil is touching me. I can feel her warmth spreading through my shirt. *Wil is touching me.*

I recognize the back door as it slams behind us. And then there's silence. Me and Wil. Alone. Lucas's backyard stretches in a sheet of never-ending white. She's close. My back is to the wall and her lips are not far from mine. She looks pissed and maybe I should be scared, but she smells like strawberries. I tell her as much.

"That's all you've got to say to me?" she says, breaking the silence with burning eyes and gnashing teeth. "Not 'sorry my family is stealing your home, Wil'? 'Sorry I'm not helping you solve your mother's case,

Wil'? . . . Seriously, though, strawberries?" Her anger dips to brief confusion, and she takes a sniff of her own hair. "I smell like BO."

I think I say something, but I'm not sure. All I know is that as soon as she lets go of me, I'm going to fall. My legs are barely keeping me upright.

"Your father's done playing preacher, huh? He wants to become God now? What does your family even want with the motel? Let me guess, you're going to demolish it? Make it into a megachurch?"

The motel?

I blink, but I can't make her words make sense. My dad's never mentioned Wil or her family since the accusation and the case. There's no way he would want to buy anything like that.

"I don't . . ." I'm not sure what sobers me more: the snarl of the wind or the tightening of my collar beneath her fist. She eases and I gasp for air. "I don't know what you're talking about, Wil."

"Liar," she hisses, and her voice is frigid. She's as volatile and angry as the last time she accused me. But this time I have nothing to fight back with. This time she's rendered me speechless. "You're telling me Sheriff Vrees knows and I know and you don't?"

I shake my head. It's all I'm capable of.

"And I suppose there's nothing you want to tell me about my mother? More specifically, where she is?" *My mind.* That's what I want to say, but even drunk, I know better. Sophie Greene has taken a permanent residence in my thoughts. She exists in murky shadows, and when she smiles, it's the same one I saw in church that day. No one new ever came to our service, and yet there she was, taking a seat in the back pew and smiling large as ever despite all the stares.

You know, my father said over dinner when she disappeared, *that woman left her newborn daughter before. She ran out on her family and when she came to her senses, she made a whole spectacle of her return. She must've missed the attention. Not everyone shares the same family values we do.*

I wonder if she's smiling wherever she is now.

"I told you before"—I fight to keep the words even—"I don't know where your mom is, Wil, but my family has nothing to do with it, okay? What else do I need to do to prove that? I don't know how you can even suggest it in the first place. They're the ones who organized the search, they're the ones who hung up all the 'Missing' flyers, they—"

"Oh, they're such saints, excuse me. It takes a real saint to abuse your child, doesn't it?" Even she seems stunned by the words. She gnaws on her lip and I wonder if she's afraid of anything else toppling out and spoiling in the air between us. "I shouldn't have said that."

"You don't know anything, Wil." I twist away from her prying eyes. I can't believe the words that come out of my mouth next. I guess that's a common theme between us tonight. "Is abandoning your own daughter any better?"

She holds her glare a while longer before breaking away with a hiss. "Fuck you, Elwood."

I was right—she lets go of me and I collapse to the frozen pavement. The patio door rattles behind her. I'm not sure how long it takes for me to find my footing. I wobble on my feet, a growing sickness climbing its way up. The world outside is freezing, but my skin burns still from her touch.

I feel sick.

It's already become far too hot to breathe. I feel like I'm about to purge.

I take the stairs two at a time.

Upstairs, the walls are lined with smiling faces. Grins that grow wider the longer I look at them, eyes that become more pupil than white. My skin feels like it's going to ooze off my bones like paint.

I need to find the bathroom.

I swing open the doors, one by one. The knobs twist open easily enough as I look for an escape. An empty office with sterile, crisp walls. A storage closet where everything is tucked away neatly in compartmentalized boxes. The third door swings back to reveal the moon. Silver streaming in, casting down on a bare back. Spine curving like the bones in the woods; wounded, guttural cries; bodies bathed in blue.

Harvey and some girl, hooking up on the bed.

The image of them washes away. Just two creatures, arms and legs and limbs. Blood and bone and the flesh sealing over them both. Pounding hearts, the heavy drumbeat of youth. "What the fuck, get out of here!" she screams at me, chucking a pillow toward my chest. I scramble over myself. The door slams shut beneath me, my legs carrying me away. I run fast down the hall. The nausea grows stronger with each passing second. I creak open the last door, audibly sighing at the sight. I'm at the toilet in seconds. The burn of bile rises in my chest, clawing up to my mouth, leaving a bloody mess of my throat. I heave and heave and heave. My eyes sting, already welling with tears. It's disgusting, all of it. The taste of it, the sound of it, the fact that my hands are gripping a grimy toilet seat for dear life. People have sat on this. They have done more than sit on it. God, god, god. I need to disinfect my hands five times over. I need to bleach them. My mother can't know about this. My father can't know about this. No one can—

I throw up again.

Sinner, sinner, sinner.

My nails drag down my tongue, clawing away the layer of filth with equally filthy hands. I need to get the taste out before it roots itself inside me and stays forever. I'll pray and I'll pray until it goes away.

I stare into the bowl.

It's full of snapped twigs and clumps of grass. Pine needles peppered all around, a stark forest of green against the white. In the very center of it all, I see the broken, crumpled body of a moth. Fur as red as dried blood, no longer fresh and vivid and bright. Crescent moons are carved out from its wings, two identical sepia-stained splotches. Eye spots black like marbles, mimicking the hawkish, beady gaze of a predator. It's a Columbia silk moth.

It buzzes in the middle of the water, not quite dead yet, squirming with the last flickering of life.

The flush of the toilet takes it away.

I stagger back to the wall and wonder what it was that I saw. I'm drunk. That's it. I'm just hallucinating because I'm drunk and tomorrow it will all be a bad memory.

Stumbling my way toward the faucet, I let the hot water run between the cracks in my fingers.

"This isn't real. This isn't real. This isn't—This isn't—"

The words clog my throat and block out the air. I gasp, but I can't breathe. *I need to get out of here.* But I don't get far.

Stars burst from the lights until they're all I see. They take the world with them, shattering my vision into a deep, dusky black.

CHAPTER FIVE

WIL

"So, how did that go?" Ronnie asks. I lean into her, not quite trusting my legs to keep me upright. Elwood's driven a stake through my heart and I'm doing my best not to bleed out on the floor.

Of course he wouldn't say anything. He doesn't give a shit about you. He made that clear a year ago.

Months have passed and the past is still festering and raw.

I give Ronnie's hand a squeeze. The night has taken a toll on her makeup; her eye shadow is starting to crease in the folds, lipstick transferred from her mouth to her cup. Even when she's messy, she's beautiful. Her presence helps, but it's not enough. Nothing is enough.

"I wish you'd talk to me, Wil," she begs. "Really tell me the truth about things again." One day she'll leave me too. Everyone does.

I try to say something, but when I open my mouth, everything comes rushing to the surface.

My nails sink into my arm, deeper, deeper, distracting myself with pain. Pain is better when I'm the one in control.

"Whoa, Wil?" The sound of her voice forces me to look up. She's standing there, concern etched deeply in her face.

Tears trickle down, seeping into my mouth until all I taste is salt.

"Can we leave? I don't want everyone to see me like this," I croak into her ear. My fingers clutch greedy fistfuls of her—her hair, the back of her dress, anything I can do to get closer.

Her thumb swipes my cheek. "This party is boring anyway. Tell you what, let's head back before the roads go to hell."

Hell isn't some burning, fiery pit beneath the earth. Hell is stepping out into the cold and having Mother Nature sucker punch the air out of your lungs. Hell is a scraping wind so intense that you check for blood on your cheek.

Thank God Ronnie dried the tears from my face. I have a horrible feeling they would freeze onto my skin otherwise. On particularly nasty days, I've gone outside with damp hair only to end up with hardened clumps of ice.

The car rumbles to life. Windshield wipers scratch against the frozen glass and ice-cold air blows out from the vents, doing very little to fight the chill slithering across my bones.

Embarrassment has already begun to creep in where the grief was. It's one thing to cry alone—teeth clamped on a pillow, smothering sobs behind paper-thin walls. It's another thing to cry openly, to let the whole world see how vulnerable you've become.

"Here, let's see how worked up they're getting over this storm."

Ronnie presses a gloved finger against one of the radio buttons. All the stations are hours away from us, our own town too small for much of anything. "Huge storm front moving through tonight, folks. I've got to tell ya, it's rough on the map. There's a squall advisory from one to five a.m." Our local weatherman's got the heaviest Yooper accent you've ever heard in your life. "Real monster of a storm. We're getting our first taste of it tonight. Hopefully, all of you listeners are staying safe—"

Meanwhile, Ronnie's death-gripping the wheel and we're barely creeping along. There's bound to be some kid in a ditch soon. Scratch that: there's bound to be several. By tonight, the winds will be wild, and you won't be able to see anything in front of you. Just blinding white everywhere. And tonight is mild compared with what's to come.

We weave our way out of the world's smallest neighborhood and past Earl's—which Ronnie may or may not have a job at anymore because of me.

All the buildings in this town are scattered among the trees like stray billboards on a rural road. Ronnie's car crawls past the only bar we have. Despite the weather, there's still cars parked in the lot. Mill workers treat drinking at Tail's Tavern like a second job. Thanks to them, the Ramirez family must be rolling in cash; they've certainly got enough to plaster pennies all over the place.

I resist the urge to tell Ronnie to swing over there. They hardly card as it is, and I'd love to scrape some of the coins off their resin floor. Dad's so behind on his bills that I'll take whatever I can get.

"So," Ronnie starts. If the roads weren't trash, she'd probably be drumming her fingers against the wheel like she usually does. Outside, the snow has picked up even harder. It's going to suck to shovel later. With the motel being sold, I'm almost tempted to give up on it completely and let the snow bury us alive.

No.

I'll figure something out. The motel isn't going anywhere.

"So," I parrot, but I stare at the road in favor of making eye contact. Silence.

She makes the mistake of rubbing her eye with one hand and her eyeliner smudges even worse. "Please offer me a sliver of what's going on. I'm begging here."

My mouth's gone dry. The fortress I've built around my secrets is steep, but I force some through the cracks for Ronnie. "They're closing Mom's case. Vrees practically told me that when I came in today. He's done dealing with me."

I see the effect instantly. The awkward ripple beneath her skin. The gears turning rapidly in her brain, trying her best to offer up the right thing to say. I really hope she doesn't tell me she's sorry. I've had my fill of that.

"Seriously?" she asks instead, and I could almost sigh in relief. Her brows furrow, and I watch the curl of her lip as she scowls. It's hard to tell how much is genuine and how much is her mimicking me, serving whatever emotion she thinks I'd like to see. "It's only been a year. And now it's all over? Just like that?"

"For them," I'm quick to chime in. "Not for me."

Ice gusts carry flurries across the half-eaten road. Snow's devoured any lines we had. She wets her lips. The lipstick from earlier has all but disappeared. "I could help."

"Unless you want to hang out in Elwood's bushes with me—" Shit, I didn't mean to say that much.

Her laughter is short-lived. When I don't join in, she whips toward me, and I have to swat at her to keep focused on the road. *"You're serious?"*

"It would be one horrible joke," I counter, and the thought of someone else knowing the truth sours my stomach. "I need dirt on them."

She's never been one to hide her nerves well. "Wil, you could get in actual trouble, you know that, right? What if they send you to juvie or something?"

"Pretty sure they don't send eighteen-year-olds there." I shrug.

She doesn't ease up. "I'm not well versed in the law, but . . . God, Wil, now you've got me paranoid about this. Next thing you're going to do is tell me you've actually broken in . . . you haven't, have you?"

I shake away her concern. "No, Ronnie, you can relax. And I'm not really worried about me. I'm worried about Mom. I need proof."

Ronnie offers me a sympathetic look, but I avert my eyes to the radio.

I don't need pity. Pity won't pay the bills, and pity sure as hell won't fix things.

"Did Elwood give you anything?" she asks.

"That's the worst part," I confess, and luckily my hands are out of sight. They've begun to shake a little. I sit on them to fight the tremble in my fingers. "He acted like he didn't have a clue what I was talking about. Again. I guess it doesn't matter if he's drunk or high or on truth serum."

"Do you believe him?"

"No. I should've known better. I don't believe a word out of Elwood's mouth."

We sit in silence for the rest of the drive. It's a full fifteen minutes to the motel from Lucas's place. Typically, it takes half that time, but not before some Good Samaritan decides to plow the roads.

The green from this morning has vanished without a trace. Ice gusts whip past the main entrance, spinning the VACANCY sign in dizzy circles. Any faster and it might fling right off and crash into the parking lot.

Above it: GRE MO EL.

The surviving lights cut through the gray night, a fluorescent lime green that should spell out "Greene Family Motel" but hasn't in a year. Now it's an eyesore, but at least it's hideous enough to match the rest of the building.

"Does it ever get any easier?" I ask. It's a quiet question, barely there in the dark.

I don't have to explain myself. Grief stitches an impenetrable bond between us. "I've missed my dad since I was eight. I think about him all the time, I really do, but . . . time helps. You learn to take the world day by day. You pick up the shattered pieces of yourself and move forward."

I link my pinkie finger with hers and she gives me a reaffirming squeeze. "Do you need me to spend the night? I can make up some lie in the morning to my mom, but if you need me, I'm here."

I don't want to be alone. I really, really don't. But try as I might, I can't bring myself to ask.

Not when it's so easy to fake a smile, give her finger a tighter tug, and say, "Don't worry, I'm okay."

She squints. "Are you sure?"

"Positive," I lie.

She abandons my hand to pull me into an actual half hug. "Text me if you need anything, all right?" She's a lot stronger than she looks. "Anything you need. I'll be here. Anarchy Sisters, remember?"

Mrs. Clearwater dubbed us that shortly after she started hanging out with me. After I started "influencing" her to be her own person. It was never meant to be a compliment, but it sounds too cool to be anything but.

"How could I forget?" I grin—a real one this time. "Anarchy Sisters for life. Drive home safe, okay?" I smile until her car fades from view. Then I'm left with my own racing thoughts and what Sheriff Vrees lovingly described as the "money pit."

From an outside perspective, I definitely see why. The family motel is a portal to the seventies. Everything in this place is determined to stay old. No amount of Febreze chases away the musty scent hanging in the air. Wipe off the furniture all you want, but the dust will always come crawling back.

You can hardly even see us from the main road anymore. With every passing year, the Morguewood creeps closer. Vines tangle up the walls, scratching the sides like it might tear us apart if it tries hard enough.

We didn't always live here. The idea of having an actual home is so long gone, so distant now, that it doesn't even seem real. The memories are there, but they feel transplanted, fed to me. Like a story you heard all the time growing up. You might remember it by heart, but the story itself doesn't belong to you.

The only employee we can afford to keep is nursing a cigarette at the door.

On second thought, I'm not sure if we ever pay her. Dad doesn't pay for a lot of things.

Maybe Cherry's here out of the sheer goodness of her heart. Maybe it's pity. My mother and her were so close, you'd think they were mother and daughter. With my real grandma dead and Cherry's son in jail somewhere, maybe that's what they became to each other. Family.

"Before you ask, no, you can't have one," she says without even looking at me. I'm surprised the strong winds haven't blown her cigarette right out. She protects it with an ungloved hand. Each finger is jammed with rings, and her nails are yellowed where the polish has chipped.

"What makes you think I was going to ask?"

"Because you always ask." There's a faint smile on her lips.

"Touché." I snort.

She may be older than dirt, but she's never got gray hair to show for it. She dyes her locks a fire-engine red, sprucing it up every week. She told me once she swipes the box colors from the corner store by distracting the cashier with a bone-rattling cough and "accidentally" knocking them into her purse. *If I gotta put up with growing old, I need to have some fun every now and again, right?*

At the moment, though, she looks exactly how I feel: frustrated, worn out, and in dire need of a yearlong nap. Her signature red lipstick looks like it was reapplied in the dark with her left hand. She's bundled so tight in a sequined scarf that it makes my own throat itchy.

Her nose scrunches, and I'm sure she can smell the heavy stench of alcohol riding along my breath. "So, what's a girl like you up to on a Friday night?"

I shrug, carrying my eyes over to the sign. The neon lights burn. "Drinking. Partying. Making reckless adolescent decisions."

"All that, huh?" she prods before laughing and taking another puff. I watch the way she holds the smoke inside and shudders with it like a dragon's breath. It reeks.

"Nah, I had one beer and then Ron and I drove home. That was it."

"Shouldn't be drinking."

"You shouldn't be smoking."

She grunts, but I see the hint of a grin. "Touché." One more puff and she's tossing it in the ashtray. "So, your dad finally told you, huh?"

"He didn't tell me shit. I read the paper myself." My body burns at the memory and the anger is almost enough to warm me up.

"Your father isn't the best at handling things, but can you blame him for being nervous?" she asks, her words breaking in a telling smoker's cough. "You're not exactly sunshine and rainbows around him. You're a real spitfire like your mom. Let me guess, you ripped into him for it?"

I avert my eyes. "A bit."

You're selling to the fucking Clarke family? How could you?

What else would you have me do? There's nothing left for us, Wil!

I might not be good at much, but I'm great at drawing out rage. For a couple wonderful seconds, he came alive. He was more than a hollow husk of himself. A guy who was a father to me once but nothing to me now.

But then he disappeared again.

I tell her the same thing I told him: "This is all we have left of her."

The look she gives me is nostalgic at best and tragic at worst. Eyes drooping low, lips pressed tight. I dislike pity, but I'll take it any day over the way Dad reacted. His emotions wiped away as easily as they came, soaked up until there was nothing left.

Cherry sighs. "Your mom was never too thrilled about Greene's. Sure she would have sold it, too, for the right price. This place has always been your father's child."

Goes to show how much he cares about his "children." I almost say it, but I bite my tongue. At this point, Dad's the least of my concerns. "I don't care. After this, it's all over. We already lost the house. We've lost so much, Cherry. We can't afford to lose anything else. Besides, what are you going to do?"

She makes a face—hard to say if it's over the smoke riding the air or my sudden interrogation. "I'll manage, kid. I always do, don't I?"

"It's not fair."

"Life's not fair."

I grind my teeth. How many times do I have to hear that from people who've already given up?

"I hate to say it, Wil, but it's too late. I'm not sure how you'd weasel your way out of a contract unless Ezekiel Clarke drops dead or lands himself in jail. And even then, who knows?"

Her voice is distant, foggy, even. "Growing up means learning to roll with the punches."

I refuse to accept that. "Then I'll never grow up because I don't plan on taking this lying down. If they're punching me, then I'm punching back hard."

I clamp down on my lip hard enough to draw blood. Ronnie's words spin in my thoughts. *You haven't broken into their house yet, have you?*

SKYLA ARNDT

No, but maybe it's time. If Vrees isn't going to help me and I'm not going to get any answers from Elwood, I'm going to need to double down on my investigation.

"Wil. Promise me you'll leave that family alone." There's a desperate edge in her voice that isn't lost on me. Cherry rarely begs for anything.

"I promise," I lie.

Her eyes rest on me for a moment longer. But then she nods, musters a weak smile, and leaves.

"Dad, I'm heading out. Try not to choke on your own vomit, okay?"

I squint to make sure he's only passed out and not actually dead. It can be hard to tell some days.

When Mom first disappeared, there was still a bit of life left in him. He'd comb his hair, trim his beard, make sure he wasn't covered in literal ketchup stains. He even got a second job as a chef in the neighboring town of Hartsgrove.

Those days are gone.

Today, he's whiskey-stained, and his room is a hoarder's paradise. Our old microwave sits unplugged in the middle of the floor; next to it, there are boxes of old plates wrapped in newspaper; a vacuum ironically catches the majority of the dust, sitting neglected in the corner. He hoards all this in hopes we'll move out one day and need it all again.

Without Mom, the two of us alone couldn't afford to pay for the house and the motel, so here we are.

I check the nightstand beside him. There's a whole medicine cabinet's worth of prescriptions—some to make him less depressed and some to make him less of an alcoholic. He's used none of it. His drug of choice is a bottle.

"The things I do for you," I snarl, flipping him to his side. Not like he hears. He barely hears me when he's awake. "If you need me, I'll be saving the motel. Saving *us*."

I leave him with that, and slam his door shut behind me.

Without Cherry here, the whole motel has grown darker. The place feels especially haunted tonight—there's a quiet sputtering somewhere, a faucet dripping, pipes creaking. Walls grown tired of holding their weight, floors shifting and crying beneath my feet. Shadows find their way in from the outside. Wind slams at the glass doors in violent gusts. The parking lot lights tear through the darkness, but beyond them the world has grown pitch-black. Snow blows in from the east, ripping out from the sky in sideways gusts.

With an aggressive storm like the one outside, I should be happy I'm in here. Cozy and safe with a roof over my head and the blankets raised to my chin . . . but my mind is set. Whether she wanted to give me the idea or not, Ronnie was right. I'm done camping out in the bushes and waiting for something to happen from the outside. I need to find out what goes on inside their carefully held walls.

I only barely remember to layer up before I charge out.

The doors scream their complaints, swinging open to reveal the snow-drenched forest, newly barren branches, the moon held captive between the clouds.

It's a ghost town outside. There's nothing but the snapping of twigs under my feet and the cloud of my breath and the warning whistle of the wind. It tugs at my chin, inviting my eyes toward the tree line.

Tendrils jut out onto the road, inching out from the forest, breaking only to claim new land.

I stand on shaky legs, my eyes drifting back and forth between the peeling doors and the white-capped forest. I've cleared a decent path, but

I can't go back yet. I wince against the onslaught of snow, doing my best to look out even when the flurries get into my eyes. The quickest way to get to their home is through the trees. There should be a path by now, but it's obscured by mounds of fresh snow. I've walked this route many times before, my eyes shot from tears and my blood coursing like acid in my veins.

I'm getting answers today one way or another. *Ready or not, Clarkes, here I come.*

CHAPTER SIX

ELWOOD

The world returns in fragmented pieces: burning white fluorescent lights, a gaping crater of a room, and a wicked bruise forming on my temple. It all bleeds back together.

Kevin gapes down at me, a cup of water sloshing in his hand as Lucas hoists me upright. I try to help him, but I'm nothing more than dead weight.

"I was really scared you were out cold, man. Do you feel like you have a concussion? Do you feel like you might start to have one? I mean, you don't seem to be bleeding." Kevin's questions sober me in seconds. "Should I call your mom?"

"No!" I hate the slice of my voice when it meets the air. It's too brutal to belong to me, too frigid and unforgiving.

I try again, softer: "No, please. My parents can't know about any of this. I-I'm fine. Maybe I drank too much, but everything is good now. I threw up most of it anyway." I force a chuckle. "I guess I'm more of a lightweight than you guys bargained for, huh?"

They don't laugh.

"Give him some space, Kev." Lucas frowns. "It's my bad. I should've eased you into it. Here, drink some water. You'll probably want some Tylenol, too, in case you wake up with a wicked hangover."

Condensation drips down the glass and slides off my fingers. There's so much I should say, but I can't. I should tell them about the moth spewing from my lips, the creeping sensation that I'm losing my mind.

I should tell them that I'm terrified of losing them, that every time they share a laugh or smile without me my world cracks further. But I don't say any of that. I only mumble, "Thanks." The water scratches my already-sore throat.

Kevin takes my empty glass and sets it down on the counter beside him. I'm grateful, if only because my hands have grown weak. I'm not sure how much longer I could have held it without it toppling and shattering to the bathroom floor.

Lucas's smile is bittersweet. "Sorry if this night wasn't all I'd hyped it up to be. There's always next time when you're back, yeah?"

The somber look in his eyes says it all. Next time is ages away, buried under a million maybes. Maybe I'll come back different or maybe they won't come back at all. Maybe this night is the last we'll ever have.

We're still quiet in the car.

I burrow into myself, rubbing my arms together like I might spark a fire. It's freezing cold, but one click of a button and the leather seats beneath us begin to warm up.

Kevin clears his throat and his breath leaves an imprint in the frigid air. "This is the exact reason I'm studying down south." His nose has gone nearly as red as Lucas's hair. "I'm going to become a Popsicle at this point."

"Roll Tide," Lucas snickers at Kevin's school of choice. "I don't know, the cold's not so bad. Alabama will be crawling with bugs all the time and humid as hell."

"Bugs? Maybe you should tag along, Elwood. You'd love that." Kevin winks and I try to smile, I really do, but I'm not sure if it comes across that way.

He purses his lips after a thick silence. "Do you have to become a preacher like your dad? Can't you go to college, too? I'm sure there'd be a program for you."

Almost. I almost clicked submit on an application. I don't think I've ever stared at a computer screen that long. University of Michigan in big menacing letters, the form fully filled out, my heart racing.

Then with a shaking hand I dragged the mouse up to the X and washed my hands. Buried the dream away.

I don't think he realizes how much his words burn. "I chose this path."

Lucas's face scrunches. "Sure, that wasn't that 'hard' of a choice." He decorates the word with quotation marks on either side, lifting his hands off the wheel long enough for the car to slide. Kevin jabs him in the ribs, and he scrambles back for the wheel, regaining control.

It's my duty, I almost say, before realizing exactly how that sounds. "It doesn't matter what I want anyway."

Lucas's disapproval is poorly concealed. "So, it's what, your life burden? The consequence of being born?"

For as much as they butt heads, Lucas and Wil have the same heart. Lit coals, burning and blazing in their chest. I've learned the hard way that some fires can't be put out.

"I want to," I argue, and I hope if I repeat it enough, I'll believe it. "I have to."

I remember the last time my father scolded me. His face was unnervingly blank, chest rising and falling with a measured breath. The light went out in his eyes—much like a hand snuffing out an open flame, first the sputtering wisps of smoke, and then the darkness. He stalked my way, the soles of his shoes barely making a noise against the wood. Hand swinging back, delivering one dizzying, sharp slap to the face. Just a taste of the pain to come.

My fingers brush the yellowing bruises beneath my sleeves. Unlike butterflies, scars are so very easy to catch.

What will he do to me if he finds out I was gone?

The conversation turns alongside the screech of wheels, diverging into unfamiliar avenues. I sink into the back seat, getting lost in the background. There's a whole world between them that I don't know. Days crashing at each other's house, late-night drives, and inside jokes. Their friendship sinks into my gut as sharp as any blade.

I scratch idly at my thumb. My mom's never been successful at stomping this out of me. I pick and pick at my thumb until my skin is as raw as I feel.

The air changes as we get closer to my house. Everything changes. The rest of the town might've progressed with the times—telephone poles and wires strung like stretches of ivy—but my home and the church feel more like a page ripped from a history book.

Lucas and Kevin are like the cars flying through our unchanging expanse of wood. They come and go as they please, but I'm rooted here forever. It hurts for a second, but in the end, it's better this way. When I leave, they'll forget about me. I won't hurt them, not as much as I hurt Wil.

My family would never kidnap someone, Wil. Do you hear yourself?

She'd looked off to the forest's edge, staring past the thick veil of pine. *You're siding with them?*

They're my family, Wil.

She'd huffed, incredulous. *Family only goes so far.*

I stare out the window and let the snow bury what's left of the memory.

Through the hollow parts between the trees, the shadows take shape.

Darkness twists like a writhing eel, a curious ripple in the night air. I don't only see it; I feel it deep within my chest.

"You really need to stand up to your parents at some point," Lucas says abruptly over the murmur of the stereo. I can tell he's been sitting on it for some time now.

"It's not right to go against your parents," I say, as if I haven't done precisely that.

Lucas is unrelenting. "My dad was pissed when I applied for Chicago. Absolutely red-in-the-face, foaming-at-the-mouth pissed. He had this whole make-believe fantasy in his head that I was gonna spend my life here in town and work at the mill. Here I am, doing it anyway. You're not just their child. You're your own person."

The words fly from me untethered. "You have *no idea* what it's like with my family. I will never get what I want. I don't even know what I want in the first place. But at the end of the day, it really doesn't matter."

The silence that follows is suffocating.

My anger gives way to a cold, crushing fear. I shouldn't have said that. I really, really shouldn't have said that. Thou shalt honor thy mother and father. Thou shalt—

"I think we're all tired," Kevin says, though I'd be a fool not to notice how weak his smile has become. "We shouldn't have pried about it."

Tired. Is that it? Maybe. My exhaustion manifests itself in deep black bruises beneath my eyes. Just looking at myself in the rearview mirror is enough to make me yawn. Nothing sounds better than warm covers and a waiting pillow. I long to watch the woods fall asleep with me. The wind tamed back to a lull, the moon breaking over the trees, drowning the world in cold, pale blue.

But the woods show no sign of falling asleep.

The car slows against the gravel, and Lucas shifts into park. Behind us, the forest spreads out thick and unyielding.

"Thanks, guys," I mumble, at a loss for something better to say. I've never enjoyed goodbyes. The guilt of leaving doesn't help.

"Get some sleep, Clarke," Lucas jokes. "See you . . ." His voice cuts off, uncertain.

I swallow. "Yeah. See you."

I watch their car until there's nothing left to see.

Beneath my coat, a shiver works its way up my back.

I glance toward my window in the distance—fear wriggling inside my chest for the first time. What will the consequences be this time? How many more scars can I acquire before I'm no longer a person but one large blooming bruise?

No. I focus on my breathing, on every wicked, whistling breath in. Maybe my parents won't even notice. I'll slip back into my window, go back to bed, and everything will go off without a hitch. For once, my dad's hand won't lurch back to strike me. He'll lower it gently on my shoulder, proud of me for once.

The late-night Mass is over. My parents are asleep. I chant the words like a mantra, something I can manifest and make true. There's no reason they'd be awake. My father's life is one never-ending routine. He goes to sleep as soon as his sermon is over. He'll take as much sleep as he can before the morning bell rings.

I hold on to the belief as I shimmy the latch. The window creaks louder than I'd like and my heart lurches in my chest at the sound. I pause, wait, and then raise it up some more and climb through. The bedroom is steeped in darkness, but I suck in a breath as the shadows collect on a silhouette.

I hear the click of the light switch first before I see him. My father stands in my doorway, his face the picture of rage.

A stillness overtakes us and we're suspended in time, caught between the Before and After and trapped in the miserable Now. My father's green eyes burn black. It's no use backing away. When time catches up, he slaps me, and it's enough to make my eyes well with tears and my teeth rattle in my mouth. I heave for air, but it's been knocked right out of my lungs.

"Where on earth were you?" The threat in his eyes is more than a warning. It's a promise of more pain to come. That's when I notice my mother watching in the wings like a vulture waiting for a kill. Perhaps she will swoop in to feast on what's left.

I open my mouth, but my voice won't come.

"I smell it on you. You're drunk," he snarls, his words striking me harder than the sting of his palm. On the floor I see the smashed remains of the Tracfone Lucas gave me.

"I'm not, I—" Thou shalt not lie to thy parents. The proverb pushes the words right out. "I mean, I was, I—I'm sorry, sir." My words plummet like anvils. They crush through the silence and echo back in my ears.

"You would disobey us like this?" His fists tremble at his sides. "Tonight, of all nights? We prayed over you, Elwood. Have you forgotten that, or do you simply not care?"

"I care!"

Neither of my parents have changed out of their church attire. Did they know I was missing before the sermon even started, or did they find me here after? Either way, they've been standing in my room waiting for quite some time.

I should've known better.

"You just what?" my father demands. "Care about those boys more than your family? More than the church?"

I think of the Lord's eyes burning on my neck as I heaved up my sins. "I wanted to say goodbye."

"Those boys shouldn't matter to you. We aren't like them, Elwood. *You* aren't like them. Their families don't even attend mass."

"They're my friends."

"Your friends?" My father laughs like it's the best joke I've ever told. "Those boys are worthless. Worm food at best."

"Don't say that." I surprise myself with each word. Every muscle in me wants to tremble and cower beneath his stern eyes, but my mouth has a mind of its own. Perhaps it's some of the rage, the bubbling leftovers spewing from the core of me.

It takes my father a moment for the words to catch up with him. His blank face pulls back in a disgusted sort of disbelief. "I'll say what I please, and as my son, you will shut up and listen."

I swallow and it hurts. "Are you buying Wil's motel?" My treacherous tongue will see me dead.

Father is momentarily quiet, but the silence doesn't last. "Don't say that viper's name in this house."

Wil, Wil, Wil, Wil, my thoughts sing. Wilhelmina Greene. I feel her fingers latch onto my chest, the snarl of her breath against my skin. I remember the anger swirling in her eyes and the pain buried beneath.

"But are you?"

My mother looks between us both. I know if it was her, she would have struck again already. Her eyes drop to Father's swaying hand and I know she's counting the seconds in her mind, but my father doesn't move an inch. "What I do doesn't concern you. What concerns you is not affiliating yourself with a good-for-nothing snake who publicly smeared our family name, or have you forgotten that?"

"No, sir, but—"

My father's voice smooths over and it's ten times more dangerous than before: "Tell me, what does the Bible say about children who disobey their parents?"

I clear my throat, already dreading the outcome of my words. "D-do not withhold discipline from a child . . . If you punish them with the r-rod, they will not die." I can hear my heart in my throat. "Punish them with the rod and save them from death."

"Then you know that you have earned this punishment."

I flinch, but my father isn't reaching toward me. Instead, he lifts one of my butterfly displays from the wall and the sound that rips from me is hardly human. More like a desperate croak. I'd take the beating. I'd take it gladly if it meant—

"No, please!"

His face scrunches and he sends the first piece of my collection flying. It hits the wall in a deafening shatter. Broken glass no longer looks like stardust. It looks like flying shards and vision blurred by tears. Like sin and punishment and God's ever-watching eye. More and more of my collection is hurled against the wall. I've covered every bare inch of this room in framed displays, and one by one they fall in a deadly kaleidoscope.

My butterflies lie crumpled and broken, wings torn and bodies bent. My swallowtails, my monarchs, my glasswings. I've spent years tucked away in this room with pins and forceps. Prying the wings open, stabbing through the thorax, lining the wings up neatly to make them new. Alive.

Now the only thing they are is dead.

"Let the pain be a lesson," my father sneers. "And don't even dream of leaving again. You don't know the extent of my wrath." I watch as he retreats down the dark hall with my mother in tow. Inch by inch until there's nothing left of him.

I am alone.

Time blurs with the ticking clock. I sit there for so long, staring at the damage, squeezing my eyes shut, praying it away—but God still isn't listening. It's all the same. There's a graveyard at my feet, a sea of glass and corpses.

I scoop the remains of a moth. Glass slices through my fingers, but I hardly feel it. In my hands lies what used to be an *Acherontia atropos*. One of my most prized creatures, body split between a punch of bright yellow and a deep speckled brown. A death's-head hawk moth.

Next to it, I see my comma and my emperor moth. The antennae are torn off and the wings are a shredded imitation of their former glory. There will be no putting any of them back together again. The tears pour before I can stop them. They gush from my bloodshot eyes, raining down my cheeks and trickling off my chin to the floor. I imagine them scorching right through the wood. All that's left is a sticky, consuming grief, and I worry I'll drown beneath its waves. I'll sink so deep that I'll never come back.

No more school. No more Lucas. No more Kevin. No more butterflies or moths. No more anything.

Try as I might to snuff out the ache, it lingers, heavy in my ribs. It weighs down my lungs until breathing is a chore.

A sound breaks me out of my thoughts. Beneath the floorboards, the front door creaks open. There's a flurry of movement, a shuffle of feet and whispered words. I press my ear to the floor, straining to listen.

Sheriff Vrees's voice is gruff and low. "We need to take care of that boy sooner than later. If you can't keep an eye on your own son, Ezekiel, I'll do it. Got a nice little cell with his name on it."

Cell? Oh God, it's the drinking, isn't it? I broke the law and now I'm going to get fitted for handcuffs and spend my life in an orange jumpsuit and—

"Prudence's due date is soon. What would we have done if she went into labor and your boy was frolicking off somewhere?"

Huh?

My dad's voice enters the mix. "It will do you well to not speak to me in my own home like that, Mark. You forget I'm still the Right Hand. Nothing has changed."

Vrees snorts darkly, not a lick of fear in his tone. He stands his own against my father in ways I could only dream of. "Nothing *yet*, Ezekiel, but the clock is ticking before we need to cut out the seed for the next Alderwood."

What?

My fear and confusion act as puppet strings, carrying me toward the door with a dark, insatiable curiosity. The voices grow more muffled as the visitors retreat into the living room, but my mind is clear.

Go look.

I'm careful to step around the broken glass to avoid the loud, telling crunch of my feet. My mouth has become painfully dry. I try to swallow, but there's nothing left.

I'm used to being quiet. I've mastered the art of blending into walls and keeping each step as soft as possible. Years of walking across eggshells will do that. Even so, I'm terrified that the flurried beating of my heart will break the silence. I'm worried my father will sniff out my pulse and hurt me worse than he ever has before.

If that's possible.

But I have to know what they're talking about. The hallway stretches downward into a steep staircase. I creep to the second step and peer beyond the wall of railing. The lights haven't been switched on, but candles cast shadowy silhouettes.

The smell hits me first. Thick and rotten like curdled milk, potent as poison. It's always lingering in town like a vile aftertaste, spilling out from the thawing woods. It's never been pungent inside my own house, though.

This is much, much stronger. It stretches in every direction, soaking into the floor and pushing back out like weeds.

My own thoughts briefly return, snapping back with a painful fury. If I thought this through, maybe I would have thought better of it. My dad will see me. I know he will.

None of that seems to matter. I'm already here. I bend against the side of the stairs, running a careful hand along the banister.

The Pine Point police stand behind Vrees like disciples to a prophet. There's a whole swarm of them here in the living room, badges on and faces stern.

My father's broad shoulders stiffen. "I am more than aware, *Mark*." Dad runs a wild hand through his hair. "But we risk a spectacle with you driving him to the station. If anyone sees him—"

"Everyone has already seen him." Vrees shoves a finger against my father's chest and I have to bite back a gasp.

My father looks equally stunned at the gesture, unaccustomed to a challenge and despising every second of it. When the shock ebbs away, he swats the sheriff's arm back to his side. "If you insist on playing the role of a small town jailer, you may station yourself around the perimeter with your men, but I will not have you risking our plan. I know Elwood.

I have struck more than enough fear in him for tonight. He will not cross me."

Vrees sneers. "He already has. Elwood is a curious boy, Ezekiel, and curiosity is a dangerous thing. That behavior should've been snuffed out sooner."

It's true. My curiosity started early on. It was born in books. Old encyclopedias my father deemed harmless enough to allow me to scour. Before I could read, I traced the photos on the yellow-stained pages. Curved wings and antennae. Butterflies. That's when it all began. My father always curled his lip at every new crate that came to the house. He never minded so much as I stayed in my room and left him alone. One butterfly pinning turned to several, several turned to hundreds. It's hard to be lonely when you're surrounded.

"*He. Will. Stay. Put.*" Each word is a bullet fired through his teeth. "Patrol the perimeter if you must, but don't overstep your station. Nothing has changed yet."

Sheriff Vrees glares in my father's direction. With the room so dimly lit, the shadows nearly swallow his eye sockets whole. "That boy takes after his uncle."

My uncle. Dead before I had the chance to know him. There's a lash on my skin from the time I asked about him. I'd found a picture of Dad standing side by side with a boy who looked an awful lot like me—there was a certain softness in him not found in the rest of my family. It made my heart pang, a wash of grief for a man I'd never know. I was crying long before my father snatched the photo and beat a lesson into my back. *Never bring him up in this house.*

My father says the same thing now as his fist latches onto Vrees's collar. The sheriff doesn't budge.

"Do you love Elwood?"

"No," my father is quick to deny, his voice too quick and too harsh. He doesn't pause to think about it. I'm not worth the wasted second. "I don't love him. He is only a means to an end. Now be done with me."

I smother a horrible keening noise as it threatens to rise from my throat. *I don't love him.* I've suspected it forever and yet the words brand my heart like white-hot iron. *He is only a means to an end.*

The rabbit was a means to an end. So was the thrashing white-tailed deer, throat slit in a grisly red path, glassy eyes reflecting my own. Every creature skewered on a pike and gutted. The severed head of a black bear rolling in the snow. So many sacrifices my father made me watch.

This forest is God's gift to us, Elwood. My father's face was grim when he said it; he hadn't bothered to look at me. He was too busy wiping the stain from his blade. *We only prosper because He allows us to. The Lord has always called for blood.* My fingers brush the still-smooth skin of my throat.

I don't wait to listen to any more of it. I push my way back to my room, eager to place a door between me and them. Questions buzz in my head like biting gnats. They search for answers I don't have.

I was never going away, was I? At least nowhere in the mortal world. My curiosity gives birth to a fear so potent that I can't dream of shaking it off. The Garden of Adam has something planned for me. Something that involves my blood spilling out onto the snow. My "holy mission" was always destined to be six feet below the earth.

No . . . They wouldn't.

Would they?

I slide down my bedroom door. The shattered glass and the audience of the dead beg to differ.

Butterflies torn apart to oblivion.

I think of my father praying over me, his hand resting on my shoulder like I were a prized pig. He knew. He knew my fate when he uttered the last haunting, damned words:

For with life there is death, but with sacrifice there is eternity.

I envision my blood spilling. Glassy eyes heaven-bound, tongue lolling from an open jaw, my heart sloshing in a bowl.

I stumble across the floor. The carpet skins my palms, but I ignore the pain. It holds no weight against the pain to come. I try to imagine the light bleeding out, the very last seconds of consciousness before I die. And then I imagine the wrath I'd face in hell. All my sins are catching up to me at once. I'm not going to die. I can't.

Don't dream of leaving.

Tonight, we will have men all around the perimeter.

I conjure my remaining courage. One deep, bone-rattling breath. My lungs wheeze as I slide the window back open. I steady myself and then I jump. My knee scrapes against the rock-hard ice. Blood drenches through the leg of my jeans, but I don't stop to think about it. I can't stop.

My mother never bothered enrolling me in the Boy Scouts. I might have been glad as a child, but I'm not now. Other boys liked to kick and punch and break, they liked to laugh at tears and dump soda on anthills, they liked to run wild and howl like wolves.

All I wanted to do was carve out a spot for myself in a garden patch, sit with a book against the ledge of the fence, study the sprouting plants and all the little bugs that lived beneath us in the soil. Now I wish I had been meaner, crueler, stronger—I wish I knew how to run and how to fight and how to get myself out of here.

The moon hangs above like God's eye. He will follow me to the ends of the earth. Everything slides out of focus, a muddy world of green and brown and deep, dark black.

The snow picks up, gusts of white obscuring the world in front of me. Every stride forward is met with the scrape of a branch or a near-collision. Trees blocking my path, a frozen prison entrapping me here. The woods root for my death like spectators of a cruel sport.

But I run and I run and I do not stop.

CHAPTER SEVEN

WIL

There's a stillness in these woods that only exists in cemeteries. No chatter of birds or scurrying in the branches, no creature watching me among the shadows.

Only death.

These are the dying months. The time when winter runs its frozen fingers along the world and murders everything in its path. It feels wrong for me to be here at all, living and breathing in a place lacking a heartbeat.

It's not like I have much of a choice. I'm too far gone to abandon my plan now. You can't stop swimming after you've waded into the deep end. You have no choice but to make it to the other side.

I've made this bed. I'm going to need to lie in it.

This is the absolute worst time to think about warm beds.

I curse myself under my breath and trudge forward in silent frustration. It's hard to say how long I spend drifting through the trees.

My plan feels hazier, more impulsive with every step. I only thought about getting to the Clarke house; I hadn't considered how I'd break in when I got there. "When" being the key word here. With the blizzard, my trek feels twice as long.

The forest stretches forever in the distance. My labored breath hangs in a dense fog in the air, and I've lost all sensation in my toes. I only remember that I have toes in the first place when my good-for-nothing laces unravel and the soggy edges slip beneath my heel, tripping me with my next step.

The world slips beneath me as I fall and I brace for impact. For the only time in my eighteen years of life, I'm thankful for the snow. Without it, my knee would be shredded by a snaking root or a jagged rock underfoot. All I meet is a plush carpet of soft white.

That being said, I'm not fully relieved. The cold drenches through my jeans and I get a face full of ice. As if I hadn't already been worried about losing my nose to the cold, now I've got a one-way ticket to frostbite city. I guide myself upward, my one hand massaging feeling back into my face and the other sliding up the base of a tree beside me.

Something sticky is on the bark and curls around my fist. Black blood drips down my skin like sap.

There's a body nestled among the branches.

Two empty sockets caked in darkened, dry blood. Sallow, tight skin, a fist-size hole ripped through her chest. A gut full of leaves and skittering, crawling bugs. My mother.

"No." That's all I am capable of saying. My mouth hasn't caught up with my mind and my mind hasn't caught up with my eyes and there's no possible way—

Dinner drags up my throat, but before I can spew, the image of her vanishes with the shift of the wind. She blurs away until she isn't my mother but a rabbit. Eyes no longer bright blue but a hollow black. A flayed hare hanging in the tree, white fur tinged black, entrails escaping from an open chest.

I scream myself hoarse. Until my throat feels bloody. I scream because I know the woods will swallow it up. I'll bottle my fear, my grief, my frustration, and I'll hide it here in this forest. I let it all out until I have nothing left.

With the last of my screams, I crumple inward, falling to the ground. My nails dig past the snow, all the way to the dirt beneath. I'll root myself here. Some nights I think I can hear her screaming. Some nights I think she never really left.

My eyes lift up, soaking in the cold scenery. The dishwater-gray sky, the dark pine, the never-ending white. I'm not like Cherry or Mom, but even I can't deny that the Morguewood is cursed. It's been tainted forever. Mom spent so many days with her cheek to the glass. *You feel it, too, don't you?* she'd ask, eyes trained on the tree line. *That forest is a graveyard.*

I never felt it then, but I do now.

Your mother isn't missing, my thoughts sing with the wicked vision of her still burned into my mind. *She's dead. You've always thought you could save her from the Clarkes, but how can you save someone they've already killed?*

"They haven't," I chant to myself, and I don't care how loud or frantic I've become. "She isn't dead. She's not, she's not. *She's not.*"

My breath hitches in my chest. I'm no longer alone. I sense it before I even see the silhouette breaking through the trees.

They've come to kill you, too, that same awful voice croons. For an awful, fleeting moment, I believe it.

I only have a second to regret coming out here. Only a moment in time to imagine my father's grief when his family is fished out from the trees.

The shadow focuses, the shape clearing into a boy. He runs toward me, his green eyes wide, all my fear reflected back in him tenfold. His hair is whipped wild, a deep chestnut brown.

All my fear, all my numbness twists and turns in my gut, boiling into a sharp hatred. Elwood Clarke.

I shake my vulnerability off with the snow. No one can see me like this. Especially not him. Why is he here? The thought flutters briefly through my mind, rushing past like the wind. Why isn't he back at the party?

"What the hell?" I snap, hoping he doesn't catch the hitch in my voice. I wait for him to hear me, for his eyes to land on me for the second time tonight, but they don't. They're blurry and unfocused, trained on something beyond me. He breathes in noisily, his legs moving for dear life.

My hatred ebbs for a moment, giving way to confusion.

Elwood nearly mows me over but stops dead in his tracks. The terror dials back on his face and a strange hope takes its place. "W-Wil?"

"What the hell do you want?" I snarl.

You'd think I tased him by the way he jumps. He stands there, whipping around like something might leap out any second and sink its teeth into his neck. God. I ease myself up, running my fingers along my legs.

I gawk at him, soaking in everything I missed. His skin is scraped from branches, and he's shivering profusely. His fingers are a raw, blistering shade of red, and his lips are tinged blue.

I clear my throat, purposefully looking away. Mom's image is carved into my mind; it takes everything to keep my voice level. "I know why I'm out here, but what about you? What's your excuse?"

He looks out in the shadows again, and then lurches back toward me, snatching my arm. "It's—" He shakes his head. "We need to go."

"We are not going anywhere." I yank my hand back, throwing a skeptical look over his shoulder. Nothing. No glowing red eyes, no sharp glint of a knife. His fear is contagious, sinking into me even after I try to swat it away. Maybe it's all the cuts on his skin. The blood is enough to make me squeamish. But I won't give him the satisfaction of seeing me tremble.

"You don't understand."

I steady myself. It's easier said than done. My body acts on muscle memory; my traitorous arms long to wrap around him, my traitorous face keeps wanting to go soft. Thank God for my iron will.

"You're right," I bite through my teeth, "I don't understand."

Frustration wears differently on his skin. Mine manifests in clenched teeth and quivering fists. His is a quiet beast, built less on rage and more on desperation. A shiver works through him, his eyes wide. "Please. I'll explain later. My family is—" But he doesn't get to finish.

A sound breaks through the night: several feet wading through the snow, their boots crunching hard against the ice. Elwood's body stiffens, freezing to stone. He doesn't so much as breathe. He grimaces, and I watch his eyes bulge from their sockets. The darkness shields the strangers in the distance, but each step forward places them closer.

"My family," he mouths.

Here in the shadows of the forest, the words feel heavier. They strip what little air is left from my lungs. Flashlights tear ribbons through the darkness. Light catches in the space beyond my shoulder, a perfect spotlight on the bark. Elwood doesn't need to say anything. We need to go.

I give a dazed nod and my body burns with adrenaline. He yanks my arm, throwing me to his chest before the next beam can reach me. With my skin flush to his, he shields us behind the bloodied bark of the rabbit's tree. Red drips from the branches, slithering a grisly path down his scalp. It rolls like a bead of sweat on his cheek. My eyes dart above him, training on the glossy wet stare of the corpse.

I wonder if it felt anything when they slit its throat. I decide I don't want to know.

Time passes like half-dead roadkill: each second slow and agonizing, an eternity trapped waiting for the end to come. I'm not sure how long we stand like that, chests thumping in tandem, waiting for the lights to click off and the footprints to change course.

Eventually the yellow beam turns elsewhere, cold blue pouring in its place. The footsteps stop altogether and the silence is worse. I clamp a hand over my mouth to soften my breathing, hyperaware of each sputtering breath leaving my lips. My free hand finds Elwood's and there's nothing gentle in the latch of our fingers.

One second. Two.

Just like that, his family retreats. With the last muted step, Elwood peers into the darkness. It takes a swallow, a nod, and a tighter grip of my hand for him to decide to move.

The path I made earlier with my sneakers has been buried over. The snow is up to our knees, but that doesn't matter. We race all the way back, dodging branches and wincing against each pummel of the wind. Ice sprays sharp streaks across my face. I have to wipe the snow from my eyes to see the motel in the distance. It's an ugly finish line, but I'm sprinting toward it.

Minutes blur and I'm only slightly conscious of the change from forest floor to asphalt parking lot. Then the motel door is creaking open like a mausoleum vault. I squint against the yellow lights. They're barely a comforting presence. They seem dingy and unstable, at risk of blinking out. The heat hits me hard with the doors slammed behind my back.

"Jesus." I breathe, for lack of anything better to say. My body has thawed out, but I don't think my brain has.

"I need to hide," Elwood blurts, clearly more alert than I am. "Can you barricade the door? We can . . . uhh . . . push that desk in front of it." He juts a finger out toward the lobby desk—all two hundred pounds of it. I know for a fact I can't move it. I doubt he could, either. Together, we make a useless combo.

I swallow and wait for the words to come. Then I wait a minute longer to find my edge. "Yeah. No. We're not doing that. You honestly look like you're about to collapse, so I guess I've got to make sure you don't keel over. As much as I hate you, if I let you die, the sheriff will be after me. We all know how much of a sweet spot he's got for your family. And then as soon as you're done, you need to get the hell out of here."

"No," he groans, more desperate than I think I've ever heard him in my life. He shakes his head, his skin growing paler by the second. He's starting to look like he's got tuberculosis. That, or like he's a ghost already. "Please."

That's the last thing he says before he slumps to the floor. There's a pooling snow stain on the carpet already, grimy gray ice working into the fibers.

Cherry is going to have a conniption over that when she sees it. My chest aches. Cherry would know what to do here. She wouldn't be racing around like a chicken with its head sliced off. She'd figure it all out. I breathe in—one tight, deep breath that stings when I release it.

There's an untouched first aid kit in the first drawer. I sweep off the thick layer of dust, propping it underneath my arm.

I guess this is it. I'm going to have to play medic and hope to God Elwood pays up in information.

"I don't owe you anything, but fine. God. Just don't die in this motel, got it? Here, Lord knows I can't carry you. Help me out if you can. I'm going to bring you to my room . . . for now." I lower myself beside him, offering a shoulder for him to lean on. He hesitantly takes it. His fingers are frigid against my skin. Almost corpse-like. We wobble and sway down the hall.

We make it to my room after a frustrating five minutes. The plaque reads 103, but I've taken a blade to the metal and carved my name beneath it: WIL.

I prop him to the side, kicking the door open with a grunt. The air in my room is heavy with must. The once-white walls have grayed, the paint peeling in odd spots. Burnt-red carpet clashing with olive-green drapes. A combination that is only festive this time of year and hideous the rest.

Luckily, I have a room with two twin-size beds. One for him to bleed over and the other for me to collapse on later and wonder what I've done. We shuffle awkwardly through all my junk. The broken stereo, a box full of useless old tapes, and other relics of the past.

I kick my trash off the spare bed, knocking it to the floor without the slightest concern for grace. Currently, I don't have the mental capacity for shame.

"I can hear your heart," Elwood comments out of nowhere as I get closer. Each word is breathless.

"Don't say weird shit like that." I sneer at him. "Shut up and let me fix you."

The words feel too heavy on my tongue. It's never been this way. I remember all the times I'd skinned my knee or bruised my knuckles in a fight. The reckless blood in me demanded I scale each tree to the highest branch. Elwood's fingers were always so nimble after. He'd cluck and fuss over me, spinning gauze over my cuts and pressing Band-Aids to my cheek.

But that was then, and this is now.

I hope I don't look as nervous as I feel. Lord help him if he needs stitches. It's not like I can even google it with my prehistoric Tracfone: "WikiHow to save my estranged former friend from dying of hypothermia."

This isn't how I thought we'd meet again after the party. I thought our reunion would involve me backhanding him at our motel's demolition. Cursing him out. Doing something. Not nursing him like he's made of glass.

I walk over to the bathroom, swiping a towel off the rack. The water pours from the faucet, running ice-cold. I wait for it to heat up, hesitantly meeting my own reflection. My hair is slick with snow, my eyeliner smudged from tears. Black ink streaks down my cheeks. I smear myself clean.

Get a grip, Wil, he's not going to die. A little cold and exhaustion won't do him in. I shut the faucet off and head back over to him.

His chest rises and falls faintly. It's enough to propel me forward. I run the towel over his cuts—there's one against the base of his throat and another blooming out of the ripped patch of his knee.

Most of the scrapes are shallow, but there's a couple nasty, deep ones. Specifically, one on his cheek. My fingers linger longer than necessary. I expect him to feel like a stranger, but the touch of him is unnervingly familiar. I'm not sure how long I'd stay there if I could, but I break in seconds the moment I hear him clear his throat. What the hell am I doing? I busy myself with rummaging around in the first aid kit. I'm not sure if antiseptic goes bad or not, but I don't bother looking for an expiration date. I pop off the cap and he winces as it meets his wound.

I throw the towel to the floor along with the first aid kit. The cloth used to be an eggshell sort of white, but it's smeared now with dirt and blood. I swallow. "Here. I'll get you some clothes from my dad. They'll be big on you, but at least . . . erm . . . Just stay alive until then, okay? Can you manage that?"

He looks over at the window. His face has gone unbelievably pale. "I don't want to be alone."

"I'll be back in a couple minutes. Trust me, you still owe me an explanation for . . . all of this." I wave at the air.

For a minute, it looks like he might try and fight me. Like the thought of being alone is too great a burden to bear. It doesn't last. He clamps down on his lip, giving me the world's weakest nod. "Okay."

"I'll be back," I mutter, waving him off. "In the meantime, don't look at or touch any of my shit."

The door creaks shut behind me and I brace myself for what's to come.

CHAPTER EIGHT

ELWOOD

The cold twists around my bones.

My ribs have been replaced with shards of ice and my breath pools out like frozen pine. I twist and turn under Wil's blankets, but nothing will chase the feeling away. It grips greedy talons into my skin.

I wasn't cold in the forest—not when I was running. I've never been athletic; my limbs always felt like twigs, fragile enough to snap in two, but I ran like hell. I ran as fast and as far as I could.

Stronger than the fear, stronger than the cold—a bitter seed blossoms in my gut. My parents were going to . . . what, exactly? Kill me? I know what I heard, but separated from the moment, it feels like fiction.

Only, I know it isn't.

Somewhere deep within the trees, my family is still searching for me. Wil doesn't know the danger I'm in. She doesn't know anything—

Wilhelmina.

Another emotion stirs inside me. Not anger, not fear, but the same guilt I felt back at the party. It seems like ages ago, but the flashing red numbers on her clock suggest it's only been two hours.

I've never been in her room before.

It's cramped, packed so tight with belongings that there's hardly room to breathe. There's a layer of dust over everything. Beneath me, the patchwork quilt is dingy and old. There are cobwebs in the corners and the lingering smell of ash.

My room is a crisp white with very few personal touches aside from my pinnings. All of my shirts and pants are folded neat in the drawers, steamed to get out the wrinkles. Here, she's got clothes wadded everywhere. There's some on the floor, some shoved haphazardly in drawers.

I fight the ache in my bones as I lift myself out of bed. She's right. I need to change out of these clothes. But first, I've earned myself a shower. A real one.

Each step forward is a struggle. *Sleep,* my bones sing, *return to the bed and sleep.* I refuse to listen.

My limbs are no longer so weak that I can't carry myself. In fact, a strange new energy propels me forward.

Don't look at my shit. Don't touch my shit. Wil's voice buzzes in my skull. I shuffle from the bed to the bathroom, awkwardly dancing around all of her things.

The bathroom opens with a rusted groan. The lights take a moment to flicker on, but when they do, I smother a scream. The bedroom doesn't hold a candle to the bathroom. Drawers swung out, piles upon piles of garbage lining the counters; half-empty bottles of shampoo, tipped over into permanent dried goo; shelves collapsing under the weight of all the contents crammed inside; hairbrushes, combs, curlers, an overflowing bin of trash.

I push through it all, grabbing what I hope to be a clean towel off the rack. More of her laundry has migrated in here from the other room. Mismatched socks and a belt that looks suspiciously like a snake in the corner.

The shower floor has a disturbing streak of rust that resembles black mold, but I force myself to step inside anyway. I crank the dial to scalding, but the faucet has other ideas. Ice water spews from the showerhead and it's cold enough to throw me back a step. I grip the tile to keep from toppling over completely. With another gurgle, the water gradually transforms from torturous to bearable. By the time the temperature is finally what I want, I'm already shivering.

The burn is miraculous on my skin. I let it run down, drip off my hair and my brow to the floor. The bliss doesn't last for long.

My life is over.

The realization hits me. I can't go home again. Everything has changed. I need to get out of this town. My father said it himself: next time I sneak out, I'll see the full extent of his wrath. Now that he knows I'm gone, there's a countdown. Seconds ticking away to my last breath. When I become the rabbit in my father's sermon.

The blood beneath my nails has darkened from red to black. My father's hand had gripped my shoulder, and he'd beamed for the whole church to see. For one fleeting moment, I thought he might've been proud of me.

I don't love him, he'd said. No hesitation. *Elwood is a means to an end.*

I fall to the grimy floor and cling tight to my bruised knees. The water rains over me, scalding hot to ice-cold. The tears racing down my cheeks blend seamlessly with the water, blurring together. I'm not sure how long I sit here crying with the pelt of ice on my back. It's an eternity before I lift myself and fumble with the knob to shut it off.

I expect to freeze the second the air hits, but my whole body is burning up.

A splitting migraine shoots throughout my skull. Two knives stabbing through my temples. I massage it, but nothing is enough to drive it away. My mother would know what to do.

She's got an entire arsenal of medicines at home, enough to blur away the slightest bit of discomfort. Wil's got to have something, right?

I swing open the medicine cabinet, but there's nothing tucked away aside from neglected combs, bobby pins, and a bottle of expired melatonin. I let it fall shut and stagger back.

The mirror shows a strange reflection. I see myself—rigid and frozen over, my body heavy like cement, eyes as wide as they'll go. The pain only magnifies each time I move, growing and growing until I feel on the verge of passing out. Wings beat against my ribs. The sound of it travels to my skull, a cicada scream blocking out my thoughts.

My reflection burns in and out of focus. Back and forth like the hypnotic spin of a watch. It clears for a dizzying second and I spot a peel of dead skin on the bridge of my nose. I lean in, close enough to fog the glass, and I pull. The strip doesn't end. I unravel myself piece by piece.

The colors spin and drain off my skin, replaced by a dewy, vivid green. My skull cracks, my already-sharp chin elongating into two pointed pincers. Eyes exploding out of my sockets, growing large and buggy with two inky-black pseudo pupils.

This isn't real. This cannot be happening again. First the moth in the toilet and now *this*.

The whole room transforms with my thoughts, wallpaper bubbling and peeling, bugs scurrying out from the interior—writhing maggots, thick, milky-gray worms, fur-covered tarantulas. A garden full of squirming, buzzing insects.

I scream, jaw unhinging to let out a shriek that tears like a knife's path up my throat. It doesn't even sound human. My voice pitches. Higher and tighter until it's no longer a voice but the smacking of a wet tongue and the clacking scrape of teeth. My humanity chips away, and all I'm doing is chirping. Screeching like an insect hiding in tall grass.

I fall. The ground is buzzing with beetles and the tile breaks to let the dirt in. Squirming roaches and ants that scurry up my legs in a thick black swarm. The vision breaks with the slam of the door.

"What the hell?" Wil asks, and I don't want her to look at me. I don't want her to—

"Dude, are you okay? I heard screaming." Her eyes catch on my slicked hair, and she twists away with blooming cheeks.

I trace the curved path of my jaw and feel around for any monstrous qualities hidden beneath the skin. Nothing. The room has gone back to normal, too. The wallpaper has glued back to the wall and the tiles beneath me are grimy but relatively intact. Swiveling around, I search my reflection in the mirror. I see nothing out of the ordinary. No more bulging, buggy eyes or sharp pincers.

Everything is back to the way it was. Just like last time. "I—I'm sorry. I thought . . ."

"You thought?" she prompts, but I only shake my head. "What? That the world was ending?"

Yes.

"I-it's nothing," I insist, and I marvel at the sound of my own voice. So very human. "I—I don't know."

She furrows her brows. For a second something strange crosses her features, but like the vision, it fades just as easily as it came. "God, Clarke. You're not supposed to take a shower when you've got hypothermia . . . Whatever. Here, I snagged some of Dad's clothes for you. Put something on, for Christ's sake."

She offers me a wad of clothes and I use what little energy I have left to change into them. I lift my arms through the sleeves and pull on the pair of too-loose sweatpants and a hoodie with Bass Pro Shops on the front. "Th-thank you."

I try to follow her back into the room, but my legs have grown weak. They barely feel like they belong to me. Left foot, right foot, left—

I hit the ground face-first. The pain comes in an explosive, short burst. I grimace, cradling my nose and hissing against the pulsing flare of heat.

"Dude, what is with you today? You're weirder than usual. Are you still drunk?" She gets close—too close—and her nose scrunches like an alcohol-detecting bloodhound.

With her face inches away from mine, I catch all the little things I missed before. The clump of mascara, her lashes sticking in odd places; a tiny mole in the middle of her cheek, another one grazing the skin of her jaw; sharp teeth, a few of them bent inward. Things that shouldn't be endearing but are.

"No, I don't think I am." I shake my head and marvel at how normal my fingers look. "Something's wrong, though. Really, really wrong."

I don't realize my knee is trembling until she grips it tight. "Tell me." No longer a question but a demand.

My mouth is unbearably dry. The only thing I taste is the sharp bite of blood. "I turned into a bug," I confess. "I thought I did, at least, but I shifted back."

She squints. "You took something at the party, didn't you?"

"No! I—I know how it sounds, but it happened, I swear. I'm not on drugs. This isn't the first time. I threw up at the party, Wil."

That breaks the silence. "A keg stand will do that," she quips, offering me a hand so I can get off the grimy floor.

I take it with another desperate shake of my head. "No, not like that. I threw up a moth." Anything she had planned to say dies on her lips and she clamps her mouth closed. "And now in your bathroom I saw my . . . my skin peeling and . . ." The words aren't coming, so I mimic pincers with my fingers.

"I'm going to stop you right there, wonder boy." Wil hisses in a deep breath and nods for me to sit down on the bed and shut up. "I don't know if you're hallucinating or tripping or what, but I can promise you that you didn't turn into a praying mantis in my bathroom." She sets a mug beside me on the bedside table. "Here, drink this and sober the hell up. I figured I'd brew you something warm. It's coffee, sorry. I know you hate it, but it's all we have. I dumped the last of our sugar in. You're welcome."

I cradle it in my hands and shiver against the heat.

The first sip is brutal, but I barrel through it. Dad drinks a cup every morning.

He allowed me a sip once. It took all of my focus and concentration to even get it down in the first place. He snorted at my sour expression, drawing it back for a hearty gulp. "You can soften it with cream and sugar, but that would make it into something it isn't. It needs to be harsh to rattle you awake." My father grimaced down into his cup then. "You don't need to like it; you just need to drink it."

I swallow a bitter gulp.

Wil settles on the bed beside me. Her inky-black hair barely grazes her shoulders. When we were younger, back when I knew her, it fell down past her waist. She'd twist it into a tight braid, and I'd often be responsible for picking out the twigs and leaves caught inside.

I still remember the way it felt twisting around my finger. I swallow.

A dozen studs and hoops litter each of her ears. She only had three last year. I would know.

You don't know her now. She's become someone else. Before her sneer, I remember the smile that stretched cheek to cheek. The subtle indent of dimples on both sides. I remember her laughter—soft and lyrical and at odds with everything you'd expect from a girl so tough.

She pulls a face, her brown eyes narrowed.

"So, can you tell me what's really going on? Aside from the . . . erm, *bug* thing, what's up with your family?"

I shake my head. "I don't know."

"Why would a Goody Two-shoes like you run away?" Her voice is as sharp as the branches in the forest. Maybe she'll draw blood, too.

I can't bring myself to admit it. Not out loud.

The silence that hangs between us is enough to make her curse. "I'm going to start charging you extra for wasting my time."

"Charging?" I parrot.

"Yes, Elwood. Charging. You don't get to waste my time for free. Of course, I also have to factor in room service"—she points at the steaming cup beside me—"emergency care, staying in the luxury suite."

This? The luxury suite?

"I don't have money," I blurt, and for the first time in my life, it's true. Without my parents, I'm alone. No money. No belongings. Nothing at all. Nothing but the fear brewing in my gut.

"Of course you do, Clarke." She draws out my last name like it's a scathing insult. "Your family has enough money to buy our motel and demolish it for fun."

I've never liked being called Clarke. The name doesn't fit. It's too large for someone so small. I clear my throat and taste the tang of blood. "Fine. You're right. I ran away from home." There. It's out now. The words take shape in the air and I fear they might lace their fingers across my throat and throttle me. There's a sharp finality to them. Nothing I can take back or fix. I ran away from home and now the sin of it will brand itself on my skin.

"My dad caught me. The one time in my life I sneak out and he catches me. He catches me and he—" Stalks toward me, his rage spitting off him like embers, lips pulled back in a snarl as he shatters everything I love. "He called the rest of the church over. They were talking about me like I didn't mean anything . . . I'm sorry. I don't know. Sheriff Vrees was there and my dad said he didn't love me and—" My voice cracks, hitching up like in puberty.

Silence spills like lake-born fog. It hangs over us, heavy and thick and unyielding. "What?" Wil asks, breathless.

"They were talking about making sure I don't escape again before Prudence gives birth." I hiccup and burrow deeper beneath the covers. "Wil . . . I swear I didn't know my dad was buying your place. I had no clue. Believe me."

Muted, dull moonlight pushes across the room. It can only do so much, though. "Prudence? Vrees's wife?"

"Yes." I breathe in—deep and full—and I feel the swell and rise of my chest. "They want me dead. They talked about cutting something out of me and putting it in the baby and—I'm sorry, this is too much."

"It was all so obvious," Wil whispers, and it's unlike her to be soft. "The Garden of Adam is some fucked-up cult. And this whole time with Vrees I thought he was inept or bribed, but I never stopped to think he and his wife were in on it. Holy hell, Elwood, *Vrees is in on it!* This is big. This is incredibly big."

Outside, the snow rages onward. Wil's words whip across my bare skin as cold as the wind rushing beyond the windowpane. Father always said the cold makes you feel alive in all the worst possible ways. It sparks an energy in you, a desperation that you didn't even know you had. The cold shows you who you truly are.

I'm afraid of what it says about me. "Did they say anything about my mom?"

I shake my head. "Nothing that I heard." My fingernails carve into the flesh of my arm, sparking the comforting bloom of pain. I am alive. I am very, very alive.

Beyond the curtains, the woods have crept closer. They hum and murmur among themselves, and I worry my words will carry back to the church. I want to bite each word back.

I tuck myself smaller and throw my arms over my knees.

Wil's eyes burn in my peripheral vision, but I don't turn to look. I can't.

"I'll help you," she says, her tone shifting. "I won't let your parents find you, I promise. You help me get dirt on your family and find my mom, and I'll hide you as long as you need. Free of charge or whatever. Then when your parents get fitted in orange jumpsuits, we'll both be happy."

Betrayal is a family of scars on my skin. Every time I made the mistake of uttering Wil's name aloud under my parents' roof. "I can't incriminate my family."

She looks exactly as I expected her to: massively frustrated. "You said they were going to kill you." It's so black-and-white coming from her, but in my mind, it's as muddled as the snow, one indistinguishable blur of right and wrong.

"I've never gone against my parents."

"There's a first for everything, isn't there?" She doesn't miss a beat. "Besides, you don't have much of a choice here, do you?"

I hate it, but she's right. If I had a choice, I wouldn't have run and when I got here, my first instinct wouldn't have been to burrow under a bed and pray it all away.

Home is a knife slash across my throat and a collection of shattered, torn wings. "Okay." One little word weighs more than everything. "I'll help you."

With my sinful path cemented, I fall back completely.

The bed groans beneath my weight. I wish the mattress would swallow me whole and take me away. I haven't lifted the corner to check for bedbugs, but I'm too worn out to get back up. Maybe I'll help spruce up tomorrow. Maybe I'll give this place a top-to-bottom cleaning for my own sanity. Or maybe the terror will catch up to me fully and I won't be able to do anything at all.

"It's settled, then." Wil's eyes are locked on her patch of the ceiling. It's like we're looking up at the stars, tracing constellations with our fingers. An entire peel-and-stick universe hangs above us, glowing a faint luminescent green.

"You still love space, huh?" I mutter to distract myself.

"I'm not as obsessed about it as you and your bugs, but . . . there's something appealing about getting as far away from this place as you can get," Wil mumbles, tracing out the Big Dipper with her finger. "If it wasn't for Mom, I'd be out of this stupid town. Buy a bus ticket and go wherever it takes me and never come back." She sniffs, looks away. "Mom did this for me. It would have been so easy to paste all the stars and be done with it, but she made them into constellations just for me."

"Your mom loved you a lot." The words slip out on their own. I blink at the popcorn ceiling, keeping the tears from trickling down my face. I wonder how much asbestos this place has. I wonder if the walls around me have lead paint. "I shouldn't have said that back at Lucas's place."

She's quiet—just the steady up-and-down of her chest, the beating of her heart.

"Please don't speak about her in the past tense."

I open my mouth to say sorry, but she shuts me up with a look. "You don't need to comment on it, Elwood. I've already got my collection of sorrys." Her expression is rigid. "If you told someone what happened to you, would 'sorry' help?"

Sorry your collection is smashed. Sorry your family doesn't love you.

Sorry for what's to come when they catch you. "You're right, I'm sor—I'll shut up."

"I lost everyone in the same week. My mom, my dad in every sense that counts, and you."

"I didn't have a choice." There's a desperate edge to my voice that surprises me. "You accused my family."

"And now look at you. Here." She bites the word out, and her voice is harsher than I've ever heard it. Or maybe it's the truth that's harsh. "Do you think I would have burned that bridge if I didn't have to?" Her voice is the one breaking now.

"You made me choose."

"And you chose," she trails off, swatting tears off her face. "God, I hate you." The wind rushes harder outside, banging against the glass.

There's so much venom packed in those four words that even she recoils. Each word hits like a bullet, planted deep in my chest. There's nothing to say after that—even if I wanted to, the pain is too much. I've deluded myself this entire time. Deep down, I always knew she hated me, but if I kept my distance, I could pretend she didn't. I could fool myself into believing things would be good again one day.

My eyelids grow heavy, worn down from holding back tears. The blanket feels like a coffin door, trapping me underneath its weight. Luckily, when I sleep, I see nothing.

I am thankful for the darkness.

CHAPTER NINE

WIL

I don't wake up to the sun shining and the birds chirping. I wake up to Elwood Clarke losing his shit.

He launches himself upright, his chest heaving with every turbulent, noisy breath. The shirt I gave him clings tight with sweat. Some of it trickles down the side of his face, sticking to him like morning dew on the lawn. His bedhead gives mine a run for its money.

"All of that was real," he pants.

"Good morning to you too," I grumble, throwing a less-than-enthusiastic look in his direction.

Even mid-freak-out he manages to look decent. His eyelashes are ridiculously long and I don't see evidence that he's had a pimple ever. Maybe his parents have him on Accutane as a preventative. I follow the slope of his nose and the curve of his jaw.

When I first met him, his ears were far too big for his face and his arms were comically long in comparison to his body. He was a puppy growing into his paws. The last year has changed us both. He's gotten better-looking, and I've steadily gotten uglier. My hair is . . . well, my hair. I wouldn't say I've broken out recently, since it would imply I've ever had clear skin. Stress has made a home in my brain and in my oil glands.

The black bags are a bonus. I'm a mess.

A shiver sweeps over me, and I turn my rage over to the heavy draft spilling in from the window. Every winter I try to fix it with a good roll of duct tape. I'm not a handyman and I don't know the first thing about draft repairs, but I do know duct tape. Unfortunately, my polka-dot duct tape is doing nothing today. I've got a smatter of probably permanent goose bumps along my bare arms.

I swing my legs over the bed and use my feet to fling back a crumpled hoodie from the floor. It passes the five-second stain-and-BO test, so I bite the bullet and throw it on. It's got PLANET HOLLYWOOD—ORLANDO scrawled across the front.

Spoiler: I've never been to Planet Hollywood, Orlando. Someone from Goodwill has, though.

"My dad is going to kill me," Elwood moans into his knees. He's exaggerating, but it doesn't take long for him to realize that he isn't too far off. His dad might literally murder him.

I can't think about that, though, because that feeds into a different fear I don't want to believe—that my mother isn't trapped and waiting for me somewhere but long dead. There's always been a part of me kept smothered, a nagging worry that my instincts aren't far off. All the times I've looked to the trees and the world around me and grasped for a connection—*I am here. I am alive*—but never finding anything. The line between us is pulled so taut, frayed and worn, would I even notice if it had been severed?

I force the idea away for now because it's too big a truth for me to swallow.

"Your dad won't get the chance," I say, and mean it. "You forget I hate the man more than anyone else on this planet. I'd gladly fight him on your behalf."

As infuriating and awful as Elwood is, I have to admit I need him. Cherry's words cycle in my head on a constant loop. With enough evidence and with a witness, I can fix this. Mom's disappearance, solved.

The motel, saved. The Clarkes and Sheriff Vrees locked behind bars for the rest of their lives.

Elwood stares at me. His eyes are unnervingly green. I break away on instinct.

"Before we figure out how the hell to go about this, let's figure out breakfast," I suggest. He doesn't reply; he's too busy stress-clawing at his skin. He did that freshman year too. Whenever he got really nervous back then, he'd start worrying his fingers and scratching his skin bloody. Good to know some things haven't changed. Altogether, he looks thoroughly Off His Shit, so I wave away the idea of him following me to the kitchen.

"I'll grab something. I guess stay put. If your dad jumps out from under the bed, give me a holler and I'll come back and kick his ass."

In a miraculous feat that only Jesus himself could perform, my dad is up before the wee hours of one p.m. Well, he's kind of awake. He looks half dead at the kitchen table, but that's kind of his "look." His hair is wild and spiky, and he's wearing the old robe I "got" him when I was ten. Really, Mom bought it for him, but she let me sign my name on the card. His eyes are blurry and unfocused, his breath reeks of whiskey. It's nothing new. He carries the scent like it's his go-to brand of cologne. Whiskey and Trash, the signature edition.

I make a noise in my throat. He won't get a good morning from me, but he'll get a humph. "I know you're upset, Minnie," he mutters as I sweep right past him to the coffee maker. I throw a glance his way, but he isn't looking back at me. He's too busy fiddling with the tear in his sleeve. The robe looked great when I was ten. Now it looks like something he fished out of the garbage.

He clears his throat, and it sounds like a fork going down a garbage disposal. "I thought I heard you talking to someone last night. Did you have a friend over?"

"Must've imagined it." I shrug. It's not technically a lie. He said "friend," not "estranged former best friend." And even then, I would shrug him off. It's none of Dad's business. He doesn't get to pick and choose when to care about me.

"I could have sworn I heard—"

I'm about to say *you're hearing things*, but then Elwood decides now is the best time to show up in the doorway. Dad might not be looking at me, but he's certainly looking at him.

Elwood shuffles forward like a newborn calf. I wait for the wrong gears in Dad's head to turn. The two of us. Here. In pajamas. Clearly disheveled. Elwood absolutely drenched through with sweat. Dad chokes on his own breath.

"H-hello, Mr. Greene." Elwood's breaking out in stress hives already. The color rises from his neck to his face to the tips of his ears. He shrinks in on himself, his shoulders slouching like he might vanish if he puts his mind to it. He must not try hard enough, though, because a minute stretches by and he hasn't evaporated into thin air.

He opens his mouth, but he doesn't get the chance to finish.

The sound of the lobby door echoes down the hall, and Elwood jumps faster than I can blink.

I watch all the red bleed away to a ghostly white. His eyes bulge and a full-blown shiver travels beneath his skin.

"Hello?" The voice is deep and familiar and aggravating. It's followed by the rush of wind and the harsh slam of the door falling shut on rusty hinges. I'd know it anywhere. Elwood's father. Everything that comes out of Mr. Clarke's mouth sounds like it's spoken in italics. He sounds like Siri if Siri only talked about the Lord.

"I'd be surprised to find him here, Ezekiel," another voice grunts. On the flip side, Sheriff Vrees can't be bothered to enunciate. He talks like his mustache is choking him. I wish it would. "They have a hard enough time finding actual guests. Frankly, this place would look better as a parking lot."

"He's not here," I mouth to Dad. "Make them go."

After a full second of me mouthing obscenities, Dad sighs and sits up. What comes next is a weak gesture for us to scramble into the walk-in pantry and another quick motion to be quiet about it.

Dad doesn't need to tell Elwood twice. Elwood would gladly sink into our floorboards and never come back out if presented with the option. Elwood sneaks in first and I follow suit. Between the cracks, I give Dad a slight nod before slowly pulling the door shut. "Good morning, Sheriff Vrees," I hear Dad call out. I can't imagine how he must look, strolling out to the lobby in his pajamas. His voice is formal enough, but anything pleasant saps from his tone as soon as he says, "Good morning, Clarke. Suppose the two of you aren't looking for a room?"

I shuffle where I stand, looking around at the shadowy imprints of shelves. For a walk-in pantry, it's pretty barren of actual food. We've got some old Cheerios and a couple trays' worth of ramen. Aside from that, I spot a can of spinach that expired two years ago.

It's a far cry from the past. Before depression mowed Dad over like a semitruck, he doubled as a chef. We weren't the run-down pit we are today. Dad's whole dream for this place was a bed-and-breakfast. He'd rise at the crack of dawn every morning to start cooking for guests, and the wildest part was he loved it.

Now, unless Cherry's the one cooking for me, most of my meals are of the microwavable variety. Frozen nuggets, withered and limp "lasagna," ribs that both taste and smell like dog food.

With Dad's ambitions shot dead, he's used this pantry as yet another storage space for all our old junk. It's packed to the brim with boxes sealed over in both tape and dust.

There's hardly enough space to breathe. Elwood's chest is smashed into my back and I can feel the rampant drumbeat of his heart. It sounds ready to jump ship into my ribs. I grip his hand tight.

He goes perfectly still.

"We're looking for my son," Mr. Clarke announces. "Is he here? Snuck off with your daughter, perhaps?" He says *daughter* like it's the worst insult imaginable. Maybe it is. I'm not exactly the darling of Pine Point.

"Last I checked," Dad counters, his voice shockingly smooth, "my daughter stopped talking to your son over a year ago." His words hold a much heavier punch. I'm sure it isn't lost on anyone in the room. A year ago—when Mom disappeared and the first accusation was flung Clarke's way.

"I don't appreciate your tone, Mr. Greene," Mr. Clarke returns, and his voice is cut sharp. I imagine him huffing and puffing in our lobby. A navy-blue scarf twisted tight around his throat, a matching coat clutched tight to his chest, probably sneering at all the dust. "He could have come here to spite me."

I can't imagine Elwood doing anything to spite anyone.

"Do you see any room keys off the rack?" Dad asks, and I have to hand it to him. He's carrying this act better than I anticipated. "He's not here."

I'm sure that little tidbit will come back to bite me later, but for now it works.

"Doesn't matter," Elwood's dad insists, though he sounds like he's losing some of his earlier steam. "We still need a top-to-bottom search of the place."

Elwood's fingers tighten against my own. Any tighter and he's going to break my hand in two. I jab him in the ribs and he loosens up.

"It'll be much easier for you to search the rubble after you've demolished it, Clarke," Dad says. He's reining in a temper much better than I would. If I were out there, I would have decked Elwood's dad in the face by now. "You're wasting your time. Until then, you can't go through here without a warrant. Sheriff Vrees, you, out of everyone, should know that much."

There's a snort on Vrees's end. "You a lawyer now, Greene?" Silence.

"Sure, that won't be hard to work up," Mr. Clarke says. "This place is a walking health code violation."

Dad snaps something, but it's too soft to hear. A quieter argument unfolds, followed by the angry stomp of heeled dress shoes. Then comes the sound of creaky hinges and wind whistling in. The blizzard is cut off midscream by the slam of the door.

One second passes. Two and three and four and five.

My father returns and the kitchen door slides to a close behind him.

"Okay," Dad says, and I feel Elwood's hand jolt back to his side. "The two of you can come out now."

CHAPTER TEN

WIL

Elwood looks ready to purge, so Dad, oblivious as ever, starts cooking pancakes.

It's weird having *Dad* and *cooking* in the same sentence. I'm used to *Dad* and *takeout* or *Dad* and *Lean Cuisine*. I haven't had an honest-to-God meal in ages.

"Sorry, I'm a bit rusty." Dad gestures down at what should be pancakes. It looks more like gristle and chocolate. "Forgot they were cooking for a second there."

I scrunch my nose at the heavy cloud of smoke. I'm surprised the alarm hasn't started screaming at us. God forbid the sprinkler system kicks in. After he whipped his last platter, Dad threw the pan with all the other dishes in the sink. There's a whole leaning tower with the pan on the top like a Christmas tree star.

"Thanks," Elwood mutters, accepting the plate without so much as a curl of his lip. He sounds so shot, so absolutely dead inside, that I can hardly fend off the feeling it stirs in me.

"You're welcome." Dad pushes the remaining air out from his lungs in a long-winded sigh.

"I used to cook all the time, right, Wil?"

I remember him serving me and Mom breakfast in the morning—pancakes fluffy and oozing with chocolate. He'd always have a glass of orange juice waiting for me on the kitchen table (the same one collecting past-due bills now). Things were, dare I say, normal.

If you marry someone one day, Mom said once, licking hollandaise off her fork, *make sure they can cook*. If Dad was in earshot, he'd always follow up with, "So that Elwood kid in culinary class?" which would earn a swat and blush on my end.

"Mm-hmm," I deadpan, slicing through a miserable chunk on my plate. Chocolate goo spurts out from the center. That's all he's going to get from me.

Dad clears his throat and tries again. "I didn't think the two of you were friends again."

"We're not," I reply, with a mouthful of pancake.

"Oh . . . Okay. Um." Dad drums his fingers against the wood. If he's looking to connect with me, the father-daughter bridge is burned to hell. Any chance now involves treading through gator-infested waters, and we all know "effort" isn't in Dad's vocabulary. Sure enough, he twists away from me and turns to Elwood. "You know you can't hang out here forever. I ran away once as a kid. Eventually, your dad will—"

Elwood bristles at the mention of his father. The pancakes slide down his throat hard, and he has to gulp some juice to keep from choking. "I know," he says, already panicking. The color's all but sapped completely from his face. "I know he's going to find me."

Way to go.

Unable to close his mouth for all of five seconds, Dad starts back up for the third time. "So, uh . . . about the no-keys-off-the-rack thing, erm, I assume you're staying in Wil's room." He looks between us both, his eyes shifty and uncomfortable. I can already tell what awful, embarrassing direction he's planning on taking this in. "I can trust the two of you not to . . . um . . . do anything you shouldn't."

There it is. I knew that was coming.

"*Dad*," I howl. Now I'm the one choking on pancakes. My sick subconscious throws back an image of Elwood fresh from the shower, towel hung loose to his hips, hair slick and dripping down his chest—

I need a lobotomy.

"I mean, your mom and I were young once, so I know how things are," Dad backtracks, though he pushes his plate forward like he's lost his appetite. That makes two of us now. "I don't want any accidents."

Elwood's cheeks burn bright crimson.

"God. No. Gross, Dad." My chair scrapes the floor as I stand up. "Elwood is here to hide from his family, and that's it. Why do you have to make things so weird?"

It's Dad's turn to go red. He sucks in his lips, clamping down with his teeth to keep from saying anything else. He should've done that sooner.

So much for breakfast.

Neither of us talks back in the room.

I mean, honestly, what does one say after that? Sorry that your dad's on the hunt for you. Sorry that my own dad implied you might knock me up if you're not careful. Sorry you didn't disappear into thin air like you wanted. If you figure that one out, let me know.

Silence with Elwood is the worst. It's so hard to weasel myself into his thoughts. Borderline impossible. He's got a fortress of a mind, and I've always been left at the gate. He sits there at the foot of the bed and stares down at the grimy carpet at his feet.

When he does open his mouth, fear drips off every letter: "Your dad's right. It's only a matter of time before my father catches up with me."

Dad really shouldn't have said that. I cough, crossing my arms over my chest and trying to look tougher than I feel. "My dad is rarely right about anything. I told you I'd keep you safe and I'm not backing down on that. You better not back down on your side of the deal either."

He doesn't acknowledge that at all. After five seconds of staring at the floor, he buries his head in his hands. "The whole town's looking for me and it hasn't even been a day. I'm doomed."

"You're not doomed." I snarl. Jesus, he's melodramatic.

"I feel doomed."

Sympathy isn't easy. Expressing it, at least. The words get jumbled on my tongue and I have no idea what to do with my hands or my face or anything. I plop down beside him and rest my elbow on my torn-denim knee. "Well, you're not, so shut up."

Okay, maybe that wasn't very sympathetic. I cough and try again. "You're going to be okay. I promise." There, that sounds mildly convincing.

Except I guess not, because now he's crying. He tears himself away from his self-pity cocoon, and I see that his eyes are red-rimmed and watery.

The sight carves through my chest. Makes me feel weird and hollow and gutted. I don't mean to, but my fingers reach out in a fit of muscle memory. They twist through his hair, my thumb tracing slow circles against his scalp. I used to do this back when things were different. Back when he'd hold in tears for too long, his emotions flooding all at once. When it was just us against the rest of the world.

I lurch and sit on my traitorous fingers. I no longer trust myself.

The bridge of his nose is flushed soft pink, and I watch as he smears away his emotions with a sleeve. *My father told me boys shouldn't cry,* Elwood confided to me in sixth grade, his face puffy from fresh tears. *But it's so hard to hold it in. How do you do it?*

I make myself go numb, I told him. I do that now. I soak in everything and tuck it away. I recenter myself with the task at hand: get answers.

I clear my throat, feeling strangely sheepish. "We need to start searching for answers today, and we're sure as hell not going to find them in the motel. I was planning on breaking into your house when we bumped into each other."

His eyes go buggy, and as ridiculous as he looks, it's a welcome change from crying. "Wait, go back, you were going to break into my house?"

My nightly escapades never sound that great coming from other people. "Something like that, yeah. You wouldn't have noticed, though. I'm stealthy when I want to be. Have you ever seen me taking photos before?"

Luckily, I'm too busy rummaging under the bed to see his reaction. I'm sure his eyes have popped right out of his skull.

"Wil, are you trying to tell me you've been stalking me? Wait, I thought I saw something in the bushes two weeks ago. I thought you were a raccoon."

"Eh, honest mistake." The space under my bed is packed with shit. It doesn't matter, though. I know exactly where my box of evidence is. It used to hold size 7 Skechers, but now it's home to a million incriminating photos. "You're a boring guy to stalk, Elwood."

"I'm . . . sorry?"

"You should be, but don't worry, my Saturdays weren't all wasted." I dump the contents of the box beside him, and he jumps. Hundreds of blurry photos of his family spread across my duvet, and I gotta say, it looks pretty damning together like this.

"Holy sh—" He stops himself with a bite of his lip.

"Were you about to say *shit*?" I snort. "I've never heard you curse. Kinda assumed you had some parental-control chip in your brain."

I expect him to squawk and squabble, but when he doesn't do anything, I'm forced to shift gears. The humor drains right out. "Okay, okay, it's not the most ethical thing I've done. God. Don't look at me like that, Clarke. I never peeked into your windows or anything." Both of our faces burn crimson at that and I swat the idea away. "All of these were taken from the outside. Your father sacrificing animals in the woods, your mother wearing Mom's jewelry, your dad walking into the church and literally never coming out one night. The next morning he was back at your house. I swear to God I didn't fall asleep, but—"

"And this one?" Elwood asks, his fingers deftly lifting the one photo I should've burned. "Give me that." No amount of slapping my face will beat away this blush, but I'm determined to try when he lifts it out of my reach. If my face gets any hotter, the Smokey Bear fire danger sign outside is going to have to be bumped up to "high."

"I didn't mean to take this one. Give it back."

Elwood's photo captures a rare smile. Genuine and blooming wider in the summer breeze.

He'd been sitting outside of his house by his mother's garden, and in true Disney Princess fashion, there'd been butterflies fluttering overhead . . . and if I'd liked the way the afternoon glow settled upon his skin, that's my business, not his.

He can be frustrating when he wants to be. "How long were you watching me?"

"Oh, you're one to talk," I quip, and this might only embarrass me further, but I'm bringing out the big guns here. There's another shoebox I've kept under my bed. One I should've parted with, but never had the heart to. I dredge it out in the open, and by God, does it work like a charm.

"Y-you kept all of this?" he stammers.

My own face stares back a thousand times; I exist on torn parchment paper, notebook margins, and the crinkly expanse of a napkin. Elwood left these little doodles for me like cats offering fresh kills to their owners.

"Evidently." I swallow. "You think you would have gotten tired of sketching me over and over again. How many different ways can you draw greasy hair and a permanent scowl?"

He opens and closes his mouth like an airborne fish. I wait for him to deny any of it, but he doesn't breathe a word. What did I expect—him to sing my praises? Have some flattering, wonderful reason for drawing me so damn much? I was the only person who talked to him for years at school. Obviously I'd be his only muse. It's not like it meant anything else.

I kick the box aside and if I'm being honest with myself—which I rarely ever am—it stings more than it should.

"Whatever. We're not here to talk about that or the stupid photo in your hand. We're here to talk about your lunatic father." I thumb one photo off the top. I don't care what I grab as long as it acts as a distraction. I glance at the image and I'm in luck: perfect segue achieved. "There's a handful of photos of him at the library, too. That seems to be one of his haunts aside from church and your house. Didn't think a place like that would be his scene. I doubt he's checking out Stephen King. Does he have a permanent hold on the Bible or something?"

Elwood has miraculously regained his ability to talk. "Libraries aren't just for books, Wil. There's records there too, you know? He's probably checking out the town ledger or something."

Town ledger. The two words blow the dust off the gears in my head. "What sort of things would be in a ledger like that?"

He's the same Elwood as in class, always so eager to lift his hand and prattle off answers. "Everything. Anything. It's the best way to preserve our history. Important dates, births, deaths, you name it. My father is very good at record keeping."

Those same gears start spinning. "It's settled, then."

For as quick as he was before, he's slow on the uptake now. "What's settled?"

"We need that book."

"If it's even a hair out of place, Dad will know I've taken it." El-wood scratches his cheek, his eyes darting to the window. I've swung the blinds closed, but some of the Morguewood manages to peer through the cracks. The once-familiar land has grown wild in the storm. "Besides, what if he sees me?"

I shake off his concern. "It's the perfect time to go. You said it your-self. You can't risk anyone seeing you. What's better than an empty library on Christmas Eve?"

He mulls that over, and I can see the indent from him gnawing on his cheek. "How are we going to get there?"

"I've got a bike."

"So you're suggesting we skid down icy streets totally in the open?"

Damn him for making sense. I massage the tension between my eyes and rack my brain for anything useful. Walking is an obvious no, and Dad's car is a rusted hunk of junk, and loud, at that. The horn might as well honk Elwood's name into the streets. They'd see it immediately. How else could we possibly get there?

Seriously, Wil, anything you need. I'll be here. Anarchy sisters for life, remember?

"I think I've got an idea."

My fingers glide over Ronnie's number. With the numbers punched in, I count each ring. "Pick up, pick up, pick up."

"Yello?"

That is most definitely not the voice I wanted to hear. Lucas yawns into the other end, his voice thick with sleep. I hear the rustle of bed-sheets, the swipe of a hand to his eyes.

Goddamn it, the two of them hooked up.

"I'm sorry, I thought I called Ronnie's phone. If I wanted to talk to you, I would've chanted NFL three times in the mirror." I'm genuinely pissed now. Elwood goes full deer-in-the-headlights at me. I wave him away.

Lucas's whole tone shifts. "You've got some nerve. I still can't believe you shoved me back at Earl's."

"Yeah, whatever, I didn't call to talk about your bruised ego," I interject.

"Asshole," he huffs. Luckily, he doesn't hang up on me right then and there. "What did you call for?" It's less of a question and more of an accusation. An interrogation lamp swung my way. I envision his face tensing, his brows pushing inward.

"To talk to Ronnie. This is her phone, after all."

He can't argue with that. I hear the click of a speakerphone.

"Who is it?" Ronnie mumbles in the background. I can picture her face smashed into one of Lucas's pillows. Her makeup is probably smudged from last night, and her hair is frizzy the way it always is in the morning before she smooths it out.

"Wil," Lucas grumbles.

My name's as good as coffee to her. Hell, it's better than cocaine. It wakes her up fast. "Wil! Hi! Sorry! I can explain. Lucas and I . . . After I dropped you off, I mean, well . . . He texted me and . . ."

"Yeah, this isn't the first time y'all have hooked up. I know the drill." Ronnie's one of those people who has to make a mistake a million times before she gives something up. Same with her prehistoric straightener that kept singeing off her hair. Took her ages to throw that thing in the trash, and by then she'd lost entire chunks of her hair.

"Um . . ." She still sounds guilty as hell. She strains for a subject change. "What's up?"

Elwood scooches in closer to listen, and I have to inch away from him to keep his shoulder from touching mine.

I highly doubt the police are sophisticated enough to tap phones, but I'm not gonna risk it.

"I was hoping for a ride," I say, which, in all honesty, isn't a lie.

"A ride?" she repeats. "To where?"

"The library."

"It's Christmas Eve. The library's closed, duh," Lucas says, only to immediately get punched in the shoulder. He winces, letting out an "Owww" underneath his breath. I nearly forgot the two of them were on speakerphone.

"Don't be a jerk."

"Lucas, if you want a black eye, all you had to do was ask," I snap, and I hope he knows I mean it. "I don't care if it's closed. I need a ride."

"Can't it wait?" Lucas tries again, probably wanting to get back to whatever godless act he was in the middle of before I called him. On Christmas Eve, of all days. Though I do have to commend Ronnie on her sneaking-out ability.

"No," I respond, with all the fake sweetness I can muster. "It can't."

Ronnie gulps. I can hear the rustle of sheets again as she sits upright. "Okay, Wil, we'll be there in five."

"What do you mean 'we'——?"

Lucas hangs up before I get an answer.

CHAPTER ELEVEN

ELWOOD

Lucas and Wil decide the perfect time and place for World War III is right here in the car. "What part of 'subtle' did you not understand?" she gripes, her finger launching in Kevin's direction as soon as she opens the door. He sits like contraband in the back seat and his smile slips clean off his face. "Are we stopping along the way to pick up Brian Schmidt too, or is he already hiding out in your trunk? Might as well schedule a town parade while we're at it."

Kevin coughs out an "Uh, I can leave," but Lucas is having none of it.

"Ignore her, Kevin. Sit down and shut up, Greene. You said you wanted to go to the library." Lucas hurls her attitude right back at her. "Ergo, I brought Kevin. The guy who literally works at the library and has keys. What? Did you expect us to break in?"

She huffs, and when it's clear she's got no intention of buckling up, I snake a shy hand across from her and pull the belt into place. She throws me a withering look before returning to Lucas. "It would've been easy."

"Yeah, no. Some of us have futures to think about. Speaking of . . ." Lucas finds my reflection in the rearview mirror. I could be on the FBI's Most Wanted list and he still wouldn't stare any harder than he does now. "What the hell is going on with you, dude?"

The sight of him has my teeth chattering. His blond curls are smashed beneath a red knit cap and the rest of him is zipped up in a thick Patagonia jacket. Red plaid manages to peek out from the zipper, and I'm sure even that is thermal.

"Um," I start. I don't finish. The wind punches at the glass, hungry and clawing for what it can't have.

"I'm going to need a little more than an 'um' here. Your dad and Sheriff Vrees barged into my house looking for you. You've got 'Missing' posters, for Christ's sake. I'm surprised they don't have helicopters out yet." He glances at the sky like they might swoop down any second. "What happened after we dropped you off? And why are you with her—? Don't tell me the two of you are a thing again."

"Jesus," Wil says, and I try not to think too hard about how disgusted she sounds. "Once again to you and the rest of the universe: we were never a thing. Also, that's real bold coming out of your mouth."

"We were going to tell you," Veronica insists. Her foundation is a shade too dark for her skin, applied in a way that suggests she threw it on in a hurry. She's wearing one of those bubble vests over a long zebra-striped shirt. Lucas talks about Vee almost daily. When he isn't talking to her, he's blatantly staring at her down the hall. "I swear."

"Oh, I'm sure," Wil grumbles to herself at the same moment Kevin places a hand over my shoulder.

"Seriously, Elwood, are you okay?" he tries. "We've been worried about you."

Saying the words aloud to Wil was hard enough. Repeating them for the rest of the car proves almost impossible. I clear my throat. "I ran away."

Lucas blinks from the steering wheel and his frustration seeps back in. "When I told you to stand up for yourself, I meant apply to college, not run away from home. No wonder your dad was so pissed at me. He practically accused me of kidnapping you."

My father's face flashes in my mind. I see him with his finger wedged tight in Lucas's chest, shorter yet still finding a way to loom over him.

"There's more to it than that," Wil says on my behalf. She grinds her teeth as if just being in the same car as Lucas is enough to set her off. The two of them have always been oil and water—identical ends of a magnet, repellent in their similarity. Kevin joked once that Lucas was the only one who could properly fill the hole Wil left, but I don't think even he could fill her shoes.

When she opens her mouth again, the whole story comes pouring out of her lips. It sounds exceedingly worse hearing it from someone else.

Lucas is quiet for one shell-shocked minute. He shares a look with Veronica and Kevin, pleading with one of them to speak first. When no one does, his eyes settle hard on me. "And you believe all that?"

If I close my eyes, I'm still running, branches whipping across my skin and fear sloshing in my gut. The forest has never left, and I see it on the back of my eyelids. Trees splitting the clouds, trunks wider than homes, roots ripping like fingers. The deeper you go, the less light there is. At its heart, not even the moon can penetrate through the leaves.

It had been real in the moment, but here in the car doubt gnaws away at my memory. "What's that supposed to mean?" Wil interjects.

"Not talking to you, Wil. I know what you believe."

"Oh, you think I put him up to this?"

His fingers tense on the wheel. "Quite frankly, yes. You ran off with him at the party, said God knows what to him there, he comes out looking thoroughly off his shit for the rest of the night, and now suddenly everything has gone off the deep end." His eyes find mine in the rearview. "No offense, dude. You were drunk and Wil put this wild idea in your head. It was my bad. I should've eased you into drinking, so you left with a clear head. But you're all trying to tell me that after a year of Wil auditioning for *Dateline*, now we all believe her tales? We're talking about your parents, man. They're all holier than thou and overbearing, but murder? Cults? This isn't a TV show. This is real life."

"Last I checked, a small group of secretive people with strange rituals is the textbook definition of a cult," Wil scoffs. "Ronnie, Elwood, tell me why you've never told me anything about the church services before. I was under the impression that religious people loved talking about their faith."

Veronica and I share a glance. "It's this whole 'keep it to ourselves' thing Elwood's dad preaches," she says. "Everything runs on a need-to-know basis in the GOA"—she abbreviates Garden of Adam like it's text slang—"where only adults have access to certain things. Basically up until you're eighteen, you're just sitting there twiddling your thumbs and listening. Then, suddenly, once you're an adult, you're magically super devoted like Mom. I never questioned it before. I thought it was just getting older and suddenly wanting to pal it up with Jesus. It's weird, for sure."

"Weird but not homicidal, Vee." Lucas drums his fingers against the wheel. "I guess your mom is magically in a cult too now. Wonder how she juggles the bake sale and dancing naked under the full moon."

"Gross visual," Veronica gags. She turns to me, and despite her boyfriend's snark, her face is surprisingly sincere. "Did they say my mom was in on it too? I know she's super into the church, but I never thought she'd murder someone."

"Veronica, it's not real," Lucas gripes. He massages the bridge of his nose with one hand before Veronica swats at him to keep both hands on the wheel.

We take a turn and suddenly the town is alive with "Missing" posters. They're everywhere. Stapled to telephone poles, taped to store windows, probably slid under every residential door. I've sprung up as the unofficial town mascot overnight.

"So . . . is that why we're going to the library? Looking to see if Mr. Clarke checked out any books on Charles Manson lately?" Lucas asks.

"He hasn't," Kevin offers readily. "If anyone was wondering."

"There, mystery solved." Lucas claps, and he's once again yelled at for not keeping his eyes on the road.

"No, asshole," Wil bites. "We're looking for something else. If this is such a joke to you, let us in and then wait out in the parking lot. No one wanted you here to begin with."

He huffs. "No, I'm coming. I don't entirely trust you to not ransack the library . . . and I'm here for Elwood." His eyes lift to meet mine in the mirror, and I'm flung back to our first meeting, those pensive eyes landing on me for the first time.

"Did we both get dumped at the same time?" he'd asked, his back sliding against the cinder-block wall. He'd tried to smirk, but his expression wobbled. He blew at a wet clump of hair, his scalp sticky from a dumped milk carton. "What a day."

I'd wanted to open my mouth and blurt out some rambling retort about Wil and me not being together, but my shattered heart made it too difficult to speak. My throat was lodged with the pieces of it.

He'd taken my tears as answer enough. "To think, it's only lunchtime, huh?" His stomach had grumbled then, and the noise sent his head slamming back into the lockers. "Lesson learned: never date a girl who breaks up with you food fight–style."

He was in luck. My stomach cramped so badly, I never thought I'd eat again. I rummaged for a brown paper bag from my backpack and gifted it to him.

Lucas had smiled weakly and looked at me—really looked—for the first time. "You're Elwood, right?"

My attention drifts back to the world beyond the window. The wind has torn some posters free. They float in the air. Staring up from sewer grates, punctured through a tree branch, nestled way up high on someone's roof.

Wil's mom comes to mind instantly. In the early days when my father first printed them off, it was impossible to walk a step without being assaulted by her face. She littered the town with her black-and-white frown, not a scowl like Wil' but something somber and distant.

"That woman was never happy, was she?" my mother asked at the dinner table after we'd put the first batch up. "Her mind was always on something else. Probably dreaming of her next grand escape."

Those words carried with me as I stapled the next stack of flyers. I thought the wind had carried away all of my previous work, but I was wrong. It had been Wil. Every time she found her mother's face, she crumpled the flyer into a ball. "Mom hated this picture."

It felt like such a silly reason then, but I'm reminded of it now, seeing my face. Each photo of me is exactly the same. My hair is slicked back with gel, my smile is less of a smile and more like clenched teeth. Red ink stretches across my face, a single haunting word obscuring my features: MISSING.

I always hated that photo.

Pine Point Public Library is tiny. A barren parking lot circles the perimeter, empty spaces one right after the other. At the front door, the glass is covered top to bottom with scribbled-in paper trees and rainbows. Something you'd find in a kindergarten class. Each one is colored outside of the lines. Another "Missing" poster of me is wedged between it all, held on with a heavy slab of gray tape.

I shiver, and it's hard to tell whether it's from the wave of heat or the absence of cold. The wintery world waits, caged behind the door. The storm howls for us. Around us, the room nuzzles in on itself. The shelves are crowded from wall to wall, and the books themselves look worn and tired.

"Well, we're here." Lucas shoves his hands in his pockets. "What now?"

"Now we grab the book we've been looking for," Wil says, her hair flung wilder by the wind. "Lead the way, Elwood."

She's looking at me like I'm some sort of bloodhound. Her brows furrow the longer it takes for me to lower my nose to the floor and scout out a trail for us to follow.

Where was it that Dad always went? The specific memory is tricky to hunt. It burrows behind other imprints of this place, moments hellbent on taking center stage in my mind. My father yanking a fantasy book from my hand and sliding it back onto the shelf, watching another kid check it out minutes later; eyeing the row of prehistoric computers along the wall and wondering what it might be like to log in without my father's vigilant stare.

The day I almost, *almost* applied for college on the one farthest to the left. Beyond it all, the memory I'm looking for arrives at long last.

"Here," I whisper, and I'm no longer toeing the edge but diving deep into the past. It leads me through the stacks and beyond the service counter, past carts and catalog cards and tacky posters adorning the walls. Beneath our feet, the carpet is a turf-grass green. "Dad always went in here."

Unfortunately, the door reads SUPPLY CLOSET in bold lettering. Those two words summon a massive blush.

"Isn't this where they keep the janitor's stuff? Did your dad have a side gig or something?" Lucas asks. "Well, Kev, what magical books do you keep in the custodial closet?"

He scrunches his nose. "I don't have keys for this." He jangles the keys in his hand, four separate pairs conjoined on the same rusty loop. Kevin fumbles with the ridges of each one, muttering to himself as he does so. "Front door, back door, conference room . . ."

"I'll kick it down," Wil volunteers readily.

"See, this is why I came in," Lucas groans. "If I was back in the car, you would've punched a hole through this door or something."

"And?" she challenges.

"And you can ruin your own future all you want, but leave Elwood out of it."

"Lucas, for the last time, stop being such a jerk," Veronica snaps. "Wil's my friend."

"Well, Elwood's my friend. He's smart and—"

"Wait!" Kevin's done muttering to himself and has resorted to shouting at all of us to get our attention. It definitely does the job. Everyone shuts up at once, and he waves the fourth key in our face like it says it all. "Front door, back door, conference room, and then this." He taps his nail against the ridges. "Guys, this is Mrs. Beasley's set. I—I have no idea how I mixed them up, but I definitely did. Mine only has three. But this should open it."

"Your call, Elwood," Lucas tells me. If he's wondering what career to go into in the future, I think he's got the "concerned principal" expression down pat. "I don't know if this counts as breaking and entering or not."

Wil meets that with a roll of her eyes. "I don't see how it can be breaking and entering with a goddamn key."

So this is what it's like to have a devil and an angel on my shoulders.

I swallow down my nerves. Here goes nothing, I guess. I give my consent with a shaky nod and Kevin puts the stolen key into the lock.

Lucas might be right. This feels . . . illegal. I shift my weight from one foot to the other. The world around us seems empty enough, but I know it isn't. There's got to be a camera tucked away out of sight, eyes on us somewhere, a sensor that will start blaring the moment we step foot inside.

I already know God's watching.

I sniff, digging my own nail into my thumb. I scrape away the skin and shift my weight again. Would this merit jail? A fine? A slap on the wrist? Libraries count as government buildings, right? So breaking into one of those is even worse than breaking in anywhere else? Is it really breaking in if we've got the key?

What is my family going to do now that I've run away from home and broken into a library? Then, that same dark voice: *Does it matter?*

The door creaks open like a mausoleum vault or a centuries-old tomb. Either of which is probably riddled with curses.

"Guys . . . this doesn't look like a janitor's closet."

CHAPTER TWELVE

ELWOOD

"Maybe they keep their supplies in the basement," Lucas offers with a flip of the switch. Muted, dull light floods the room, but shadows still cling to the far corners. The wooden steps leading down from the door shift to accommodate my weight. They're flimsy and rotting, dark sludge spread across each board like a layer of film. Abandoned spiderwebs litter the gaping crevices in the stone.

"Yeah." Wil snorts. "That's where I hide my Windex. In a secret lair under lock and key." Lucas says something under his breath in response, but I'm too busy shivering to hear it.

From the lens of my childhood, it always felt . . . normal for something so important to be locked and hidden away. Now it's the same as crawling into the mouth of a beast in search of its heart. Sinister and deadly and exceedingly foolish.

"Dude, you may need to talk your boss into a better security system," Lucas says to Kevin.

"I'm sure that'd go over well. Hey, I accidentally stole your keys and broke in, Mrs. Beasley . . . You should really be more careful next time. In my defense, Lucas Vandenhyde pressured me into it," Kevin retorts. "Easy scapegoat, since she doesn't like you."

"*What have I ever done to that woman?*"

"You've got fifteen dollars in library fees. Pretty sure you've had the same book checked out since you were ten."

I've stopped listening. They're still chatting behind me, but the world has grown silent in the book's wake. It's encased in the distance, likely kept behind glass to feebly protect it from the damp chill of the air. It lures me forward, a moth to a flame.

Wil beams ear to ear at the sight of the terrifying subterranean room. "I'm sorry, what were you saying earlier, Lucas? I forgot."

He swallows. "Okay, so it's not a custodian's closet, but that doesn't mean anything. What exactly is that book?"

I run a careful finger along the title and he reads it over my shoulder: *Pine Point—Past and Present.* Our history stains the pages and I have always dreamed of the day I would pick up the pen next. Yet here I am, prying apart the cover before my time, my finger wisping along the worn spine years too early.

I carry the book with me to the other table in the room. It's nearly as old as the ledger itself and blackened from time and splattered pots of ink. I recognize the fountain pen immediately; Dad's got a nearly identical one back in his office. It's a tarnished gold engraved with twisted foliage and the same Latin words that are recited in the church. My father sat here last and now I'm here, viciously disobeying him.

I try not to think about it.

"It looks like it could fall apart if you blow on it," Veronica comments. "It's got to be a hundred years old. Probably older."

Past the title, the first handful of pages are yellowed, the script a thin, slanted cursive, tight and hard to distinguish. Kevin looms over my shoulder and recites each line below his breath as he reads.

"Mrs. Beasley acted like this book didn't exist. I can't believe we've had it down in the basement this whole time. I also can't believe this place has a basement." A gulp. "Do you mind if I . . . ?" His sentence lingers, the rest of his question unspoken.

I nod, but I can't shake the guilt as he lifts the book. It feels too intimate for someone without the Clarke name.

He brushes a careful finger across the page. "You're right, Wil. I'm not an expert, of course, but this book is definitely old. You can tell by the paper alone." He eyes the deckled edges and hums to himself. "It's missing pages. Hard to say if they were ripped out or if the book's that delicate and the binding came loose. Regardless, we should be careful with it."

"Okay, so it's a history book?" Lucas asks. "A really old history book. That's what you're getting at, yeah?"

Kevin nods, and his response might be good enough for Lucas, but Wil's hardly sated. "What do you mean, Mrs. Beasley acted like this book didn't exist?"

He returns it gently to my hands and buries his own in his pockets. "Your mom never told you?"

"Told me what?"

"I had my suspicions when you brought up the library, but I wasn't sure about it until now. Your mom was in here a ton. Drove Beasley crazy. Kept asking for town records and stuff. She gave her a file of old newspapers, but your mom was never satisfied. Kept insisting there had to be something else. Let's just say Beasley wasn't exactly a fan. But here she was, right all along."

I return my attention to the page, and Veronica flashes her phone light overhead to help.

It opens with a grim prognosis for the Upper Peninsula. The federal government deemed our part of Michigan "forever a wilderness." Never mind the Native populations that had called this land home for ages, the country thought it uninhabitable and harsh, no place to create a settlement.

But then copper changed that. It tells of the greed and desperation that sent men here to strip whatever they could from this land. I trace the image on the page, a black-and-white illustration of early Pine Point. It was somehow even more remote than it is now, a sparse assortment of timber-framed houses hidden among the trees.

Winter stole almost everything. Food rations slashed to a critical level, lives lost to disease and starvation. The season had been abnormally cold, no doubt slipping well into the negatives. Winter was greedy, too. It stretched its fingers into May, the snow only beginning to melt after one last brutal storm. "Led by religious leader James Alderwood, the villagers did what they had to in order to survive."

"Wow, what a totally normal, not-creepy-at-all way to end things," Wil grumbles under her breath. "Nice touch with the ripped-out pages, too."

She's right. Just beyond that unsettling last line, the following passages are torn right out of the book.

Veronica's attention trains elsewhere. "Alderwood, huh?" She fidgets with her tongue piercing as she speaks. I remember back when she walked into class every day with a golden cross strung around her neck. "It sounds a lot like your name, doesn't it?"

I clear my throat. "It's my legal name, Alderwood. I go by Elwood, though." I gnaw on my cheek. I got bullied hard enough for having an old man's name. I can only imagine what sort of hell my classmates would have put me through if they knew I was named after a man from our town's founding. "My uncle had the same name."

I don't think that makes it any less embarrassing.

"And what happened to him?" Kevin questions. From the tone alone, I know it's more than an innocent question.

I answer it delicately. "He's no longer with us. He died young." The earth hums and murmurs below my feet, the world waiting for me to uncover the truth it already knows. My stomach burns as I flip through the pages. My uncle's name is printed alongside my father's in the birth records, yet only one brother is still breathing. "Right before I was born."

Prudence's due date is soon.

"That doesn't mean anything," Lucas insists, but there's an edge to his voice that wasn't there before. It's hard to be the voice of reason when doubt slithers from your core. "He could've died from anything. Was he sick?"

"I honestly don't know."

I flip through the ledger some more until I make it to the death records. So many lives are reduced to lines on a page. There's relatives and old churchgoers, neighbors and people I never had the chance to meet.

Everyone and anyone, but nothing for my uncle.

"He's not here. I don't see a burial plot or death certificate or anything."

Lucas shakes his head. "The guy's got to have something on him." He whips out his phone. "Here, I'll google it. Can you spell the name for me?"

I clear my throat. "*A-L-D-E-R-W-O-O-D.*"

He mumbles back the letters, his fingers moving overtime on the keyboard. He scrolls through the length of the page with his thumb. "You don't happen to have a year or something I can add, do you?"

I offer it up to him and listen to the four resounding clicks of his nail against the screen.

He groans. "No dice here either. I'm checking this graveyard site. This thing's got grave photos and death records and all that stuff. I can't seem to get a hit. No obituary, no nothing." I shake my head. "He was my father's older brother. There should be records of him somewhere.

I'm sure there's medical or hospital records at least. There's got to be something."

I'm hyperconscious as Wil looms over my shoulder. "Could it be another set of pages ripped out?"

"Doubt it," Kevin offers. "It only seems like there's two parts torn and neither line up with the death records at all. Here, let me show you."

He flips through the ledger again and leads us to the other missing passages. I hadn't noticed them on my own, but he's right. There's a handful of rips toward the beginning of the book, pages upon pages lost.

The surrounding passages deviate from the stiff historical retellings and note keeping.

They're Old Testament in nature, one long, unforgiving scripture. "Well, what's it say?" Wil demands.

Kevin clears his throat, his fingers going white under his intense grip. "When thy God calls for blood"—his words break, the confidence sapping the further he reads—"thou shall offer your sons unto him. The blood shall water thy crops and the bones shall nourish the earth. For with life there is death, but with sacrifice there is eternity."

I stiffen to my very bones. I'm a caterpillar helpless to my father's parasitic prayer. His words lay their eggs under my skin and devour me from the inside out. He read my death sentence aloud and I smiled.

I smiled.

Lucas's face goes ashen. "What the hell does that mean?"

"It means Wil was right. I'm nothing but fertilizer. They knew this from the day I was born. My mother marked me the moment I came out of the womb. They're going to sacrifice me." I stagger away from the book and the horrible truth inside. "And Prudence's child is next."

How many people have died? How would they have done it? Would they have woken me early and dragged me into the trees kicking and screaming? Or would they have taken mercy on me and laced my food with poison and let me die in my sleep?

No, mercy isn't something this town knows.

"Whoa, buddy, we don't know that for sure," Lucas tries, but he wasn't there in church with me. My father's hand didn't rest on his shoulder and Sheriff Vrees didn't threaten to lock him in a cell. "What reason do they even have to kill you? To kill anyone?"

Kevin coughs. "I mean, we never read what they 'had' to do to survive. All of this probably stems from whatever sick thing they did in the past."

I fall to my knees and bury my face beneath trembling fingers. The dark thoughts have returned. There's no pushing away from them now. Images flash on a loop in my skull. Different ways my father will find me, my mother holding me down as my father drags the knife.

What's another scar when the alternative is bound wrists and a cutting blade in my ribs? The ground pulses alongside my heart. So loud, it's all I hear. They're speaking, all of them, lurching up from their seats as the ground quivers. But I don't hear them.

Ba-dump. Ba-dump. Ba-dump. The noise flares through me like a second heartbeat, a creature living and breathing just beneath the skin.

"Elwood!" Wil shouts, and the sound of my name is enough to send me spiraling further. "Get it together. You're not dying on my watch. On any of our watches."

Lucas is frantically shaking his head. "Elwood—This isn't—None of this makes sense." He's taken to pacing. "Wil has hated your family from the start, and Kevin—y'know I love you to death, man, but you're the biggest conspiracy theorist I know. Your dad mowed the lawn weird one time and you thought it was a crop circle. I know you're all eager to believe this, but are we all forgetting how far-fetched it is? The Bible is filled with batshit sayings like that." He grips the ledger for himself and taps on the photo beside it.

It's a black-and-white newspaper clipping of the Pine Point Lumber Mill. There's a factory's worth of men standing dutifully outside of the building.

"You know the saying: blood, sweat, and tears and all that. That passage could mean a million other things and we're all here freaking ourselves out in this spooky basement." He wets his lips. "I'm sorry. Things like this don't happen in Pine Point. It's weird, but . . ."

"Typical," Veronica says. "You always turn a blind eye to things you're too scared to face."

"Is that what you think?" He grits his teeth. "Fine. It's weird, okay? All of this is weird, but I don't want to incriminate a whole church due to superstition and hearsay. Your own mother goes there, Veronica! In case you forgot." That last line has him squinting in her direction. "Elwood, if you're really worried, we need to do the sensible thing and take this to the cops."

Wil scoffs. "Oh, good old Vrees. I'm sorry, did you forget that he's in on it? We're on our own on this one."

Lucas looks ready to throw a barb back at her, but Kevin clears his throat. "Do you have any idea where a ripped page could be, Elwood?"

I can hardly form coherent sentences, much less pull anything of substance from my scattered mind. It's as big of a mess as my room, all fractured glass and broken thoughts. It physically hurts to examine my past.

Everything is sharpened from this new revelation, made twice as jagged. All the times my parents never tucked me in at night as a child, the bedtime stories lost, grim-faced Christmas mornings, the pride I so desperately craved from my father. Just once I wanted to earn something real. To be worthy of love.

I thought I'd earned it for once, but I'd been wrong. Standing beside my father as he opened the tabernacle, pushed past the folded yellow page inside for the chalice—

"I know where it is." I struggle against the bob of my throat. "My father has it hidden with the sacrament. I saw a torn-out page in there."

Veronica waves her phone and the flashlight shines across the table. "We could go at night."

Lucas massages the bridge of his nose. "Oh yeah, because nothing screams 'Christmas Eve' like breaking into a church," he mocks.

Kevin's the first to look over at him. His eyes spark. "Actually, you know, a peek wouldn't hurt. We'll never be a hundred percent sure unless we look."

"That wasn't an actual suggestion." Lucas's jaw drops. "Do not look at each other like that. We are not breaking into a church."

CHAPTER THIRTEEN

WIL

"Is this the right type of crowbar for this?"

Kevin walks with his chin on the curved handle like he's some sort of tap-dancing showman. Well, he would be if I could think of any Broadway performance as morbid as this one. The five of us have gathered here under nightfall fully prepared to break into the church of a potentially murderous cult. The only musical coming to my mind is *Grease*, and I'm pretty sure Sandy and Danny didn't sing about ritualistic sacrifice.

It's been a while since I've seen it, though.

"Did they drop some new version of a crowbar while I wasn't looking?" I ask, wedging my hands deeper in my pockets with every chattering word. It's hard to stay warm when Lucas has us walking this far, his car "safe" and hidden in the Morguewood. "I didn't realize it was like the iPhone. *Yeah, I'm sure it'll work.*"

"There's tons of different types, Wil," Lucas says because he gets off on not only making us walk forever but being a know-it-all, too.

"I didn't realize I was in the presence of the God of Crowbars. Please do share your infinite wisdom with the rest of us ignorant fools."

I shiver and the surrounding trees do the same. With their skeletal trunks and barren branches, they look an awful lot like hands breaking from grave soil.

He bites out his words. "Listen, I don't even want to be here."

"Then do us all a favor and leave." My frustration does the talking for me. It lashes out before my brain has the chance to catch up.

"I'm here for Elwood, not you." He curls his lip and shoots a look at Elwood like he's his dutiful little golden retriever. One measly year and I'm no longer the most important one to Elwood. He's strayed to this asshole.

Everything with him has changed. The baby fat has all but disappeared and left him hollow and oversharp. Beneath his green eyes, the skin has purpled with sleepless nights. I'm not the only one who's become a shadow of myself. I try to meet his eyes, but he's decided a much better use of his time is staring abjectly at the ground and worry-picking at his skin.

"Elwood doesn't need you." It's a childish thing to say. But too late; it's already out of my mouth.

Elwood freezes at the sound of his own name and I can feel his eyes burn on my skin. I can't look. Can't meet his eyes with my cheeks this hot. "Wil."

Lucas's voice is loud enough to drown him out before he even begins. "Oh, and he needs you? He survived a year without you just fine."

Yeah, that's what I was worried he'd say. Now I've got to grind my teeth and hope my exhaustion doesn't douse my heart in lighter fluid.

"Is this what custody battles are like?" Ronnie wedges her gloved hands beneath the pits of her jacket. She's always been the worst with cold weather, and it shows in the freezing back-and-forth shuffle of her feet and the ruddy red of her nose. "Wil, you get Elwood on alternate weekends and—"

"Guys, we're here!" Kevin hisses. "Shut up before we all get caught."

That breaks *whatever that was* and allows us to think clearly. We are all very much outside in a blizzard and in enemy territory to boot, so it would do us well to zip it, like he said. The rest of the world is silent, too. The only noise comes in the way of stray ice gusts as they rack past the sides of the church. They skirt around the wooden beams, the white paint tinged gray in the shadows.

We're suddenly conscious of every step, the crunch of ice and frozen dirt beneath our heels as we cross from the cemetery to the back church door. I'm trying my damnedest not to freak out—though I'd sooner die than admit that to anyone here. With the moon overhead and the fact that there's literal graves surrounding us, it's hard not to get the creeps. I sneak a worried glance over my shoulder.

PINE POINT CEMETERY is written in iron right behind our heads. The dusky charcoal letters hang high to signify the shift in the air. The possession of this land passed from the living to the dead. Snow gusts rack past the headstones, burying them to the very top. The tree line encroaches on the gate, inching nearer with the years. With a forest full of dead things, perhaps it feels entitled to our dead, too.

"This was way less terrifying in theory," Veronica whispers as we weave our way to the back. Her whole dress code might revolve around fear—scaring her mom when she catches her walking out of the house, scaring the elderly as she passes them on the street—but beneath it all, she's a softie. She's one of those tiny little Chihuahuas with the spiked vests, and I have the sudden, inexplicable terror that I'm guiding her toward a hawk's nest.

We make it to the world's most ancient door, and we might get lucky and be able to huff and puff our way through.

"Show of hands, how many of us have actually done this before?" Kevin's directing the question at all of us, but his eyes are trained solely on me. The one person here reckless enough to have experience. Except, unfortunately, I don't.

I tell him as much.

"Maybe it's unlocked," Lucas says, and even he doesn't sound hopeful. He rests his hand on the knob and recites something under his breath that might be a curse or might be a prayer, and then wiggles the knob.

Nothing.

After a moment of stubborn resignation, he abandons it for the crowbar. "Fine, give me that. You guys would probably break the door for real or something. Guess we're doing this the hard way."

He breathes in, all doctor's-office-stethoscope-style, and readies himself to commit his first-ever crime. Beneath his shallow breath, he's started up a count.

One, two, three—

On "Go!" he makes the loudest noise I've ever heard in my life.

The slam of the crowbar wedging into the doorframe freezes us all over. An owl goes flying off a high branch, and the world reverberates with the sound, echoing back like a scream in a cavern.

"They definitely heard that one on the *other* side of Michigan," Kevin says under his breath. It's pointless to whisper after the sound we just made, but no one wants to admit that. Because admitting that means admitting the fact that there's the potential someone already heard us and is now on their way over. "We need to go fast and get the hell out."

"I think I'm going to throw up," Elwood contributes uselessly.

In an attempt to be *actually* useful, I peer into the shadowed gap he's made through the door. There's a century-old radiator inside and a massive table holding a single cross and nothing else. I can't say for sure what I was expecting, a dead body rolled up in a rug or what.

Satisfied that there's nothing immediately horrifying on the other side, I slip my wrist through the gap and unlock the door. Once I hear the click, I yank my hand back, and Lucas lets the bar go slack against his side.

I move to take a step forward, but in a shocking feat, Elwood beats me to it. I didn't think he had it in him to make the first move. All his life, he's waited for my lead: letting me pick our lunch spot every semester, giving me first pick for group assignments, sitting there limply sophomore year for our first and only kiss . . .

Jesus Christ. My cheeks give the radiator a run for its money. This is *not the time to dredge up that memory.*

I'm thankful it's dark as I follow Elwood's lead. I slap the blush right off my face and focus on the task at hand. I'm not frolicking down memory lane; I'm stepping into a holy war zone.

Even being here is surreal. The church has always been a constant, something ominous in my peripheral as I ride through town, as familiar as the frozen sun above my head. I've never stepped foot on the sun, and I never thought I'd step in here, either.

"So, what's the plan?" Lucas asks finally. His eyes dart to every barren corner of the office like he's willing some shadowed deity to appear out of thin air. Every shift of our weight against these wooden boards feels explosive, our labored breath a battle cry in the dark.

"The plan is don't get caught," I answer, and I'm relieved I can get the words out at all.

My body's all live wire, my tongue short-circuiting with the chattering of my teeth. I nod at Elwood and pretend that I wasn't imagining his mouth on mine five seconds ago. "Lead the way."

He nods, his arms an impenetrable barrier across his chest. He's made a locked box of himself, but for once, I know exactly what lies inside. His brows pull into one furrowed line and there's a tightness to him like a frayed rope. One wrong pull and that pretty resolve of his will snap.

He presses his ear to the barrier between this room and the next. Content with the silence, he grips the handle and pushes it open a crack to peer out. We only breathe again after he finishes surveying the church. The door swings the rest of the way open and he takes the first experimental step forward.

The pews might be vacant at this hour, but they're worn with years of use. Discolored from several hundred Sundays spent in these very seats. Swing the kneelers out, and I'm sure you'd see the imprints of bodies hunched over, bowing to a god that's never once stopped to listen to me.

My hands ball at my sides. I clasped them in prayer once when my mother went missing, but no amount of "amen"s brought her home. That's when my folded hands turned to fists. God and the law might have given up on my mother, but I haven't.

And I never, ever will.

"It should be over here," Elwood whispers. His voice is deafening in the quiet.

I can't help the nauseous tide rolling in my stomach as we walk past the pulpit. The thought of Elwood's father standing here and treating this glorified podium like it's a royal throne, some symbol of his divine entitlement—it sickens me to no end.

"The tabernacle is here behind the altar," Elwood clarifies, and he might as well be speaking in Latin. I've never felt more like a godless heathen in my life. He catches my confusion and clarifies quickly, giving me the SparkNotes of Christianity. "For the Eucharist . . . communion, Wil. The body and the blood."

"Ah, yes, *that*," I reply. That's actually vaguely terrifying in itself, but I hold my tongue.

"It's a relatively simple lock," he tells me, pointing to the little box they keep beneath the cross. It's raised high and flecked with gaudy splashes of gold paint. Upon closer inspection, I see floral markings etched into the wood. Someone really took their time on this to create a forest of ivy and sharp branches. "I've watched my dad open it a million times. There is a slight trick to it, though."

He mimes the action with his hand, the ninety-degree turn one way, followed by another counterclockwise one after that. One last shimmy and the imaginary key is yanked free. "Like that."

"Noted." I fish two bobby pins from my hair and my greasy bangs break free and spill across my forehead. I flatten the first piece and dig it into the groove, and then I create my pick. I jiggle the makeshift key in the lock and listen for the clicks of each seized pin inside it.

One by one until the door swings wide open.

"A little scary how good you are at that," Lucas says.

"Says the guy who easily broke down a door with a crowbar."

That shuts him up.

Elwood reaches his hand into the chasm. Beyond the gaudy chalice, there's a page tucked in the gloom. He frees it and shuts the door behind him, his full attention on the stolen passage. It's folded several times over and creased from the time it's spent hidden away.

He's delicate with it, his fingers brushing the paper as if it were the sacrament itself. Some holy artifact bestowed from the heavens.

He smooths it against the pulpit, pressing it out like he might read it to a congregation. We crowd behind him for a better look.

"*In the midst of the town's starvation, leader James Alderwood claims to have conversed with an angel*," it begins, the script as thin and faint as the text in the library. I strain to read it in the gloom. "*A holy messenger of God showed him the path to salvation. Like in the days of old, a sacrifice was needed to nourish the land and keep the town fed. And so they spilled the blood of Alderwood's only son in the snow and the Lord was satisfied with this offering. With their Gift, the woods took on new life and a new Eden was born.*

"Blessed are those who follow in the Lord's path and offer their sons to the earth. Feed the blood to the soil and it shall nourish the land for years to come and keep Eden holy. Spare your sons and face God's wrath."

"They've been killing people here since the very beginning. There's no denying it." My voice breaks halfway in. Elwood's not speaking, hardly moving. When my heart catches up with the rest of me, it catches up *fast*. Slamming brutally against my rib cage, a stern pounding on a frail door. The chill racks along my spine.

No one else says anything. No one knows *what* to say, and it turns out we don't need to anyway, because the world that was so painfully silent minutes prior is no more. Through the quiet, the sound of footsteps breaks.

Someone's coming and they aren't alone.

The color leeches right out of Elwood's face, and the paper is no longer smoothed in his grasp but crumpled beneath his trembling fist. He utters three little words, and it's enough to make the blood run ice-cold in my veins:

"The night service."

CHAPTER FOURTEEN

ELWOOD

Spying on a church has got to be a sin. And a dangerous one at that.

After everything we've unearthed, the sensible thing to do would be to run far, far away from here. All of us should clamber into the back of Lucas's car and speed away. Out of this town, out of this state.

But spying is exactly what we're doing. Wil's busy fiddling with her phone settings in the back office and dutifully ignoring everyone's whispered pleas for us to hurry up and leave. Once she's absolutely *positive* that the flash is off, she clenches it tight between her trembling hands and starts the video. Kevin mutters something about found-footage horror films, but she swats away his comment too.

I swallow the lump that's formed in my throat. I've never been to a night service. I always thought once I returned home in the future that I'd be deemed old enough to attend . . . but clearly that was never bound to happen. As horrible as this idea is, my dark curiosity has surfaced again. It's been showing its face a lot recently and here I am, submitting once more. It's a friend at this point. An impulsive, reckless friend leading me from one bad idea to the next.

Like Wil.

So we watch the scene from the back office, the room an echoing cavern that could betray us at any turn. One wrong move, one slight sound, and it's all over.

My father stands among monsters.

Faces cloaked by deer skulls, antlers protruding like branches on either ends of their scalp. They've split deer jaws wide open, severed the mandible and left the upper teeth behind in a grisly faux smile. Beneath their ghastly masks, their bodies are obscured by long green cassocks. Stitched ivy slithers up the sides, the fabric alive with a forest of foliage.

"You all know why I've called you here today." My father's voice sounds like a roach scuttling up the drain. For years I've been Little Red living with a wolf, marveling over sharp teeth as if they weren't meant to swallow me whole. "Elwood needs to be found, no matter the cost."

"I wouldn't be surprised if *you've* hidden him." I recognize Vrees by the gray stubble of his chin and the timbre of his voice. He gnashes the words in my father's face as he approaches him at the podium. He might've switched out of police attire, but his rigid stance is nothing he can hang up at the end of the day. "You're telling me after years of keeping tabs on him, suddenly he's running free? You'll damn us for this, Ezekiel. As far as I'm convinced, the Clarke name is a rotten branch. Your father—"

"Don't speak his name if you wish to keep your tongue," my father seethes. I believe him. At this moment, I know that he'd take the switchblade from his belt and lop it right off if given the chance.

"No one here fears you, not anymore." Vrees shifts to stand beside his wife and her face is visibly strained as she cradles her swollen stomach. "You cling to power as if it's yours to keep. Prudence is due now at any point. We cannot keep delaying the inevitable. She will give birth to the new Seed, and you will step down, willingly or not."

"I'm still the Right Hand."

"You're *our damnation*." The sheriff addresses the crowd. The whites of his eyes are full-moon bright beneath his mask. "You all remember what happened last time with Ezekiel's brother. How close we were to our destruction by delaying the ceremony. The last Alderwood started changing. Becoming erratic. Hard to control. If we hadn't gotten ahold of him, who knows what he would've become?"

"Eden was vicious," a masked woman cries. I know her, too. Beneath her monstrous false skin, I remember her sitting, smiling in the school office. She helped me with my class schedule four years ago. "Half of my siding was tangled in roots. I had thorns ripping through the floorboards."

"The woods were hungry."

"The forest must be fed."

"Where is he?"

My father dodges the church's onslaught from every direction. His fists stay firm at his sides, but I can tell from the stiffening of his spine that his frustration is consuming. "I do not have him."

I return my attention to the church members. All their pacing conjures a breeze much like the one slipping through the trees outside.

Branches titter in the wind. The woods have watched and listened, but they'll never reveal my father's secrets.

"Your brother was caught before it was too late. If you don't dispose of Elwood soon, the forest will *grow in him,* and we'll all be dead. We've seen it before. That boy is dangerous."

Dangerous?

I turn my hands back and forth and marvel at the softness of my palms. No curling talons or monstrous tremor beneath the skin. These are the same hands that save bugs from windowsills and carry them to the garden. *Dangerous* has never been a word remotely close to me. *Cowardly, wimpy, weak.*

My father grapples for control of the church once more. "Believe me, I know. That is why we're here. He must be accounted for. Mark, where are your men?"

"I've got all my guys stationed around every major exit." All eyes are on Vrees as he stands in the church with his hands on his hips. "No one gets in or out without us knowing. He hasn't left Pine Point. I'm sure of it."

Veronica smothers a gasp beside me, but it isn't my father she's staring at. Within the crowd, her own mother stands. I recognize her from the blond curls spilling out the sides of her mask. I've seen her bright and beaming at the morning service and power-posing at the school bake sale, but I've never seen her like this. "He's probably with that snake. The same one infecting my daughter. She's a scourge on this town. She will rot us from the inside out like her mother did."

They think Wil is some demonized caricature, not the girl whose face dimples when she laughs.

She continues. "Maybe he'll do us a favor and get rid of her for us."

I exchange an uneasy glance with Wil and the careful mask she wears shows its first crack. A furrow works in between her brows and her lips are overtaken by a deep scowl. "That would be a true favor indeed," my father mutters.

All my life, my father's been God. The ultimate example of wisdom and holiness, a stark reminder that God's love is in limited supply, that only a few of us will ever bask in it, and the rotten rest will endure the full weight of His wrath.

I don't see God in him now.

In fact, I don't see God anywhere.

"Guys," Lucas whispers, and his voice has become serrated and scared. No room for laughter, forced or otherwise. "We need to get the hell out of dodge." When no one immediately pounces on the idea, he rests a wary palm on my shoulder. "Elwood, we can't stay like this. We need to leave."

He isn't wrong, but I can't move.

Then I hear Wil say, "I want to see if they mention my mother."

I don't know if I'm ready for any other damning reveals, but I feel like a hare caught in a predator's sight, going perfectly, completely still.

"We'll plant something on the Greene property tomorrow," Vrees follows. He's taken to pacing around the room, and my heart stammers the closer he gets. "We will get in there; you can bet on it."

That's greeted with a scoff in the crowd. It's Veronica's mother who speaks. "And the girl, what about her? She's feisty like her mother. You think she'll allow you to easily take him?"

My palms have already grown slick with nerves. The truth stares me down. Not yet complete, but a haunting picture no less. If my family catches me, everything ends. All the Alderwoods that came before were slaughtered and perhaps all the Alderwoods that come after will be too. I've never been a son. I've only ever been a seed. And now my father has come to harvest me.

I used to think if I were a perfect son, my father would care for me more. But now I know better. He has always destroyed the things dearest to him. He loved the trees and yet he never flinched when his axe cut through them.

He might not love me, but maybe he'll praise my bones after he's burned them, too.

"She isn't a concern," my father chimes in. "We've always eliminated threats."

Those four words echo back in my head, entirely unreal. This isn't possible. It plays before me like a horrific, lucid dream, forcing me to watch and see this through to the bitter end.

He continues with horrifying clarity. "That pesky Greene woman has been disposed of. We can get rid of her daughter too. A troublemaking, headstrong girl? Who in this town would so much as bat an eye if she disappeared? Like mother, like daughter."

Wil gasps as the horrible truth is out at long last. They killed her mom. My family killed her. My father disposed of her body, smiled as he hung her face all across town, and lied to me. *How could a mother abandon her own daughter like that?* My father had tutted with blood fresh on his hands. Easily, if she's six feet under.

All this time I waved Wil away and she was right. Wil got too close to me and it burned her and now there's no body for her to bury and—

And it's my fault.

Goddamnit. It's my fault.

Her expression is a chisel carving away at my own face. True horror is something I've never experienced. So many days spent cowering from my parents, not knowing what I had to be afraid of.

I learn real fear in the seconds that follow.

Murder is fresh on my mind when the silence breaks. Wil's phone rattles to life, and the ring is a banshee call in the night.

CHAPTER FIFTEEN

WIL

Oh shit.

Shit.

My own father's face flashes on my phone. I hardly recognize his smile on my screen. I only ever see it in old photographs and his contact info is a leftover relic from another era. Right now, his dopey smile is going to get me killed. Shouldn't he be drunk at this hour? What am I doing getting a call from him?

"Shut it off!" all four of them whisper behind me, and God knows I'm trying to do that, but it's not as easy as it looks, so I tell them to *kindly get off my back.* I play a frantic game of hot potato with myself trying to turn it off, but it's so ungodly loud and the church has gone deathly quiet and, God, am I in trouble.

It shuts off naturally by the time I've muted my phone. The whole church is staring into the shadows, and if I'm not hallucinating, Vrees's hand twitches toward something in his belt.

Lucas was right. We should've gotten out of Dodge while we still could.

"Someone's here," Ezekiel whispers, and the emotion draining from his voice is as terrifying as any narrowed eyes or gnashing teeth. It's a hollow sort of evil. Rage isn't what's made a devil out of him; it's the sheer *nothingness* that has. How long has it been since he stripped away his soul? Was it before or after he killed my mother?

Oh God. My stomach clenches at the very thought.

She's dead, my mind supplies cruelly. *She's dead and there's no bringing her home again.*

The worst part is that it doesn't surprise me. It should be this staggering, earth-shattering revelation, and yet . . .

Somehow . . . somehow I knew. The hunch I never wanted to consider. The dark voice I kept at bay in the back corner of my mind. It's been whispering this whole time, telling me the truth. And now it's here in full bloom, begging me to look it in the face.

They killed her, and now they're going to kill you, too.

I'm only aware I'm death-gripping Elwood's hand when I hear him gasp at the pressure. I loosen my clutch but only barely. I turn around and face down the worst Scooby-Doo gang of all time, and I hope they're paying attention when I mouth one single word:

"Run."

Lucas doesn't need to be told twice. The back door swings open to the storm and he's yanking at Ronnie's hand, desperate to keep her by his side. She flies behind him like a rag doll, Kevin barreling in tow. It's the two of us, Elwood and me, that are left in the aftermath. Elwood's gone deer in the headlights.

I grip his arm with one hand and grab the crowbar with the other—because I'll be damned if I don't have some sort of blunt-force weapon. And thank God for that violent impulse, because we're no longer alone. Ezekiel pushes through, and it's like staring down an executioner.

But I've got my spear, and I'll be damned if I let him eat me alive.

"Elwood!" Ezekiel grabs his wrist and his face is pure desperation. "Where in God's name were you? You have no idea what you've done!"

Elwood might be horrified and distracted by his father's words, but

I'm not. I swing and he howls at impact, his fingers slacking and giving me a second reprieve. I take that moment like my life depends on it—and it probably does.

My instinct-driven lizard brain takes over as I grab Elwood and clamber out the back door and into the cemetery. Every breath I take propels my feet forward.

"You're going to kill them!" Ezekiel shouts in the distance. *"You're going to kill all of us!"*

I wonder if this is how Mom felt in the final moments. Wind barreling on all sides, flesh frozen with ice, heart slamming into her ribs.

Snow steals the road right from under us. It's replaced in the distance by a soupy stretch of fog. I used to think it was cliché when people said they could feel eyes on the back of their neck. Not anymore. I feel the burn of eyes on my skin as we run.

The car's where Lucas parked it, and I've never been so relieved to be inside of a Honda Civic.

"Oh thank God," Ronnie cries from the front seat. She twists back and grips my arms in hers, a nervous tremble rippling through her. "I told him he had to wait. That we couldn't just leave you here. That—"

I don't let her finish. We don't have time. *"Floor it."*

No sooner do I say the words than Lucas slams his foot on the gas. Ice crackles underneath the tires and I worry in this weather that one wrong turn will send us careening into a ditch.

Winter makes a lethal game of driving. We drive like our lives depend on it—and this time, they actually do. It's five minutes of gunning through the town in dead silence. Five more before anyone breathes. By the time Lucas skids into the motel parking lot, the nerves have plummeted to my stomach and two more letters are shot out from our sign.

Dad will never fix them, so they'll stay dead forever until the last light burns out and joins them.

And by that time, the motel will be buried away for good. I stare into the trees, but for now, they are quiet.

Lucas is lucky we rarely have guests. The barren parking lot gives him plenty of leeway to violently lose control of his tires. He lets off the brakes, and we jerk to a lurching finale in front of the main doors.

I feel sick, and it's got nothing to do with Lucas's driving and all to do with my mother's black-and-white "Missing" smile, her face stapled in every corner of my mind. Dead. In a sick way, I should be thankful for answers. I'd long suspected the Clarkes of foul play. I spent every waking moment accusing them of my mother's disappearance.

I should be relieved. I'm not.

In fact, I wish she were still missing. I long for the inkling of doubt burrowed beneath my suspicion. That secure sense of what-if. *Mom left on her own, but she won't be gone forever. She'll come back any day now, tanned and smiling and apologetic. It will hurt, but it will be okay again.*

There's no returning from the dead.

"I can't do this," Lucas blurts, breathless. Zero involvement in any of this and yet he's the one losing his mind. "I cannot fucking do this."

His fingers tap furiously at the wheel. The last twenty-four hours have whittled his sanity away, and it shows with every hiss of his breath. "I knew your parents were weird. I knew Vee's mom was weird. Not murder-weird, though. Not sacrifice-your-son-like-he's-the-second-coming-of-Christ weird. No, no, I tap out. I cannot fucking handle this." He jerks his head toward the clock. "It's Christmas. I should be at home with my parents, asleep. *No.* No. No. No. They're probably cult members too, because that's my luck, isn't it? Giving my grandpa his last cult-y rites."

Ronnie lets out a breath. She'd been silent the whole ride over here, but it clearly wasn't for a lack of things to say. "I forgot. Everything is about you, even when it isn't. You think you're the only one going through it?"

Lucas huffs but doesn't dignify her question with a response.

"Typical," she snaps, the word breaking in her throat. "You're somehow the one suffering. I'm the one who had to find out that *my mom* and Elwood's family—"

"Don't say it." I must've bitten my tongue at some point. I speak and blood wells with every word. "Please, don't say it."

Her anger fizzles at my request and the heartbreak that shows after says it all.

Meanwhile, Elwood says nothing besides me. He can't look me in the eyes.

Kevin is the first to speak again. "What did the sheriff mean about you being dangerous, Elwood?" he interrupts. "They kept saying that."

"Dangerous to be around, maybe," Lucas mutters before quickly backtracking a second later. Hard not to with the clear anguish breaking over Elwood's face in the rearview. "I didn't mean that. I'm sorry; it's not your fault, man. You should call the state police, or I don't know. There's gotta be a higher-up somewhere." He rests his head on the steering wheel. "But what I mean is, I don't think I can do this. Not anymore."

"Oh, I get it. You're done caring." I channel every ounce of emotion into rage. Spite is an easier companion than sorrow. "You've helped enough to earn a Good Samaritan badge on your Boy Scout vest and now you don't give a shit about us. Cool. That's fine."

Beside me, Kevin wets his lips several times and wrings his hands in his lap. "I don't think splitting up is a good idea. Anytime a group does that, they're always—"

"This isn't a goddamn horror movie, Kevin," Lucas snaps. "For the last time, it doesn't matter what they do in Hollywood." He gestures to the wild amount of snow on the ground beyond the glass. "Does this look like California to you? No. All of this is real and there are real-life consequences to it all. People are dead, Kevin. Dead."

I'm this close to punching him square in the jaw. "Dead like my mother?" His eyes bulge. "I didn't mean that. You know I didn't mean that, Wil."

Too late. I give him my nastiest grin. "I guess the rumors about you were true all along."

"What are you talking about?"

"The one about you being as shallow as you look. Always promoting causes you couldn't care less about. Befriending charity cases. Leave out the sponsorships and the spotlight and at the end of the day, you don't give a shit about anyone. Not Elwood or Ronnie or Kevin. No one but yourself." I swing open the car door and grip Elwood's wrist. "You're right, Lucas, this isn't Hollywood. You're the only one acting." Elwood scrambles beside me out of the car, and without Lucas's dramatics, silence is our only answer.

CHAPTER SIXTEEN

WIL

Dad is the only soul in the building.

The emptiness hits harder than before. Mom's absence is a deep stain in the fibers, impossible to strip without burning this place to the ground. Ezekiel has the right idea to demolish us. As it stands, we're not a graveyard but a neglected shrine for a single, forgotten woman.

But I remember.

She exists everywhere in this rotting place. I trace nostalgic patterns on the wall, all the imprints she left behind. It was abnormally hot the year we spruced up these boring white walls; we ran through with splatters of paint and pitchers of lemonade. Mom and her spirals, me and my messy handprints. Most of my additions were covered over, but she left a couple littered throughout the halls. There's one beside me now—I lift a hand, but my growing fingers eclipse it.

I rip my hand away and bury my heart in my pocket. I carry it every step to Dad's room and anticipate the moment it will become too heavy to hold. Once I tell Dad the truth, it will burst and the dam I've built will break for good.

My hands rest on the knob, but I don't linger there. I rip the Band-Aid right off and fling the door open.

Except Dad's not sitting at the foot of the bed waiting for me to cry in his arms. No. He's fast asleep on his bed, his floor littered like the one at Lucas's party, a protective rune of crushed cans circling him. Snoring.

I can't help it. I laugh. It's a strange, hiccupy noise that erupts into a sob. Tears blur my vision and stain every word. "Of course he's passed out."

It's funny how a loose fray can unravel everything. I've held myself together for so long, ignored the hole in me as best I could, but none of that matters now. It's been poked and prodded and made new, my resolve undone, my fortress unmade.

Mom is dead.

It's not a cruel whisper in the shadows of my mind anymore. It's everywhere. There's no drowning it out any longer. Mom is in the ground, six-feet-under, worms-and-beetles-and-bugs *dead*. She stuck her nose in the wrong place and had it lopped right off. Just like her daughter's doing now. That same lethal curiosity, a stubborn soul that will see us in an early grave.

My pain has transformed—no stray tears slipping down my cheeks, but a face contorted and open and screaming and a hall that feels like a closing throat. My own throat is a clenched fist, too tight for any air to get through, only a silent, soul-splitting howl. Dad doesn't even stir.

Dead. Dead. Dead, dead, dead, dead, dead.

"Wil?" Elwood's hand hovers above my shoulder. A day ago, I'd have swatted it away, but not now. I lean into the only warmth I can find. I should hate him, I should scream and rage and curse at him for his parents, for what they *did*—but I can't.

I need him.

I always have.

He breaches the distance between us and I bury my sniveling face in his arms.

It's a funeral hug. There's nothing soft to it. I cling to him like he might vanish. Grief traps him in my arms and each sob racks through me harder than the last. Months of buried emotion pushes to the surface, and my breath stammers with each wave. He takes it all, his hand finding a home in my hair.

Only after the tears have dried and I pull away do I really see him. Lamplight flickers across his features and softens the depths of his hair. The winter woods might have soaked into his roots, but the light casts the darkness back out. I catch whispers of gold and auburn mingled in with all the brown.

It takes me too long to realize I'm staring. Too long to realize he's staring right back.

I nip whatever delirious emotion this is right in the bud. My eyes stray back to my father, and in my desperation, I catch something I'd glossed over.

"What is that?" I already know the answer by the time I ask. It's not the best-looking present, but it's more work than I thought Dad was capable of. I take the gift still in his hand and dig my finger into the wrapping paper. He doesn't even stir as I open it.

Merry Christmas, Minnie, the card on top reads. *I thought you should have this after all this time.* So that's why he called.

"I thought he threw this out." I've felt this only once before, this bizarre weightlessness, this hitch in my chest where the words won't come out. The day Mom disappeared and Dad sobbed, his whole soul tearing through him, never to be seen again. I feel that way now. "It's the key to Mom's office."

The door creaks open like a crypt, rusted and nearly cemented with dust. It smells like one, too.

"We should seal off that damn room," Dad said last time he stepped foot in here. "It's infested with memories. Can't get those out."

He wasn't wrong. You can call someone to get out bedbugs, but you can't do anything about the past. You can fix the ceiling and clean the carpet, but you can't fix your heart.

The light switch doesn't work immediately; it flickers like it's forgotten how. The room is a mess after my mother's heart: shelves cemented with candle wax, battered books and a bed half-made, curtains to block out the strain of the sun.

Mom spent more time here than anywhere else. Her journalism days were never far behind her. She might've switched career paths when I was born, but that intrinsic "Why?" was always with her. Each person was a mystery, their life stories a knot of yarn to unravel. And like any good journalist, she wouldn't rest until she solved the case.

"Didn't you go to my mother for counseling?"

"Yes." I can hear him swallow from across the room. "For a while. She pulled me in when my grades slipped."

"That was so shocking to me," I confess. "You always got straight As."

He takes a hesitant seat on the floor by me and tucks his knees close to his chest.

He holds himself like he's a mess of limbs, puzzle pieces that don't fit. "I'd always known I wouldn't go to college. It was so easy to ignore until junior year. Everything changed. People were getting cards in the mail, talking about life plans and where they'd like to go. For the first time, I couldn't push it away."

There's a stretch of silence that hangs over us then and his eyes dart toward me. They hold firm as I take a seat beside him. "And then you told me how you wanted to leave too. You had all these big dreams of the world and you wanted me to come with you and . . . and for once I couldn't escape it all. I started wondering what I was even doing. Why bother?"

I tip my head upward and stare at the ceiling as his words soak through me. Unlike my room, there are no stars. Nothing to splay your fingers out toward and dream for more. I never imagined what it would be like to look up and see an empty void. Nothing beyond your life here.

"It started over grades, but our talks didn't end there," Elwood continues. "I didn't have a lot of people to confide in. Not my parents or God or the church. I had so much bottled inside, so much I couldn't share even with you, and your mom—she understood without pushing me."

I bite my lip. "Mom was always good at that."

"*You're upset, Minnie,*" I still hear her voice like honey. That soft way of speaking without any edges. Whispery and delicate. I hadn't been moping. I was laughing and she cut me off mid-joke.

Dad was oblivious at the table. I remember him gawking at me, straining to see what she saw but failing. *"She doesn't seem upset."*

"She's hiding it," Mom countered. *"You should know by now, hon. Minnie's always laughing. Even when things hurt."*

Mom saw to the heart of it all. I could have a padlock for a soul, and she'd still read me like an open book. No surprise she saw through Elwood, too.

"She really helped me." His smile scrapes clean off his face. "But then she called my parents in."

"I take it that it didn't go well."

I don't miss the wince as he remembers it. "Understatement. She told my dad that he was dictating my life and ruining my opportunity to decide my own future. Had this whole spiel about my grades slipping and how I could be applying myself so much more if they only gave me the chance. How I was bending to their rules at the expense of my own dreams."

"That's Mom for you."

His eyes lock on a cobwebbed corner of the room. "I don't think he's ever had someone stand up to him like that. He . . . didn't handle it well. There's only so much pretending he can do before his patience wears thin." His voice lowers in imitation. *"I will raise my son however I see fit. He's being raised as the Lord dictates. Focus on your own wild daughter, Mrs. Greene."*

I see my mother staring Ezekiel down, his steepled hands a barrier between his world and hers. Elwood returns his gaze to his feet. "It ended with her saying, *'The Lord isn't dictating his life. You are,'* and that's what it took for him to finally storm out. He forbade me from seeing either of you. I couldn't quit on you, but your mom? She never quit on me. She knew something was wrong. Deep down, she knew. And she never stopped trying to help."

I stare at the floor. Is that why she became obsessed with him? Her need to save anyone and everyone. It's not like the lines in the wood will magically spell out an answer. But then I see it.

There might not be an answer down there, but there is a chip. A slight indent in the floor, barely noticeable with a passing glance. I crouch down to dig my fingers into the opening. The board raises, popping up like a hidden vault. I wince against the plume of dust, setting the loose board on the floor beside me. Inside, there's a small gloomy hollow.

A crumpled box sits in the center, containing a single VHS tape and a handful of yellowed pages strung together. I hoist it out of its hiding place.

Moving back to Pine Point was supposed to be a fresh start. The choice I made after I got pregnant with Wilhelmina. I couldn't raise her while I got so wrapped up in every case, losing myself to the search every time. At least, that was the plan.

But like most plans in my life, things have a way of falling apart. My careful life shattered when I met Elwood's parents. I've met men like Ezekiel Clarke. He's not the first man with a secret, and he isn't the last. I sensed it on him as soon as he walked through my office doors.

I shouldn't have pursued it. I thought I'd learned to mind myself. Turns out I haven't learned a thing.

I went to Elwood's church. I know I'm an outsider, but they looked at me like I was a secular monster. Ezekiel's sermon was short and brief, the lesson to the point: do not interfere in another man's business. "You are responsible for your own salvation." He'd been clipped and stern, his eyes locked on me the whole time. It was a biblical threat if I'd ever heard one.

Other people know to draw back when they touch a flame. I only know how to walk through the coals.

I set down the page and turn my attention to the prehistoric box TV across from Mom's bed.

I pop the tape in and the screen fills with static. After a beat, the video plays at long last, a sunny day lost in time.

Mom's calling after me as I race through the backyard. I can't be much older than eight or nine. Back when I spent all my time outside and still had the tan to show for it, my hair lightened by the sun and my cheeks awash with summer freckles.

"Why would Mom hide this?" Such a simple video hidden away.

Grass skirts around my ankles and giggles erupt from the speakers. *"Mom,* Mom! *Watch! Look at what I can do!"* Followed by a failed attempt at a cartwheel.

"You're a future Olympian, Minnie!" It's Dad's voice, and the camera flickers briefly to his face. Young and carefree. His smile unmarred by worry lines, his eyes bright and hopeful. It makes me ache. His happiness is the most outdated part of this whole video. Another wave of static steals the memory away. A new video starts playing; summer's come and gone and taken the sun with it. The film's grainy and lit only by the moon. My mother isn't smiling. Her face is hardened, her voice a whisper in the recorder: "I am about to do something very dangerous."

Like mother, like daughter.

The camera fumbles to darkness. A circle of familiar faces grace the screen: church couples surrounding the very tree I ran from earlier—the biggest one in all the Morguewood. Its branches bleed with a fresh kill, red snaking a path from the hollow in its trunk to the roots buried deep below. Mom's breath is shallow and rough.

There's murmuring, spoken words the camera can't decipher. It builds into a chanted prayer on all sides. In response to their lifted voices, the tree comes alive.

Tendrils jut from the darkness and coil across the ankles of Prudence Vrees. They dig into the flesh and burn shackles across her skin. It's such a quick, shocking movement that even on camera, it takes my mind a second to process it.

Everything is silent. The video slides a nauseating path from my mother's hand, slippery from clammy fingers, to a mound of snow. She scrambles with the lens, but the scene is wet and unfocused.

Elwood's father is a livid blur on camera, his anger recognizable even when his features aren't. "This is a mistake!" he yells into the night to anyone who will listen, Sheriff Vrees, the church, God. "There's no way. No possible way the Lord would choose *you*."

Vrees steps in front of his wife. I know the shape of him well—broad and large and taking up way too much space. "Who are you to question the word of God?"

"I am the Right Hand! I am His mouthpiece! I am—"

"A man," Vrees finishes. "You are man in the end, and God has chosen another. The Lord is saying what we already all know—I am more righteous, more devout, more levelheaded. It's high time, Ezekiel. That boy of yours is nearing manhood. Eighteen years the Lord has offered you. And now He has decided it is time to deliver and start over."

But his words have no impact on Mr. Clarke. They brush right off his shoulders. "I will not stand down to the likes of you. We must redo the ceremony. There was a mistake, I'm sure of it."

"You're *mad*," Vrees snarls. "You know the truth as well as I do. Once the seed is dug out of Elwood, you won't have much of a say. It will be planted in *my* son, not yours. The Lord has chosen me for this honor, and you will have to accept it. Perhaps use this time to focus on your faith, hmm?"

A religious burn if I've ever heard one.

"We're leaving!" Ezekiel yanks Elwood's mother's arm, ignoring her whimper of pain. "This isn't over."

Vrees's smile is ribbon-thin, eerily similar to a slashed throat. "It's only just beginning." The scene cuts to static.

I think of all the times as a child I was genuinely afraid of swallowing a seed and sprouting a whole watermelon in my chest.

A darker corner of my brain offers a different visual. I see Elwood parting his lips and a muddy clump of roots snaking out from his open throat. Foliage breaking from every orifice, his ears and eyes and nose and mouth until he's obscured by a crop of weeds. Before I know it, I'm putting my hand on his chest where his heart should be, feeling around for the squirm of roots. There's no way he has a seed in his chest. There's no way, and yet . . .

I feel a heavy thud instead. A turbulent *thump-thump-thump* in his ribs. Not a seed but a heart going wild beneath my fingers.

Elwood stumbles backward across the floor. He's sucking in air with desperate lungs. "Shit." I'll never get over hearing him curse. "I can't handle this, Wil. Holy shit. No, no, no. What were they talking about? *Digging something out of me? Putting it in someone else?*"

I'm used to pretending I'm stronger than I am. The mask I wear is chipped and worn, but I hope it does the trick now. "They're out of it, Elwood. It's probably just your heart, right? That would make more sense than having some demon seed inside you."

He freezes at my voice, eyes bulging wide at my last word.

When he speaks again, there's a strange understanding splayed across his skin. "They said I was dangerous. Sometimes I get these thoughts . . . I try to brush them off or pray them away, but they keep coming back. Things I'd never do. Violent, terrible whisperings in my brain. I . . . I saw Brian days ago, and for a terrible moment, I thought of his body mangled."

I clear my throat. "I'm pretty sure everyone's fantasized about killing Brian Schmidt." He doesn't laugh.

"Wil. I've had visions, too. Remember the bug incident back in your bathroom?"

The rippling change in his voice is enough to shake me. In the light, he's the Elwood I know, but here in the darkness, I'm not quite sure who I'm looking at. There's something undeniably feral flickering off him like a sputtering flame.

"I think they put something evil in me."

"No." I jolt to my feet, hyperconscious of every change in him. I meet his eyes and notice the explosive burst of his pupils. His irises have been overtaken by black. Beneath his skin, the veins are tinged green like the coils of vines. Night casts him in a darker light.

He looks monstrous.

"Have you ever thought about killing me?" I ask, my voice unbearably small.

His eyes widen and he breaks from his own stupor. "Never! I'd never—" He catches the look in my eyes and something breaks in him. I've seen that same grief on my own face. He shivers with the change, a severe undercurrent running through him and breaking in a cry from his clenched teeth.

It happens then.

The floorboards scream. Elwood digs his nails into the wood, his lips sputtering for words that won't come. That same dangerous energy as before ripples off him. Right beneath his skin—so potent I can sense it without even seeing it. A lot like a carcass in the woods. Like maggots and beetles beneath the bloated skin of a dead deer; you don't need to see to know it's true. You just know.

Beneath his fingertips, the room explodes in color. Weeds rip through the cracks in the floor and erupt all around us in one violent burst. Drywall caves in with an infestation of ivy. Foliage carpets the ceiling in an impossible upside-down lawn. Parts of it cave in and collapse in chunks. The corner of the room where Mom's old desk used to be has bowed in and begun to break. The ceiling hails patches of itself down on us, and a jagged clump of it slices a path down my cheek.

The sight of my blood breaks him free.

"Will!" Elwood cries, finding his voice again. He races toward me, and his fingers are cold against the flush of my neck. "Are you okay?"

I don't mean to flinch from him, but I can't help it. Here he is, the boy I know, but seconds ago he wasn't. I had no idea what he was.

His fingers fall back to his sides, and the tears welling in his eyes break through me.

He tries to back away, but I grip his wrist.

I haven't yet figured out what I'm about to tell him, but it doesn't matter. My voice is drowned out by another fierce rattle of toppling walls and wavering foundations. The ceiling is going to give out soon. This whole wing of the motel is being demolished in one freak act of nature. Elwood's midnight-black pupils have begun to recede, but they still eclipse the true color of his eyes. Somehow, someway, he did this. The fear and anger burning inside him is enough to wreak havoc. "We need to get the hell out of here."

I barrel out of the room and down the stairs with him in tow.

I've got tunnel vision on the door. I grip the knob and it swings open with a rusty cry. The blizzard embraces me with open, hungry arms.

We've only made it a couple steps into the snow and Mom's section of the motel is destroyed. I hear the deafening crash of the roof collapsing completely; the floors topple like dominoes, reduced to a smudge in the night. The greenery is carnivorous. It swallows the room whole. Not even the bones remain when it's done.

In a matter of minutes, everything has been reduced to rubble and swaying grass. And then, just as easily, the grass itself wilts and dies beneath the snap of cold. In its place is nothing.

Elwood did that.

He destroyed half the motel.

My mother's office is returned to the earth along with the rest of her.

I drag him far away from the rest of the building, which is still intact.

All that noise and I doubt my father has even stirred. He might not care about anything anymore, but I'll keep him safe. I have to.

Elwood's trembling fingers find my shoulder. He twists me around and for one grateful, fleeting moment, he's all I see. "I'm sorry," he whispers, hollow. "I'm sorry. I'm so, so sorry. I didn't mean to. I—"

The heat begins somewhere deep and then flashes and burns to the rest of me. My grief is consuming. There's no snuffing it out, but I'd do anything to try. Anything to block my vicious thoughts and the wrenching twist of my heart.

So I do the only thing I can think of. "Shut up," I beg, and I don't have time to explain my thoughts to Elwood, let alone to myself. He's frozen, too, staring so intently at his hands that I'm not even sure he hears me. "I don't want to think about anything right now. Distract me or I'm going to lose my mind."

Dad's got his vices. I've got mine. I think about all the ways I've dodged my grief left and right. The bottles I've emptied, the smoke I've held in my lungs, the sloppy drunk kisses with guys I didn't give a shit about. Anything and everything I'd do to feel something else.

Make it go away. Make it all go away.

"What?" he whispers, but I refuse to meet his eyes. I step forward and he scuttles back until his spine presses into the bark of a tree. He was a monster in my mother's office, but I'm determined to make a human out of him. Now he's only a boy.

There's a siren pull to seize the shrinking space between us, to abandon it all, and I'm helpless.

This won't fix me. Nothing on this earth will fix me. But if it means breaking up the grief for a couple minutes, so be it.

Elwood's lips are close. His breath spills like autumn wind.

"This doesn't mean anything." And then I smash my mouth to his.

CHAPTER SEVENTEEN

ELWOOD

Wilhelmina Greene is kissing me.

I breathe her in and my stomach erupts with heat. Nothing in the last ten minutes makes any sense. Everything keeps rushing, rushing, rushing past, and it's impossible to focus. I don't see anything save for the motion lines and the blur of the air as things pass me by. I'm aware of it all happening: the kiss, the feeling of a lit coal I had in my gut as the weeds engulfed the floorboards, the sickening crack of a building wasting away to nothing, Wil looking at me like I'm someone to be scared of.

This doesn't mean anything, she said before her lips crushed mine. But it means everything. At least, to me it does.

She's close. So close, I could scream. I revel in the turbulent beating of her heart, the flush of her chest against mine.

Her lips are as soft as I remember. The memory of our first kiss is an imprint that will never go away. Wil and I beneath the bleachers freshman year, watching the bitter sway of the pine. Her eyes glossing over mine, dark and purposeful. "Have you ever kissed someone?"

Swallowing a chunk of apple so hard, I nearly choked to death. "O-of course not . . . Have you?" I don't remember a blush ever hurting so bad.

"No. I just want to see what the big deal is. Don't you?"

It had been that easy. She'd kissed me then, just to see. It had been an awkward smash of lips. A closemouthed, eyes-wide-open, five-second ordeal. Afterward, she'd smudged away the imprint of my lips with a smear of her sleeve. "I don't see what all the hype is about."

But I did. I thought about it every night and every morning and all the times in between.

My hands must be possessed after all because I reach for a fistful of Wil's hair and drag her closer. Maybe it's my sleep-addled mind, maybe it's the hunger I'd buried deep exploding to the surface. There's no fighting this. There's no denying this.

She takes the lead, and we meld together into one dizzying blur of light, color, and sound. The ground rumbles alongside my pulse, flowers sprouting with every kiss. Planted and raised by my own desire. Petals like bruises, vines that mimic her curves. A kiss that lasts forever yet ends all too soon.

I draw back, mesmerized by the sight of her. Lips bursting red, a face that fits perfectly within my hands. My thumb darts out and brushes against her cheek. Her eyes were brown before, but they've deepened. They are limitless.

The wind whips her hair, sending it spiraling all around her. I dream of sketching her one last time, another portrait to add to my collection. She's always been an enigma of sharp lines, never a soft bone in her body. So many papers torn, the lead piercing through. No canvas has ever been strong enough to hold her.

Wil breaks away, horrified.

She takes a step back, but all I can focus on is the red of her lips. Puffy and swollen from the tug of my teeth. "Holy shit. I shouldn't have done that."

I blanch.

"We're tired," she continues, slow and purposeful.

With the fog lifting from my thoughts, I look to the moon. God's watchful eye staring down from the heavens. There's the cracking sound again of a foundation falling apart, but the walls are my ribs and my heart doesn't stand a chance beneath the rubble. I feel every puncture and bruise of the collapse.

She's scared of you, the voice inside me whispers.

"That didn't mean anything," Wil says again. The flowers wilt at my sides and die at her words. "That was a mistake."

"A mistake?" I whisper, and I can taste ash on my tongue.

She hates you.

She flashes me a look, but her eyes don't rest on mine. "Did you want it to mean something?"

She can't even stand to look at me, can she?

Don't be selfish. You're only going to hurt her. You'll ruin her. "No," I whisper, and it's so achingly untrue. "You're right. It was a mistake."

She nods, and her hands shove deep into her pockets. "Then let's forget about it. We should go, Elwood. I know someone who can help. Vrees and your dad are probably looking for us now. If we stay any longer, we might ruin the rest of the motel and hurt Dad. I don't want to get him involved in this."

Don't want him involved with you.

I should tell her to run away. I should tell her to forget all about me and let me deal with my fate alone. But in the end, I am so very, very selfish. Selfish enough to hold her tight as we bike away.

With the fire lulled between us, the cold reenters with a vengeance.

The bike groans as we crawl on top of it. Between the half-deflated tires and the ice-slicked streets, disaster waits with bated breath.

"We should be wearing helmets," I say, half out of genuine concern and half to break the silence.

"Hold tight and you'll be fine."

The streetlights offer a small path through the empty streets, the soft glow of the lamps breaking some of the blinding silver. On the bike, things are ten times colder. The wind howls against us, searching for the best way to tear through our clothes.

The road begins to wind upward, the start of a hill. We stumble to a stop, and I drop a leg to steady us. "We'll need to walk this. Otherwise we'll pick up speed on the way down and go flying to our death," she says.

"Didn't think safety was a priority of yours," I comment.

She rolls her eyes, but there's a slight smile tugging at the corners of her lips. It's the closest back to normal we can get.

We each grip onto a handlebar, lugging the bike on opposite ends. Walking down the hill proves just as hard as climbing it, if not worse. Wil stumbles with the last step, her feet sliding out from under her. I scoop her in time, and with her back pressed into my chest like this, I can hardly breathe.

"Careful," I wheeze.

"I could have caught myself." She shimmies a little, planting a hand on her hip. "Here, you fall next, and we'll be even."

"I'm going to pass on the trust fall. Pretty sure I'd break something."

She's about to mount the bike again, but I beat her to it. "Here, let me. It's only fair, right?"

She grumbles something in response, but her energy is shot. I can tell. She doesn't relent. I do my best not to hyper-focus on her arms curled across my chest and her head resting in the open space between my shoulder blades as I pedal. A perfect fit.

We can't escape the forest as we ride. We're perilously close to the trees. Its borders have Pine Point locked in from one end to the next.

This town might have scraped out a civilization for themselves, but the woods never left.

Somewhere between the dead branches, I catch a whir of movement in the distance. My father's face appears from the branches, his expression indignant and his nostrils flaring in the dark.

There's no outrunning him, is there? He's tracked me here, and I have the distinct feeling that I could run to the end of the earth and still find him standing there behind me.

"Elwood," he says, my name a command. The bike lurches to a stop, my mind and body freezing over. He takes a step forward, and I know Wil is hitting my back, begging for me to *move*, but I can't. "Come willingly and I'll make this easy."

Nothing about this is easy. Not even remotely. But there's a siren call in his voice, a desire to relinquish control and stop fighting. To do what I've always done in the face of my father: give up.

"Elwood! Don't listen to him!"

Wil's voice breaks me from my trance, her horror catapulting me into action. My reflexes are faster than either of us bargained for. The bike goes skidding down the street. I catch a subtle whiff of burning rubber as I kick it into overdrive.

"Sharp left," Wil barks in my ear, her breath spilling out hot against my skin. *"Now!"*

I speed in the opposite direction, barreling forward at her command. My father's shouting after us, but I'm faster than him. I ride harder than I ran in the forest. My muscles are long spent, but I push myself to keep going.

The snowdrifts pick up, crashing into us like frozen waves hitting the shore.

I'm not sure how long we ride, but it feels like half a lifetime. She directs me through winding streets, screaming directions above the howling wind. Straight at the stoplights ("Are you seriously stopping? Do you see any cars on the road, Elwood?"), right at the tree that's got a lady's face carved into it, so on and so forth. We ride until I think I might collapse right there in the snow.

"I think we lost him," she says once we've made it past the lights.

"For now," I counter, but my shoulders slump just a tad. Each word is labored. "Now, where is this house?"

"Uh . . . look for Abe Lincoln. You'll turn by him." She clears her throat, elaborating. "We're going to a family friend's house. One of her neighbors has a yard of junk. It looks like a dump. She's got a giant Abe. It's Christmas, so he should be dressed like Santa. She only comes out to change him into seasonally appropriate outfits."

Sure enough, we cross the street and Abe points the way with a candy-cane staff. He's snow-drenched, most of him indistinguishable. The rest of the lawn is just as horrible. The bulk of it is hidden, but a decent chunk still peeks out.

"Cherry's house is the one with the dark roof."

"You realize all of the roofs are white right now," I offer delicately. She groans.

"Follow my finger," she says instead, pointing a wavering hand over to the third house down the street: 817 Phoenix Wood Lane.

We clear the driveway and topple off the bike. I try to set it down gently, but it sinks into a sea of frost anyway.

We push a path through the snow. My jeans are drenched. The cold sneaks its way inside my shoes, running over my socks until they're sopping wet.

"Keep moving," Wil pushes. "I want to get inside before my nose falls off or your parents kill us, thank you."

We finally make it to the front step. My sneakers push past some of the snow, enough to make out a floor mat beneath us. It's a sultry purple, broken up by two little words: GO AWAY.

CHAPTER EIGHTEEN

WIL

Cherry's got a sturdy door.

If she didn't, it would have splintered in two by now. I pound on it for dear life. It's worse than cold out here. It's unlivable. The wind has whipped my cheeks a permanent, stinging red. I fuss with my hair, but it still flies around me in a mess. Even breathing is a challenge.

"Come on, Cherry!"

My phone has started buzzing incessantly since we got to her door. *One missed call . . . Two missed calls . . . Fifteen missed calls . . .*

```
Dad: Where are you? Wil!


Dad: [IMAGE_0164]


Dad: Call me this second, Wilhelmina!!!!
```

I know this puts me in the running for Worst Daughter of All Time, but I can't bear to listen to his frantic voice right now. All the missed calls on Mom's phone, the same nervous energy zapping off him like an electric current.

Later, I promise myself.

Behind the door, I hear the pads of feet hitting the floor, the *mraaaow* of Cherry's cat, Starlight, scratching against wood. There's a second of hesitation—Cherry peeping through at us, probably making sure we're not the owner of the corner store after her at long last—before the locks click open. Her makeup has been wiped off, but remnants of blue eye shadow linger on her waterline like a permanent stain.

Starlight is caught beneath her arm. He squints his buggy eyes at Elwood, trying to determine whether he hates him or not.

"Wil!" Cherry's voice cycles between startled and confused, and confused and concerned. She clears her throat, her eyes landing on Elwood for an unsteady, hard moment. Her smile drops a tad, breaking into a severe line across her face. She throws me a sharp look and I remember her warning well. By now, though, she should know that following orders and advice isn't my best trait. She coughs. "You're lucky my insomnia pills are shit."

"Come on, let us in, please; we don't have time," I tell her, throwing another hurried look over my shoulder.

She follows my gaze beyond the scope of her lawn, down to the cold, empty street. She lingers a while longer before breaking from the trees. Those blue eyes of hers land hard on Elwood, and something close to dread breaks in her face. She stares at Elwood with the intensity of a scientist ogling a specimen through a microscope. "What are you?"

"Human." There's a jagged cut to his voice.

She scrunches her face at that, unconvinced but relenting. With a crack of her knuckles, she turns to me. "If you say so. Come in. You could be bigfoot, but if Wil trusts you, I trust you." She ushers us in with a sweep of her bony wrist. The door is a welcome barrier against the raging cold.

"I promise Starlight doesn't bite much . . . well . . . he will bite you at least once, but it's a form of endearment." Her voice has an odd strain to it, but the fear has melted from her tone.

I lift my arm, pointing at a lingering mark on my skin to break up the tension. "Get bit and join the club." My attempt at a joke is weak at best.

Cherry's home is an exact caricature of her—satchels of dried flowers and herbs hanging from her ceiling, bold rugs assembled together like mismatched puzzle pieces. The wall is flooded with oddities: a mirror resembling a cat's-eye that she found in her late neighbor's garbage, a glass case of river rocks and pretty weeds, and a portrait shrine for Morticia Addams.

"Oh my God," Elwood mouths. I jab my elbow into his ribs, but really, I can't blame him.

Her house is like a sucker punch to the gut.

"Here, sit. You two look like Popsicles." She guides us to deep purple cushions. Couches are for normal people—something Cherry wouldn't be caught dead with. Instead, we sit on a chaise lounge with a twisted wooden frame. It is velvet-lined, the trims painted gold. I only know what it is because we've had a full conversation about it. "Found this little lady on her way to the dump. People have no taste."

Cherry doesn't own a TV; she claims she can hear the low pulse of static rolling off it from a mile away. Her living room consists of the chaise lounge, a dark walnut coffee table, a parlor chair, and a couple low-rise tables—only there to hold her copious amount of candles.

"Remember to lock the door," I harp at her.

"Don't worry about that, kid. I've got a protection ward," she trills from the kitchen. "Fine, I'll do it myself." I twist the dead bolt into place.

The lights above us twitch as I rejoin Elwood. They sizzle and burn within their bulbs, a tiny coil exploding into an enclosed flame. And then it's black. Shot from blinding to nothing in a matter of seconds.

Starlight leaps from Cherry's arms, and we hear a curse in the kitchen. The power has been zapped throughout the entire house. If it were any other home—especially with the blinds drawn shut as they are—we would be bound into darkness. But the votives trapped within smoky glasses and long tapering candles in alternating shades of red and black save us. A large enough collection to give any firefighter a heart attack on sight. It's soothing, though. Reminds me of Mom.

"You guys okay in there?" Cherry calls from the other room, her voice carrying in a shrill, worried way. We each mumble something to the effect of "Yeah, your ten million candles make a difference." She hums at that, content neither of us have grievously injured ourselves in the dark.

Starlight begins to sniff his way over. I prepare for him to get snippy and hiss at one of us—maybe even leap toward me and attack for the hell of it—but he doesn't.

"Ignore him and he'll leave you alone," I grumble.

With the adrenaline high gone, doubt creeps in to take its place. Elwood isn't human—not fully. There's something in him. I'd been too eager to brush off the incident at the house.

Engulfed in vines and weeds, infested with greenery. I'd seen his eyes burn black and his mouth contort. He hadn't looked like a boy; he'd looked like a beast.

I shake it away and a new fresh memory takes its place. I kissed him. Elwood Clarke. I pushed him into a tree and kissed him.

I burn as scarlet as Cherry's hair.

"Here, kitty," Elwood calls, oblivious to me. The cat paddles closer to him, leaping in one strained burst. I brace myself to see Starlight go straight for his face, but he doesn't. Instead the cat walks in circles on his lap, pawing and kneading his legs into shape before collapsing. If I'm not losing it, I hear a soft rumble, too. A deep, contented purr.

Elwood scratches the tufts behind Starlight's ears, his free hand rubbing his belly. I try to find my voice. It comes out as a pathetic squeak: "I forgot how much you love cats."

"I've spent half my life begging for one." The petting picks up at that, almost as if in defiance. He mimics his mother, his voice rising higher: "Animals are dirty, Elwood." He clears away the fake voice with a cough. "But look at him, he's not dirty. He's even wearing a sweater."

Sure enough, Starlight is sporting a scratchy holiday number that reads MERRY CHRISTMAS, YA FILTHY ANIMAL. It's no longer Christmas, and Starlight chews on the fabric like he might be able to rip the thing off with effort.

"Right?" Elwood picks back up, but when he finally—finally—looks up, I swallow, my fingers twitching in the space close to his. A blush of his own creeps up, and I watch his eyes drop again to my lips.

"I don't know if you're hungry." Cherry breaks the tension with her presence, making us both jump out of our skin.. She sets a bowl of roasted dandelion root in front of us and some questionable-looking berries. I don't know why I was expecting peanuts or a frozen pizza.

"Sure these aren't poisonous?" I ask her, eyeballing a palmful of the berries. They're as red as everything else she owns.

She shrugs, pops one in her mouth, swallows. "Haven't killed me yet."

I guess I'm willing to take those odds. I take a bite and leave the charred dandelions for Elwood. "Would you look at that?" Cherry breathes, staring right past me to Elwood. "Starlight rarely takes to strangers. Did you bribe him?"

"He's the cat whisperer," I tell her, deadpan.

She blinks. "Huh." Her hands move as she speaks, and she pops a dandelion into her mouth. Then comes the crunch. "So, you're Elwood. Notorious Clarke's son. I'm Cherry Delacroix, Wil's personal handler and fill-in grandma."

He jumps at the sound of his own name. Starlight lets out a frustrated mew, readjusting himself on Elwood's lap. He pets harder as an apology.

Somewhere in the shadows of Cherry's house, a cuckoo clock sings the time. "You match Wil's stories. Her mother's, too. I knew who you were the moment I opened my door. You were right, Wil. He is quite the looker, isn't he?"

All the blood rushes to my face. I nearly shatter the cup against the floor. "Stop lying, Cherry!"

Beside me, Elwood turns scarlet, huffing at my quick dismissal.

Cherry's lips pucker at the corners. "Don't fret, dear. The girl is stubborn, but she isn't blind." Before I have the chance to squawk out anything else, she sets her drink down on its saucer with a harsh clack. "All right, then, let's get to it."

That shuts us both up. I swallow once. Twice.

Cherry's hands are weathered and bony, the polish faded and chipped on each finger. "You're not going to believe us," I promise.

"Try me."

I fill my lungs with air and then push it all back out—I focus on that, my chest sinking and rising in rhythm. And then I tell her. It's a long spiel, broken up only by Elwood's random frenzied interjections. Cherry listens intently, not once stopping to tell me that we sound like raving lunatics. She nods along as if we're recounting a perfectly normal story.

When I've finished, or at least when I finally stop to catch my breath, she waits a beat and then says, "Your mother's intuition was unparalleled. I thought it was dangerous and I warned her to keep out of it, but that's where the two of you are so alike. Stubborn to a fault. She knew if I got a whiff of her research, I'd shut it down." Her mouth quivers with emotion. She brushes her fingers across Mom's handwriting as I drag the page out, and something breaks in her face. "Look where it got her."

Stars burn beyond the living room window, and the moon trickles in through cracked curtains.

"Mom started this, and we need to finish it, Cherry. Will you help us save him?"

Cherry massages out a brewing headache in her temples. "If you don't mind, I'd like to talk to Elwood alone. You know how it is. Too many auras in a room gives me a killer migraine. It's just the two of you, but God you both have some intense energy."

"But I—" I start.

"You want my help, don't you?" she asks, daring me to contradict her.

"Yes," I groan, shrinking down like I'm five years old all over again. And now Cherry is telling me to go to my room.

"Why don't you get things situated downstairs?" she suggests with a dismissive flip of her hand. "Maybe some shut-eye. Lord knows you need it. Your bags are worse than mine, and I'm more than twice your age."

"Love that, thanks. I guess I'll go sit in the basement alone while you try to talk to Elwood's demon."

She blows me a kiss and I roll my eyes, seeing myself out. The horror only floats to the surface once I'm halfway down the stairs.

Elwood's demon.

CHAPTER NINETEEN

ELWOOD

Ms. Delacroix is like a Victorian ghost haunting over her home. Her vibrant red hair is teased and pulled into shape. No matter how many times I look at her, she doesn't seem real.

"You can see the thing inside me?"

"Yes." She doesn't waste a second. "It lights up when you look out to the forest. Bit like a dog scratching at the door, wanting to be let out."

I subconsciously raise my hand to my chest, brushing against it like I might feel the spirit's claws. "How do I get it out of me?" I whisper. I'm still not sure whether it can hear me or not, but I've convinced myself that the threat is real. Ms. Delacroix says nothing, inclining her head over to the kitchen. I follow and sit down on the chair she swings out for me.

The kitchen isn't nearly as cluttered as the living room. It's much smaller, the space dedicated to a garden of kitchen herbs. Some are hanging potted plants, their vines snaking out toward the windowsill in search of light. Others are planted neatly in rows along the walls. She's got an army of tiny jars along her counter, each filled to the brim with freshly collected herbs.

"I'm not sure if I have the answer to that," she says, a wistful expression crossing her features.

Her answer hurts more than I anticipated. I try not to let it show, but it must be obvious. She straightens her emotions out, offering me a forced smile. "I think this calls for tea. Bolivian black, perhaps?"

She turns before I can respond and starts fussing over a copper kettle. I hear the rush of the faucet and the click of the stove turning on.

"Wil used to talk about me?" It's out of my mouth before I can think to contain it.

Ms. Delacroix doesn't turn, but her back twitches with a laugh. The warm light rains down on her hair, making it almost orange. I hadn't noticed before, but she's got a dozen little charms hidden throughout it. They catch the light, sparkling through her locks.

"Wouldn't shut up about you," she tells me. It's enough to make my insides burn. "She cared deeply; I can tell you that. She'd kick my ass for saying it, though."

Cared.

"I want things to be normal between us again," I confide in her, idly tracing the wood grain of the table with my finger. "We used to be so close before it happened. We'd never fought before, but . . . I mean, she accused my family of kidnapping. I told her if she didn't drop the accusation, I couldn't be friends with her. And . . . well, I'm guessing you can see where that went. She was right all along and now everything is ruined."

"You both made decisions you thought were right." Ms. Delacroix hums. The kettle whistles along with her. Before I can wipe the expression away, she continues: "I'll let you in on a secret, kid. I'm not an old hag yet, but I'm old enough to know some things, at least." She clicks the stove off, preparing us two mismatched cups, and waits for them to steep before bringing them over.

I nod my thanks, tracing the handle of my cup. It's painted over with toadstools as red as her hair and dark green frogs perched upon them.

"Everyone's bound to make a million mistakes growing up, but there's always going to be that one nagging one. Something you regret deeply but can never truly fix or change. You two were only thinking of yourselves. Nothing wrong in that, but nothing right either." She pauses for a large sip. "We have all seen trees grow in odd places. Bent out of shape, warped by their surroundings. You grow from mistakes. The two of you aren't the same people you were last year. You won't be a year from now, either. I'm barely the same person each morning when I wake up." She flashes me a wink. "Assuming my insomnia lets me sleep, of course."

"So, there's hope?" I whisper.

"There's always hope," she answers with a nonchalant roll of her shoulders. "As hokey as that may sound."

My finger circles the rim of my cup. The tea ripples like the skip of a stone across a pond. "Thanks, ma'am. I needed that."

"Please stop with the 'ma'am' and 'Ms. Delacroix' nonsense. It's Cherry."

I nod, and she grins for real. "It's funny," she comments out of the blue, staring down at the reflection in her cup. "When you're sad, the plants around you wilt and fade, but the moment you're calm, they burst back to life. Take a look at the room around you."

I crane my neck around, bracing myself for what I'll see. The vines have drifted off the wall, growing toward me. They reach out, their tips inches away from my skin. All of them rush out to hold me, to twist around my flesh and claim me for the woods.

As I startle, they jerk, falling limp and slithering back in place on the wall. "You'd make one hell of a gardener, kid." Cherry snorts.

I can't help it; I laugh. The plants join in. Flower petals opening and closing like tiny mouths. The sight of it shuts me up fast. I turn my attention back to my cup. It's a deep amber, warm enough to chase the cold from my bones. I cling onto it, tiny shivers running across my arms. The first sip goes down easily enough—nutty and full-bodied like the dense woods sprawled around us.

"So, I suppose we should start the tarot reading now, shall we?" Cherry's long nails tap against the ceramic cup, a series of harsh clicking noises. "Tell me first, what's on your mind?"

I have a sneaking suspicion she can see inside my thoughts already.

"Too much to put into words," I confess, trying to make sense of my jumbled head. At the forefront, though, I see Mrs. Greene's smiling face. Her notebook with the purple spirals and the bright ribbons she spun through her hair each day. I hadn't noticed her smile slipping farther off her face each day or the fear building in her eyes. She knew about me. This whole time, she knew. "I feel . . . guilty. Mrs. Greene died because of me."

Cherry's eyes drop to the table. "Sophie knew what she was getting into. She made that choice on her own."

"I keep thinking if I focus hard enough, all of this will go away somehow," I say, and I notice the flowers sighing and wilting all around me. Petals shriveling and falling to the floor. Dead. Dead because of me. Wil's old house razed to the ground at my touch. The fear in her eyes.

"Can you speak to it?" Cherry asks, drawing my attention away from the destruction I've caused.

"Speak to it?" I yelp. "I don't want to speak to it. I want it gone."

It came to me in a spark at the library, a subtle heartbeat thumping in tandem with mine. *Ba-dump, ba-dump, ba-dump.* It hadn't felt like anything out of my control. And at the party when it spun in my head and I coughed up a moth. Again, in Wil's bathroom mirror, bugs bleeding from the walls and my face transforming into one I didn't recognize. It had been a seedling then, not yet sprouted. Not yet powerful.

At the house, it was different. It grew and became insatiable; two bodies living beneath the same skin. I'd felt it flare and blossom. There was a sense of nothingness as it took over. Just a second and it had dug my fingers into the floorboards and destroyed everything in its path.

One wretched, helpless second. That's all it took.

Cherry takes a full sip of her drink. "Like it or not," she says, "it's inside you, Elwood. You should at least learn who you're sharing a body with."

Sharing a body. The thought conjures up a disturbing image, another head sprouting from my neck, half of my body mine and the other half completely beyond my control.

"I'm not doing it." I growl, and I curse myself for feeling angry. My fuse used to be one never-ending wick. Kick me, punch me, bully me. Brian Schmidt had tormented me for years and I'd tolerated it all. Bowed my head and hoped it would end soon. Now rage has flown out from the Pandora's box inside me, and it shows no sign of going away.

If Brian jabbed me in the ribs again, I fear what I'd do. Maybe I'd lose myself. The darkness would wash over me and one second is all it would take. One second of darkness and the vines would crawl up his skin.

"I think it's deeply important that you do." Cherry rolls her shoulders in a loose shrug. She seems immune to my outburst, and I suppose I have Wil to thank for that one. "Discovering what's inside of you is something I can help you with, but it won't be easy. Here, why don't you give it a try?"

I force myself to be gentle. I force myself to be the person I thought I was. "You don't understand. It's dangerous."

"It's more dangerous if you don't learn to control it," she tells me.

I whip away from her and I taste blood on my lips from the scrape of my teeth. "I don't even know how to do that."

Cherry gestures in one quick sweeping motion for me to close my eyes. "Pretend you're outside like you were with me. Ask to be let in."

On the back of my eyelids, I see nothing but swirling darkness.

I imagine the beast lurking behind a heavy wooden door, trapped within the depths of my mind. Darkness pushes beneath the cracks and curls at my feet, and beyond the barrier, I hear a monstrously large patter of wings.

It holds on, its voice one incomprehensible, insectile scream. The sound lasts only a couple seconds, but those seconds expand until they feel like minutes or hours of suffocation. I wait for more to happen, for the past to flood out and trap me under its weight. For the darkness to overtake me and destroy everything.

But by some miracle, it doesn't. The darkness recedes and the door stays intact.

I heave for air and fling open my eyes, free at last. It takes me longer than it should to find my voice, but when I do, I pant, "I'm never doing that again."

Cherry's no longer looking at me. She's spreading a row of cards down on the table. It almost looks like a normal deck, but I know it isn't. The backs of the cards are hand-painted a thunderstorm gray, a smidge lighter than black.

"Why not consult the cards in the meantime, then?" She hums. "Go on, ask a question."

I gnaw on my cheek, my fingers pushing down on my rib cage to calm my pounding heart. "What sort of question?" So many of them compete inside my thoughts.

She rests her face into her palm. "Anything, really—though, for your sake, maybe get to the point."

I gulp. "What's going to happen to me?" I look at her for guidance, but all I get is a barely there nod. Nothing to indicate whether I messed up or not.

She waves a hand toward the deck. "And now, the most important part: choose whichever cards call you and slide them my way."

Call me? I stare down at the full spread. They're all identical. No creases or chipped paint or anything. I twitch toward the one on my left, but then my fingers freeze, hesitant. What if I'm overthinking this? What if I pick a horrifically awful card by accident?

I close my eyes, drawing my hand out and sliding forward the cards at random.

Cherry tells me to open my eyes and return my attention to the deck. "Done?" she says, musing to herself.

"Done."

She flips them over one by one. In place of the cards, I watch the gradual widening of her eyes every time she sees something decidedly bad. "Holy Major Arcana, kid."

"Is—is that bad?" I ask the words I've been meaning to ask this whole time. "Do I need to redraw?"

"No, you picked these cards for a reason. I mean, a bunch of Major Arcana isn't bad, per se . . . The cards have a lot to say today. Guess a big problem requires big cards." Her nail rests on the first card she flipped over. It seems pleasant enough. A bright blue sky, green grass, two dogs barking up at the clouds.

"The moon," she clarifies, tapping at the card's title. "You picked this card for your present."

"What does it mean?" If it's my present situation, it can't be good. I wait to hear her say as much.

"It means you're spiraling. Lost."

My mother would burn this deck if she knew I was consulting it for anything. I gulp.

"Tarot never lies." Cherry chuckles, though it's got a vaguely protective sound to it. "Now on to your problem card." She flips the next one. "This one signifies the challenge you are trying to overcome."

She doesn't need to explain it. I can stare down at the miserable card and decipher it on my own. A skeleton trampling over corpses on a battlefield, *Death* scrawled underneath.

"Never mind; I hate this." I'm already wincing and she hasn't even said anything about it yet. Death couldn't possibly be flowers and rainbows.

"Death's never a fun one." She levels with me, though I catch her rolling her eyes at my melodrama. "But it doesn't always mean *death* death. It's, uh, a metamorphosis of sorts. Plus, paired with the moon, that's usually a good light-at-the-end-of-the-tunnel deal. But yeah, in a nutshell: you're dealing with an upcoming transformation."

A transformation sounds almost worse than death. I imagine my skin peeling from my bones and my mouth drawing into one sharp pincer. Eyes bulging from my sockets. Darkness overtaking every part of me.

She continues as if it's nothing. "Your past is a reversed Ten of Cups. Yada yada, broken family life. Funny you flipped this because the original way means 'happy home.' Clearly not the case with you. Then we come to the future, the Fool."

"Why does the deck hate me?"

That gets a smirk out of her. "New beginnings," she corrects. "It means you've got to take a leap toward something. You're stuck, but you need to make a choice. Choosing is imperative. Next comes your advice card, if you'll take it. The reversed Eight of Swords. You need to re-visit . . . something, now that you can see your issues clearly."

"And then the outcome?" I ask, staring down at the very last card. The Tower looks like the worst one yet. It's exactly what it says it is, a tower, only there's a bolt of lightning hitting the top and people are quite literally falling to their death out of the open window.

"Disaster. By the end of this, everything will change. Your life won't be the same."

Cherry's words stay with me as I walk down the stairs. The candles light my path, guiding me to the guest room with a trail of dancing orange flames.

Everything ends soon. The cards said as much. It all ends in chaos and flames, my body no longer my body at all. The death of my life and the start of another. The demon overtaking me.

I crane my neck into the basement. The room is painted floor to ceiling in red. Lace curtains dripping down to the floor like blood, a vanity curling in on itself like it's got a pair of horns, red-stained paintings of flower petals and Victorian-era dresses. It's almost claustrophobic.

And, of course, Wil isn't asleep. She sits on the foot of the bed, her eyes hard and expectant. "Well? What did she say?"

"I'm dangerous." My voice breaks in my throat—I've pulled the stitch too far and now I am unraveling at the seams. "But we knew that already. Running away was a mistake, Wil. Something bad is going to hap-pen soon. Something really, really bad, and you know what? There's no stopping it." I force the next words out of a painfully dry throat: "What if I go back?"

She jumps to her feet and stalks toward me, her finger wedging be-tween my ribs. "Your family wants to kill you, El. Or did you forget that?"

El. I haven't heard that in so long.

My voice comes out in a half sob, a broken hiccup of a noise that bleeds with frustration. "Maybe for good reason. I'm dangerous. You know that." Black talons stroke my thoughts, tracing teasing patterns. The demon's fetid breath whispers in my ear, reminding me that we are one.

"What the hell did Cherry tell you?"

My fingers are no longer twitching but outright shaking. "She read my cards. They were bad, Wil, really bad. Probably as bad as the deck could even get. But that's hardly what matters. You saw what I did to your motel. You were scared of me. You can't deny that."

She blanches white. "Your life is worth more than whatever a bunch of cards have to say. And about the motel . . . that wasn't you. At least, not the real you. This isn't over yet."

"It's been over from the start. Like I've told Kevin and Lucas, my life has never been a choice. It's been laid out by my parents since birth. It only makes sense that fate's got a hand in it too." My head feels heavier, so I bury it in the palms of my hands. I taste the salt of my sweat trickling down my face. "I should be used to it by now, but I'm not. I've never stopped dreaming of a normal life. I've never been to a football game, a dance, anything. I go home and study for hours, and for what? I don't get to go to college! I don't get to go off and do anything. I'm whatever creature my parents want me to be."

"None of those things would make you normal," Wil interjects, her face twisting into a grimace. "Normal doesn't exist—"

"What do you know?" The words slip out before I can swallow them back. They escape through the cracks in my teeth. I clamp a hand over my mouth, but I'm unable to shut myself up. There's that temper again. I'm not used to my words flying out like that. I've always sat and simmered on every sentence, but now my deepest thoughts fly free. "I didn't mean that—I'm sorry—"

When she speaks again, her voice is venomous enough to send me stumbling back. "Is it normal for your mother to be murdered? Is it normal for your best friend to leave you when you need him most? Is it normal to care about him even though you should hate him?"

My voice finds me again after a minute. "You said you hated me. You said what happened back there with us meant nothing."

"I lied," she hisses back. "Believe me, I don't want it to. It would make everything so much easier. I just . . . can't do it."

She steps forward; I step back. *Don't get any closer.*

I can't let myself get sucked into this. There's no staying here, not when there's a monster inside me. Not when staying spells disaster.

"Please, Wil." My eyes roam over her. Limbs as snappable as twigs, the delicate flesh of her throat—easily ripped out by the muzzle of a beast. "I don't want you to get hurt. I . . . I think I—" *Love you.*

My world shifts with the truth. It's existed inside me for so long, but I'd smothered it deep down. Now that it's in the air, I've become vulnerable. I feel like my heart is no longer within my ribs but growing from the outside. It's Wil's for the taking. She could pluck it off me and sink her teeth into it if she wished. I have become so very vulnerable.

My chest stings with her nearness. It hurts to breathe the same air. I don't trust myself. There's a storm brewing in my veins and she could get swept away in it easily. I could ruin her.

But how easy it would be to lose myself. To close the gap and let her do whatever she wants. To not be good, but to be whatever she wants me to be.

"We shouldn't," I whisper, but it's directed less at her and more at the quivering sensation deep within me. The lingering sensation of sin. I shouldn't be doing this. I've spent years trying to shove this feeling down, only for it to rear its ugly head again and again. I've never been able to stomp it out. "It's da—"

"If you say 'dangerous' one more time, I'm going to lose it," she snarls. Her body is pressed to mine, hard and fierce and too much. Way too much. I need her closer. I need her far, far away. "I was scared back at the house, you're right, but I . . . I'm not anymore, El. I know you. I've known you forever."

I kiss her and it's a brutal, terrible thing.

I kiss her and I taste blood. The iron tang of her teeth digging into my lip, of her tongue running along mine. Desperate and starving and so spine-chillingly perfect.

I kiss her and I want more. So much more than she can offer me. I'll take all that she can give.

CHAPTER TWENTY

WIL

Every second, he is changing. His body is a breaking cage. I'm a breath away from a monster; one wrong move and I could release it.

He looks at me and all I see are the blooming bruises beneath his eyes and the bloodshot veins closing in on his pupils. Beneath the tender flesh of his chest, I feel the scrape of what feels like a thorn. My lips move to his throat. I bite that smooth skin of his, covering it with years of unspent emotions. Consuming, crushing feelings I've hidden beneath the surface.

Flush against me, I feel the quiver of his arms, the sheen of sweat slick against his throat. I wonder what Cherry would think of his aura now. Swirling black, murky flashes of bright blue, rippling pulses of red.

It's easy, kissing him.

"Do you like anyone?" I asked years ago, oblivious, leaning my head in his lap and staring up at the clouds. They were puffy and full, and one of them looked like Texas. *"Any crushes I should know about?"*

My hands were calloused, his soft. I liked holding them. Feeling them brush against my hairline. He lifted up a couple strands and busied himself with a little braid. He trembled, his nerves traveling a live-wire path from his fingers to my scalp. His emotions ran deeper in me than my own.

"Do you?"

"I asked you first," I accused.

"Maybe . . ." He swallowed, and I could feel it. *"Yeah, I think I do."*

There's no talking now. He falls back and I lean forward, exploring more, claiming more. Mine. There's that word again. I suspect it's always been there ever since I first met him. *Mine.*

I lift up the corner of his shirt and his birthmark stares back at me, a perfect crescent sliced along his chest. I trace it without thinking, my finger running from one edge to the other.

The rest of him is scarred in other ways. So many slashes across his chest, his shoulders, his back. He shies away from my eyes as I take in every cut. His parents did this. They hoped to ruin him, but they didn't succeed. I press a kiss to each one and he shudders, a soft noise breaking from his lips. He catches himself on the mattress with splayed hands.

This feels like a fever dream. I'll wake up, dig a hole, and bury the memory away. Or maybe it's a nightmare instead. Either way, I'll follow it to the bitter end.

I stare at him—all the ways he's changed and all the ways he hasn't. There's a sharpness, something feral buried deep into the heart of him.

"So." He breathes, his voice lowered an edge. He makes the word far more tantalizing than it should be. The hiss of the *S*, drawn out like a serpent across a low branch, begging me to take a bite. He is the fruit I shouldn't touch, yet I find my hand reaching out regardless, wanting to grab him, to have a taste.

"So?" I repeat.

"I need you to know something." He breathes. Each word pulses against my bare skin. I draw back, and his eyes have dilated, full black.

"I told you, I don't care if it's da—"

He doesn't let me finish. He shuts me up, his finger brushed to my lips. "When I first met you," he starts, holding my thigh with his free hand, peppering kisses against my jaw. "I thought you were the most beautiful girl I'd ever seen."

"We were second graders." I snort, trying to mask how winded I've become. His confession grips my throat tight.

"I know," he whispers, his laughter doing funny things to his pulse, "but remember Valentine's Day? Where I only got you something and no one else?"

"How could I forget?" I try not to look him in the eyes. "You dropped a live beetle on my desk and asked me to marry you."

"You said yes, if I remember."

"To get you to shut up."

"Seventh grade," he continues, and somewhere along the line we've got his shirt off completely. His fingers trace an invisible path along the shell of my ear. His touch is featherlight. "When Riley Moorson asked you out, I wanted to die. I hated him and didn't know why. The relief I felt when you turned him down. I felt like I could breathe again."

My own shirt follows suit. His words lodge tight in his throat. "Then came the dreams."

"D-dreams?"

"Every single night," he says, and there's a wavering edge to his voice, desire cutting each word jagged.

His lips carry from my chin to my collarbone to my chest. "Without fail."

"What kind of dreams?" But I think I know.

"Ones that had me praying," he confesses, voice darker than I've ever heard it.

The lie I'd fed myself for years finally breaks. *Just a friend, just a friend, just a friend.*

"And then when you asked me if I liked anyone." He breathes, and his fingers reach to my hair like they did that day. But this time he's grabbing a tight fistful. "I didn't tell you, but it was you. It's always been you. And if you asked me now, I'd tell you I love you."

He cradles my face between his hands and his kiss is hungrier than all the others. I can barely keep up; my mind is still reeling from his last three words.

"You don't have to say it back," he assures me, his voice soft against my skin, "I only wanted you to hear it." And there's that dopey, boyish grin of his. A confirmation that as much as he changes, there are parts of him locked in stone.

The night carries on and the wind slashes fiercer than before. He becomes mine in every sense of the word. Mouths and hands and bodies tangled. I love him. My heart is willing to part with the words, but my tongue isn't. Not yet.

I show him in the flutter of my lashes against his shoulder, in my kiss against his temple, in the moments that follow, hearts racing, my face buried into his spine.

I love you. I really, really do.

CHAPTER TWENTY-ONE

ELWOOD

As soon as I sleep, the forest invites me back.

The woods—once beautiful—have become brutal. Screams peel from the bark and the trees are bathed in an otherworldly shade of blue. Wil's body is crumpled in on itself amid the foliage, constricted beneath masses of green tangles. Ivy bites her skin, digging deep into the delicate flesh underneath.

I search for the beast who did this to her, but all I find is my own reflection. Just like the motel, it only took a second. One singular moment of lost control and now she's mangled beyond recognition. The forest is ready to claim her. Her body is more green than pale and bathed in weeds.

The dream shifts, my subconscious floating above the scene and forcing me to stare down what I've become. My reflection is worse than I imagined—my human head bobs lifelessly on my neck, my skin an asphyxiated blue, mouth gaping, eyes rolling back in my skull. The beast has cut me off, claiming my body as its own. No longer the parasite but the host. This has always been the future, hasn't it? Either die by my father's hand or live long enough to lose myself.

Wil and I are bound together in all the worst ways—vines shoot out from me and sink into her, poised and ready to kill. One final squeeze and she will be no more. With the last of her energy, Wil musters the strength to glare up at me. "Kill me, then. G-get it . . . over . . . with."

And I do. I kill her.

The moon hangs in the sky above us and the transformation is complete.

I lurch awake. Wil's cuddled in bed still, her appearance smoothed over by sleep. She tries to seem stronger than she is, tougher and fiercer. Looking at her now, I see none of that. I see a porcelain doll with a tiny painted sneer and a furrow in her brows. And I'd dreamt of . . . Oh God. *Have you ever thought about killing me?*

There's a vine snaking toward her throat—the very same from my nightmare, but here and real and ready to choke the life out of her.

"No!" I throw my hands toward her but don't make it very far. The vine switches direction at the sound of my voice and stretches toward me, a rich, wet shade of green. A branch coils around my wrist, another snaking toward my cheek like a lover's caress.

I swat the limb away. My horror sends it scuttling back to the floor. In the span of a single blink, it dies. Curling in on itself like a dead spider. It lies there on the floor like something that clawed its way out of the depths of Hell.

Red circles my skin. That could've been her throat.

If I'd stayed asleep any longer, it would've taken her and it'd be all my fault. Her mother, dead? My fault. Her motel half-collapsed? My fault. I'm a monster no longer in control of myself, as dangerous now as the church warned I'd be. I'd lost myself in desire earlier, but I can't let my feelings get the best of me now for her sake.

I could be sick. I lift a queasy hand to my lips, resisting the urge to vomit on the carpet.

No. I will not be the one to break her. Loving her is selfish. Dangerous. I'd touched her back in the motel, and she'd gone ghost white. She'd lurched away from me, terrified. It doesn't matter how much she swears she's okay. It doesn't matter because I saw. Deep down, she's afraid.

And she's got every right to be.

My body is a ticking time bomb.

When it goes off, I need to be as far away from Wil as I can. *I love her.*

And for that reason alone, I'll do the unthinkable. I'll turn myself in, my life for hers. Because at the end of the day, what does it matter if I stay breathing if her life is in danger? My staying here would kill her. You don't keep a lion as a house cat. There are creatures that can turn on you in the blink of an eye, and now I'm one of them.

Nothing is funny, and yet I could almost laugh. My family was right. Breaking this cycle, saving myself, none of these things were ever really an option, were they? The seed's been planted, and the roots have tethered and grown. My family will dig the blade into my chest and my blood and bones will be laid among moss and earth. I don't want to die. I want to run fast enough to escape myself. Flee my life and my body and this horrible fate.

But there's no stopping the demon inside me. Once it comes to full fruition, my transformation will be worse than death. There's no outrunning it. I steel myself for what's to come, but it's not enough to stop the sickness rising in my throat. I've chosen to die.

I search the room for something to write on. I sneak over to the vanity, searching aimlessly for a pen and paper.

All I find are eye shadows in every possible shade of blue; eyeliner sticks so dull, they're rendered useless; spilling, half-empty bottles of foundation; bubble-gum-pink blush; and a couple thousand tubes of red lipstick. I grab one of the latter, popping off the top and examining the inside. The one in my hands looks fresh from the store, unused and still pointed at the top.

I lean closer to the mirror, brandishing the lipstick like a pen. It feels like a horrible cliché, one step away from scrawling *XOXO* and pressing a kiss to the glass.

The lipstick snaps off with the end of the sentence. There's so much more I wish to say, but what I wrote will have to suffice. My last look at her will have to last a lifetime.

My fingers rest carefully on the knob and I twist, ever so gently. By some miracle, it drifts open on quiet hinges. Portraits line the wall, painted eyes watching my every move. Questioning whether I'm truly doing the right thing.

I am.

Change is coming. Disaster is imminent. If both paths of fate lead to bitter ends, allow me to choose my demise.

I creep up the staircase to the foyer. Five more steps and I'll reach the front door.

"You're leaving?" Cherry calls from the couch, stopping me dead in my tracks. My breathing stops. I twist to look at her. She speaks as though she's discussing the rain, calling out a storm already brewing in the distance.

My fingers freeze on the doorknob. "Are you going to try to stop me?"

She sniffs. "Is this because of the cards?"

"You and I both know what's coming." Cherry stares at me, her eyes penetrating. "Don't let Wil come looking for me," I beg her. "You told me that we're all allowed one big mistake in our lives. Please. Don't have me make another. I don't know who I'll become soon." The words fly out from me, free at last after spending so long imprisoned in my mind.

She huffs, easing herself up from her chair and unlocking the door for me. "You are not captive here." Her words are a massive relief. "What you're doing is reckless, but it's your decision. I can't promise anything, but I will talk with Wil. We all know that listening isn't her strong suit, though."

"Thank you," I whisper, bracing myself to cross the threshold. To leave the safety of her home and race out into the night. To abandon the very last of my humanity.

"I wouldn't thank me just yet," she says, guilt spreading across her face. "I fear releasing you might be *my* biggest mistake."

I try to respond, but the woods call and I answer them instead, running out into the wild night.

CHAPTER TWENTY-TWO

WIL

"How did you sleep—?" My voice dies in my throat. I expect to see Elwood's dark hair, his sleepy eyes lifting my way, but I see nothing. He's gone.

No. He must be upstairs with Cherry, drinking a warm cup of elderberry tea, sitting at the kitchen table waiting for me to come up.

Or he left. The bitter thought drags back up, reminding me of last night. The moment where I felt like I honestly, truly loved him.

My skin runs ice-cold, my throat clenching on its own like a phantom hand has curled around it. Outside, the screaming wind has died down, and the snowfall is no longer one monstrous veil of white. It's all coming to an end.

. . . And then my eyes fall to a note on the mirror:

I'm sorry, Wil. Please don't look for me.
—E

Just like mom's, Elwood's script is distinct. Mom's cursive was open, the loops wide like bubbles or swinging hammocks in the summer sun. Elwood's writing is cramped and uninviting; the empty spaces look less like circles and more like the thin mouths of sewing needles.

"You asshole," I curse under my breath as the truth breaks over me. I slam the door open and take the stairs up two at a time. I nearly give myself a splinter as I drag my hand up the banister.

"Wil," Cherry says in greeting, though there's hardly any energy to her tone. Her eyes are exhausted and bloodshot—she's been up all night. At least long enough to see him leave. The truth is written all across her face.

"You knew," I accuse, a hitch in my throat. "And yet you didn't stop him. Do you know how dangerous it is for him?"

"You don't think I know all that?" Her mouth droops, my accusation weighing her down. I see the answer in her eyes before she even speaks. "He was determined to leave."

I storm past her, swiping my jacket and scarf from the rack. There isn't a plan in my head yet, nothing aside from running out and finding him. The jacket is damp still, but it will do. I curl the scarf across me one extra time. I don't care how cold it is out there; I don't care how long it takes me to find him. A need to save him propels me forward, stronger than anything else. Love. It's a sticky feeling—clinging to my every thought and action, pushing itself into the deepest corners of my mind.

I never got the chance to tell him.

A hand catches on mine. Cherry tugs desperately on me, yanking me away from the door.

"What?" I fume, my body freezing over. I am a statue in her grasp; my heart is equally frigid. "Aren't I free to leave? Won't you let me freeze out there like you let Elwood?"

She recoils like I've slapped her. Her hand drops. "You owe me a conversation first. Same as Elwood."

"What could you possibly have to say?" I ask, feeling massively foolish for trusting either of them.

"I have much to say if you will bother to listen to me."

Every second I wait is dangerous. For all I know they've captured him already. Still, I've never seen Cherry so intent. Her eyes burn through me, a fierce shade of blue.

"Fine," I relent. Cherry's shoulders drop with my words, some of her own tension escaping. "You get one minute."

"Good. Sit down."

I trail her to the kitchen, collapsing in the chair closest to me. The walls around us have been smothered in greenery. More vines than I remembered trail the walls, dangling in all sorts of unnatural positions. "Elwood did this," Cherry informs me, fishing out glass shards from the trash. She brandishes a sliver of what used to be a plate. It's a jagged pie-shaped piece. The design is still fairly visible on the sides of it, a looped blue spiral print. But that's not what I'm looking at. A plant has grown from porcelain. Roots spiral out in the open air on the other side of it. In a bizarre way, it looks like the flower is wearing the glass as a dress. It simply cuts right through it.

"That too." She gestures toward the open chair across from me, the one that's been swallowed whole. Not an inch is uncovered, no part safe from the devouring foliage.

"Just like back at the motel," I breathe.

"That boy belongs to the woods. I think he knew that better than any of us." She doesn't bother sitting. Instead, she leans her weight into the wall, her head falling back against the green. For a splinter of a second, I worry that she will sink through, that the leaves will entangle her and trap her there. "He cares deeply for you if you haven't noticed."

I love you, Wil.

Cherry parts her lips to say something, but I twist away from her and stare down at the kitchen table.

There's an emptied glass of tea. I peer inside it and see leaves against the bottom of the cup, pooling into one large circle. In the center, there's an unmistakable gap. A large shape carved out in the middle, broken up by three distinct splotches.

Two hollow eye sockets and a gaping crater of a nose.

"It's a skull," I whisper. A random smattering of leaves shouldn't have the power to unnerve me this much. I drop it quickly back on the table. "There's a skull in that cup."

"What?" Cherry blanches. She's no longer looking at me. Her wrinkled fingers jump out and grab ahold of the cup. She lifts it for a better look. "The leaves shouldn't have moved like that . . . When I first read his cup after he left, I saw a pattern of toads. It meant there would be obstacles, surely, but ones he could face himself. He needed to learn who he was."

"And now?" I ask, even though I'm confident I don't want to hear the answer.

"And now . . . death is coming."

My chair screams as it drags across the room. I slide it back, pulling myself to my feet with my hands pressed firmly on the table. "If that's the case, we're wasting time. He could be dead by now." A million gruesome images flash in my mind—all of them with Elwood at the center. I come up with endless scenarios, each one ten times worse than the last. What I can't envision is saving him. When I try to imagine it, my mind draws a stubborn blank.

It doesn't matter. I need to get out there. The plan can come later. Cherry doesn't give me the chance.

"Will!"

I turn one last time. "What is it now? More death omens?"

My eyes catch on the doorknob, and I envision Elwood's fingers curling around it, swinging it open and racing out into the frozen pine. It's so easy to fool myself into thinking I still see traces of him soaked into the shadows of the room, hanging heavy in the air.

"You think you'll save him by running out on your own? There's only one of you, but a town's worth of them. You'd be doing Elwood no favors by trying to shoulder this alone. Don't do this!" She lurches out to grab my arm, but I yank myself free of her.

Cherry's right, but I don't want to listen. Nothing good comes from other people.

"Mom's case dragging on is proof enough. If you want a job done right, you have to do it yourself."

She shouts something after me, but I'm no longer listening. The door slamming behind me is answer enough.

I'll do this my own way.

CHAPTER TWENTY-THREE

ELWOOD

I would pray, but I think the cord between me and heaven is severed. My roots now dig to hell. And hell is a foot away from my father.

His back stiffens at the sound of my arrival. The church doors sing a forgotten hymn, every loose board a broken harmony. Days ago I might've sung along, worshiped the very ground, but no longer. It's as rotten and vile as the man in front of me. His fox-light eyes gleam with dark surprise as he turns. All this time trying to make it into the chicken coop, only for his prey to find him instead.

Except I don't feel like prey. Whatever is growing inside me is powerful enough to bring a forest to its knees, to raise roots from the ground and resurrect plants from the dead. I could summon spruces across the forest floor, make them bow toward me like servants to a king, believers to their God. But it's precisely because of this power that I need to do this.

"I'm ready to give myself up," I say, willing my voice to be steady.

My father stalks forward with both arms held behind his back. His surprise has sapped away; he approaches me instead with a cool calculation. The world feels darker in his wake and the air is putrid with the stench of the woods.

He assesses all the wicked new ways I've grown. He's got a way of looking at someone without seeing them, his gaze slicing only skin-deep. "I knew you'd come back."

Of course he'd think that. His meek son returning at long last with his tail between his legs, ready for another beating. There was a time when I admired his confidence. I wanted to try it on, wear it like a too-big coat. Now I want to smash it beneath the heel of my shoe.

My rage calls up thorns through the floorboards. "You don't know a thing about me."

"Don't I?" His eyes snag on the brambles. "I know you're too curious for your own good. Too easily swayed by a viper's pretty words . . . Tell me, where is that little snake of yours?"

My face must give it all away—the resolve burning in my eyes, the slight gape of my mouth at the sound of her name. *Keep her safe. Keep her safe at all costs.*

"You've got me now. You don't need her."

His smile is slicker than an oil spill. "Her mother didn't go down easily. Gnashing and wild like an untamed beast. I bet her daughter is the same. They're fighters. I'll give them that."

Each word is a tremor in the soil, a crack splintered across the foundation. *"Don't you dare touch her!"*

That wipes the smile clean from his lips. I savor the lock of his jaw and the bulge of his eyes. I soak in every ounce of his fear.

He reins it in after a careful moment, his voice tense and to the point. "We only need you. Come willingly, and we'll spare her and her pathetic father. Once that motel is demolished, they'll have nowhere else to turn. They'll leave and we won't have to harm a single hair on her pretty little head. You, on the other hand . . . you'd kill her if you stayed."

I don't know if I can trust him, but I also don't know if I have a choice. All the what-ifs torment me, and I'm haunted by the visual of ivy coiling across Wil's throat. This was the right decision in the end. The only one.

It's the reason I now surrender my wrists and bow my head. "Kill me, then. Get it over with." I don't know what death they've got in store for me. A noose around my throat, a guillotine blade slicing through my skin, a million boulders pressing down on my chest. I tell myself it doesn't matter if this church will prosper off my death. I'd do anything to keep Wil safe.

But my father doesn't strike. "Not yet. Follow me."

He gestures for me to follow him with an incline of his head. We both know I'll go willingly, a prisoner walking to the executioner's chair of their own volition. It's not a long path to the altar. There's hardly enough space for the town's members and their children in this room, let alone God. My father jerks the podium out of place. It's always felt so sacred, too holy to be kicked aside with the muddy imprint of a heel. All this time, every sermon I've sat through, my father's stood with a secret chamber just beneath him.

He yanks open the trapdoor and I'm guided step-by-step into the bowels of the earth.

The floor beneath me is freezing, packed dirt; it's jarring against the flash of white-hot fear in my gut. Very little is visible, illuminated faintly by a few candles swinging overhead. They drip hot wax precariously; one splotch nearly grazes my knee. I jolt back and make the mistake of looking around me.

A skeleton lies in a useless heap to my left. The skull is ruptured, fractured in two as though bludgeoned by something heavy. I scuttle back as far as I can, only to bump into yet another corpse. The tunnel is filled with them.

"What is this?"

My father grins a nasty sort of smile, bringing himself so close, I taste his breath. He grips my chin, forcing me to look at him. I see more than I care to. Deranged bloodshot eyes, age lines torn across his skin, the grimy crescents of his gums.

"You're smarter than that." His words carry across my skin, slithering their way into my ears. The earthen ceiling drips, condensation rolling down the walls. It lands in a growing puddle beneath me. "These tunnels stretch beneath this entire forest. We own these trees and we always have."

The thought chills me like a vat of ice, spreading from the tips of my toes to the edges of my scalp. Suddenly, the smell makes sense. The cloying, rotten stench carrying in the air, mingled in with wet soil. He'll bury me in the bellows of the earth, beyond the roots and the trees, a place where the sun cannot reach.

He's brought me to my grave.

"Why?" I beg, and my fear brings a wide, knifelike grin to his face. The scales of power were momentarily tipped earlier in the church, and he's thrilled now to have it righted. "I'm your son. How could you—? How could you look me in the eyes, knowing this is how it would end?"

He's silent, soaking in my words before roaring with laughter. He doubles over, tears springing in the corners of his eyes. He wipes himself free of them, struggling to collect his breath. "You always wondered what your purpose was in life. I told you everyone had one. Now, boy, this is it. Your final purpose, Alderwood. You and all the others." The laughter cuts abruptly, his features dripping with rage. "If only you'd been worthy enough. A better son. A better believer. Maybe your mother would've been chosen for a second son, but no, it's Vrees's time now. The new Right Hand of God. Eighteen years in power gone like *that*."

He slams me into the wall and knocks the air out of my lungs. All these years I was convinced we looked exactly alike, but the differences between us seem starker now than ever. We have the same green eyes, but his are clouded over, no cracks for the light to shine through. I've done everything I can to keep the darkness at bay; he's embraced his.

"Do you know how hard I tried to make you love me?"

His face skews in the shadows as he secures my chains, traps me here in ironclad bars. It's not hurt, but it's an imitation of it. A softer sort of rage. "You remember the story of Job—I am the Lord's servant above all else." He says it like it means everything. Like I'll understand somehow. "Unlike Job, though, I knew your purpose from the day your mother conceived you. Love was never an option."

I could laugh.

"Even if you were allowed," I say, preparing myself for the fire, "I don't think you would know how to."

He doesn't answer me, but his face does. It stretches back in an indignant burst, lips curling to show a flash of teeth.

"Did I not feed you? Clothe you? Indulge your ridiculous little hobbies?" My father paces in the shadows, his fury building. "I couldn't love you, but I cared for you and that should have been enough."

For once in my life, I stare at him head-on. I want him to see the light he hasn't managed to snuff out. "Mercy isn't the idle moments between rage. It isn't just the absence of pain."

"Oh, you must think a lot of yourself," he retorts, sneering at me. He looks away, his gaze falling on my shackles. Maybe he's seen them on me my entire life. "Is this your own display of mercy, then? Dying to keep that girl safe?"

"I love her."

He spits his next words out like they're sour. "How sweet of you."

"And your brother?" I ask, egging him on. "The one who came before me. Did you love him?"

His stony expression breaks and I see an old pain slither through. It takes him too long to rein it in. "Don't speak about him. You know nothing, Elwood. Nothing."

"No one in this world matters to you, do they?"

He snarls and I hear the shifting of his robes as he pulls back the cloth to expose the marred crisscross of slashes on his skin. Each one is grislier than the last. Permanent welts that have only paled with time but never healed.

"This is the price of love, Elwood," he tells me, his tone grated and resentful. "I loved my brother and tried to delay his fate, and this is what it got me. He died anyway, and I was the one punished. The Lord gave you to me as a second chance. One final blessing and curse wrapped into one disappointing child."

I grind my teeth. "Don't talk to me about scars."

He lets his robes fall back into place. "I was teaching you the same lesson they taught me."

"No, you weren't." My exasperation is enough to break a chuckle out of me. It's humorless and dry. "You were taking it out on me. I'm not your son; I'm your punishment, remember? That's all I've ever been."

My accusation leaves him speechless. I wait for him to strike me down. I expect the harsh rattle of my jaw and the spit of blood onto the floor. But nothing happens. He shivers with unspent fury, his hands trembling on either side.

"That girl changed you," he says once he's found his voice.

I was raised on the edge of a knife, the type of life meant to chisel away at you until there's nothing left.

My heart should be as hideous and haggard as his, but it's the one thing that's stayed constant.

My fear has turned him into something he isn't. Given him claws and teeth and the power to tear me apart. But he is not the monster I've made him. He is spiteful, vengeful, and above all, weak.

I gave that power to him.

And I want it back.

"No, Dad," I return. "You changed me, but not in the way you intended."

He snarls like a wounded beast. "There will be no mercy when I return."

He blows out the candles one by one, plunging me into darkness. I can't see even an inch in front of my face. Without the light, it feels more and more like I'm trapped inside a coffin.

The floor creaks beneath his feet, and I hear the glide of his hands against the railing. Then, finally, the muffled noise of a door swinging open. Locks being bolted. Retreating footsteps.

And then nothing.

Nothing at all.

CHAPTER TWENTY-FOUR

WIL

My mind's a swirling cesspool.

Every time my world falls apart, I laugh. Eyes wet with tears and yet I'm making a joke, and no one's laughing but me.

This time, grief and love form a new hideous emotion inside me. The pain hit not a second after I realized I loved him. With my ear pressed to Elwood's chest, his heartbeat scared me. Hearts are fragile things. They stop so easily. *One day I'll lose him*, I thought. *The world will steal him right out of my arms.*

I trudge forward in the snow. Ice clings to my wet lashes. I can't see the world beyond me; it's a white fog. There's no telling what lies ahead.

An open heart is an invitation for grief. My emotions swelled last night, and they roar even louder today. I can't lose Elwood. I've never healed from Mom's loss. I'm splintered pieces held together by fragile hope. One more death and I will blow away with the wind.

I slap myself. Someone's got to. The pain is jarring, but I need it. I don't have time to brood. If I let myself, I'll fall prey to my dark thoughts and never crawl out. Mom said dark thoughts were ships passing in the night. You can choose to watch them go. You don't need to sail away with each one.

I've never been good at following her advice.

The tree line parts as I walk toward the Morguewood. For once, the forest feels empty. No cloaked figures, no pale skulls with massive antlers attached, no Elwood. The farther I get, the colder the world becomes. I wish my desperation would make me numb to it, but everything feels ten times sharper. The wind used to be a slash against my cheeks. It's since been forged into a much sharper blade.

I ran out here without a plan.

I laugh. Elwood could be anywhere in these woods. I could search for hours and never find him. What did I think I could do?

Looking at my chapped red fingers, I realize how small I really am.

My laughter breaks into a hiccup. My hiccup devolves into a full-fledged sob. My grief tears through the trees. Each gasping cry sends birds shooting off into the bone-pale sky.

I am alone.

I'm okay alone. I'm more than okay. No one can help me but myself. I recognize how bitter each lie is now. The truth has always been there, waiting for me to acknowledge it. I'm useless on my own.

Cherry was right.

Goddamnit, she was right. I can't do this by myself.

"Will!"

I lurch right out of my own skin. I swivel and I'm greeted by the front engine of a car. Lucas's Civic chugs steam into the frozen air, and I was wrong when I said I'd never been so happy to see it before.

Seeing it now is nothing short of a miracle. The locks pop and he gestures to the passenger seat. I dash into it, melting into the heat as it blasts from the vents.

Rubbing my fingers furiously together, I wonder if I'll ever feel them again.

"Lucas," I breathe, sounding way too enthusiastic for someone who called him shallow and useless hours prior. He sneers against the cold. His hair is wind-tossed and his eyes are black-bagged.

"I've been driving around aimlessly trying to find you guys." He gulps.

"You weren't at the motel and I saw the bike tracks and I—I messed up." His voice is clipped and his nails dig into the leather of his wheel.

Elwood's broken expression burns in place of any relief. Lucas planted that seed of doubt in him and it sprouted too soon. And now he's gone for good. My patience is thin enough as it is, but today's worn it away to nothing. Rage is better than grief. Rage is a monster of my own making. "You think?"

Cut the attitude. Mom's voice bites in my ear. She's not even alive and is still lecturing me in my mind. I squeeze my eyes shut and try to pretend she's hovering over me, her hand resting on my shoulder. *When you're angry,* she says, *it's like you're on fire. You need to cool off or you'll burn yourself and those you care about.*

"You're right." He deflates, but he can't look at me when he says it. He focuses on the road as he drives forward. "You're right; I screwed up. Big-time. Vee's at Kevin's place and neither one of them wants anything to do with me. And you and Elwood . . . wait." He swivels in surprise. *"Where is he?"*

A nasty response forms on my lips, but my mother's memory is vigilant. Cooling off is easier said than done. Harder yet when it's with someone I hate. *If you don't like someone, try to see them from someone else's view. There's good in everyone, if you look hard enough.*

I remind myself who Lucas is. To me, he's a jerk with a God complex, but he's also Ronnie's boyfriend and Elwood's friend. I've seen the way Ronnie looks at him when she thinks I've got my head turned. I've seen Elwood chuckle down the hall at his jokes.

"Gone," I confess softly, heartachingly. By the time the word has left my lips, we've already pulled into the lot of a familiar home.

Only days ago, the ground rumbled with his blaring stereo and cars lined every inch of the street. People milled in and out of his living room, and Elwood's change was only beginning. Now it reminds me of an abandoned wasp's nest, shriveled and dead and no longer buzzing with a hive. In place of life, there is a pervasive, haunting silence.

"What do you mean *gone?*" Lucas pries, yanking the key out of the ignition.

There goes my ooey-gooey heart. I've spent my whole life concealing it, and now here I am, tears streaming down my face in front of Lucas, of all people. "I mean he's gone," I blubber. "He ran away—" I hiccup and then surprise myself. "Please don't leave again. I need your help. I can't let anything happen to him."

Lucas shouts a curse into a clenched fist. This time his anger is directed at no one but himself. We won't get anywhere if he keeps impaling himself with it. He mellows at the sight of my tears and his hand does this weird back-and-forth dance like he's not sure how to console me.

I shake it away and swipe at my own tears. Crying in front of him is bad enough. I don't need him patting my head and telling me any of this is okay.

His hand lingers for another second in the air before he lowers it to his lap. "I'm not leaving this time," he promises, and my shoulders soften a tad. "You were right. I've been a self-obsessed asshole and I'm sorry. I need to apologize to Elwood most of all, but, Wil, I've been horrible to you too."

Apologizing to me? I've spent this entire year wishing him dead.

See? my mother's voice croons in my thoughts. *He's not all that bad, is he?*

We both break away and fixate on different patches of the floor. "I hated you," I confess. He looks over at me, startled. I keep my eyes trained on my knees. "You stole Elwood from me. Made him laugh in ways I thought only I knew how to. And even when Ronnie was with me, she was still looking over at you. I hated you not because of who you were, but because of what you had."

This is nowhere near the conversation I expected to be having with him. I hate to say it, but my mom might've been right after all. Offering this up to him is a lead weight lifted from my shoulders.

He rakes a hand through his hair and barks out a humorless laugh. "I was jealous of *you* this whole time."

"What?" I blurt, because I'm the least enviable person on the planet. My run-down life in a failing motel hardly seems covetable. I can't think of a single thing about me that I wouldn't willingly trade away with someone else.

"You think I had Elwood's undivided attention? Half of our conversations revolved around you. The other half of the time was him blatantly staring at you from across the cafeteria. And Vee? Veronica always gives me the cold shoulder whenever you're around. Things are so different between us alone, but as soon as she's hanging out with you, it's like she hates me all over again. That's why I yelled at you back at the diner . . . I was frustrated and angry and jealous. I really shouldn't have brought up your mom or Elwood. That was a low blow."

I gulp down my first choice of words. *It isn't about your first thought*, Mom always said. *It's about your second.* "You didn't say anything that wasn't true. I've got a raging horrible temper and I wanted everyone else to be as miserable as I felt. It wasn't a lie . . . I get that."

His eyes water the same as mine, and the silence that follows next isn't charged with unspoken venom like all the times prior. It's a quiet understanding.

"Truce?" he asks with a lopsided smile. He offers a hand my way and

I hesitate. It wavers in the air and he almost drops it, but I grab ahold of it at the last second. Warm.

"Truce." We shake on it, and Lucas's grin injects me with much-needed hope. "Let's bring him home."

CHAPTER TWENTY-FIVE

ELWOOD

It's been hours.

Maybe longer. It's impossible to tell. So many corpses lie littered around me, clinging onto their secrets even in death. I'm plagued with the image of them rising, lifting on skeletal legs and closing in on me. I think I'd welcome it. A quick death would be better, cleaner.

Hunger scrapes at my ribs and I wonder how long it will take for me to die. Humans can survive without food for thirty days or longer. Water, ten. But I don't want to wait that long. Can't wait that long. I don't want my chest to cave and my skin to rot. I don't want to be conscious when Death claims me. I huddle in on myself, knees drawn in as close as my chains allow. It's better down here without the bite of the wind, but that hardly makes it pleasant. Parts of me have gone numb, and I doubt the feeling will ever truly return.

If everything has gone as planned, Wil's as far away from helping me as possible. I hope Cherry took Wil as far out of this wretched place as she could get.

I claw at the hardened ground to feel something. Dirt traps itself inside each of my nails, pushing all the way back to the skin. My wrists and ankles are rubbed raw. The metal chains cut deep, along with the burning emptiness in the pit of my stomach. My resentment streams down my cheeks, dripping off my chin and scorching the ground below.

I'm Elwood. I'm Elwood. I'm Elwood.

Each time I say it, the words lose meaning. Which Elwood am I?

Am I the demon inside me, the darkness swirling in my gut? Or am I the boy—staying up late hours with forceps and pins and wings?

My misery morphs and takes shape. Grief and rage walk hand in hand and I spiral between them both. I want to thrash and scream and curse.

"Reveal yourself," I plead. There's that door again in my mind. Only this time I'm not knocking. I'm ready to kick it down. I want to see the wood splinter and collapse. I'm ready for whatever is lurking on the other side. I'm sick of waiting for the inevitable. Let it be on my own terms.

Nothing happens.

"*Show yourself!*" I howl, gritting my teeth to summon all of my remaining energy.

Then comes the first knock. A heavy hammering against a frail door. I reach for the handle, and it's no longer locked. It swings open in a violent gust, pushing open not to reveal a monster but an open clearing in the woods. A moth weaves its way through the trees, as if it's a beckoning finger guiding me forward.

I follow it. My toes crunch barefoot through the underbrush, leaves and twigs and skittering bugs. My legs effortlessly walk me through the tired woods like the forest belongs to me.

Like I've wandered here before. But this forest is far from mine.

Snow spills across my ankles. White coats everything, swimming up the night-soaked bark and curling around the highest branches. Above it all, the moon hangs in the sky, heavy and full.

Farther and farther I go. Quieter the world becomes. There's nothing but the snap of my feet and the cloud of my breath. I freeze, catching sight of the scene before me.

I see the imprints of wings against bark. The creature is biblical in size but unholy in nature.

This is where it all began, it whispers. Its voice is the rattle of the trees, the wind running along branches, the screech of an owl in the distance. Everything and nothing and all the little things in between.

A scream peels off the bark, buzzing back and forth across the forest. It's the horrific in-between: not quite dead but certainly not alive. Every inch of me goes still.

I listen.

Wet noises—like tires running over ribs, bursts of blood gushing from an artery. Dry ones too—the wicked scrape of nails across the earth, limbs chopped off as easily as a knife slicing through the throat of a hare. The noises spiral and rebound, playing around me nonstop. A melody that doesn't end, only loops over.

I see it all. Four men have got ahold of a boy. He is bleeding profusely, the red of his blood staining the green around him. Dirtying it. His scream cuts through the soul of him.

"Don't cry," the man closest to him whispers. He's got the same honey-blond hair, the same dead eyes, the same emaciated, hollow look to him. Hunger has made a home in his cheeks, in the thin strip of skin hanging over his ribs. A father bleeding his son out like a pig. Tears bubble down his aged face, dripping off his sharp chin. "The Lord wants this."

That doesn't stop the screaming.

It stops only after the boy has been bled dry. His crying cuts off with a gurgle of blood and the color bleaches from his skin. Everything ends. I wait for something to happen, but nothing does, at least not immediately.

Then he coughs. A quiet sputtering building to a deafening choke. He hacks something up and then his body falls still.

It's a seed.

The men cradle it in their hands, teary-eyed and overjoyed.

The door has returned beside me. It appears in the bark, carving itself in the tree closest to me. The knob swings open on its own, and a new scene waits for me on the other end. A familiar forest, a familiar family.

A tree plunges from the cold dirt. It's the largest in the entire forest, its tips scraping the sky, its bark bloodied and black. There's a man strung among the branches, his chest oozing like the tapped core of a maple tree. His scream isn't alone; it's tangled with my mother's shrill cry as I break into the world.

My late grandfather plunges a hand in his son's chest, ripping a seed right out of my uncle's rib cage. It's a small brown husk with a body the size of a wood tick. He brandishes it between his fingers before turning to me.

My parents hold their infant still as he carves a crescent in the skin. Blood trickles from the cut, but as soon as the seed is buried in my chest, the wound smooths over.

My fingers brush the same scar on my chest.

"Rejoice," my grandfather calls out to my parents and the rest of the curious woods. Last time I saw him, I was six and he was dead. Cold in the casket; my father's knuckles the same unearthly white as he dropped the first handful of dirt. "The next cycle has begun. We are seeds in the wind."

The scene flashes out of being, my consciousness violently thrown back into my body, head slamming onto the hard dirt wall. Fuzzy spots swim in my vision, white flickers of light as my skull pounds.

I look down at the scar on my chest, my breath hissing in my lungs. The skin's grown translucent and a seed is wedged in place of my heart.

CHAPTER TWENTY-SIX

WIL

"I don't think we need a crossbow."

"Are you sure?" Kevin asks, and I'm secretly relieved to have both him and Ronnie here. The fifteen minutes spent waiting for them to show up didn't result in a screaming match or anything, but it was . . . awkward. Lucas and I spent the time walking on eggshells and making small talk, neither one wanting to ruin the shaky alliance we have with one another. Thank God for Kevin and Ronnie diffusing some of that tension.

Lucas's living room is spacious enough, but none of us are here to get comfortable. We skip the La-Z-Boy and the plush couch in favor of the cold, hard floor. With all three of us here, Lucas doesn't waste time dragging out all of his dad's hunting gear. It's like a miniature Cabela's.

Kevin digs his hands out from his coat pockets and I see he's wearing useless fingerless gloves. Beneath his jacket, he's got a tie-dyed St. Ignace Mystery Spot shirt tucked into his jeans. He continues with a slight smirk, "We don't want to be the only ones there without one. You don't bring a knife to a crossbow fight."

I stare into the case. "Can't say I've ever been in a crossbow fight."

"Well, I can tell you there weren't any knives there."

I always found his humor annoying in class, but it's growing on me now. My coping strategy might be screaming into a pillow or punching a mattress, but his—no matter how obvious of a strategy it is—is strangely soothing after staring into the Morguewood alone.

"We can't point something like that at my mom." Meanwhile, Ronnie doesn't know what coping means.

She's been steadily losing her mind with every passing second, and I can't say I blame her.

Lucas tries to place a soothing palm over her shoulder, but she lurches away from him. He tucks the offensive hand in the depths of his pocket. "We don't know if she's all talk. Your mom might try to seriously hurt us. It's better to be prepared in case she comes swinging. You can always use it as a bat or a shield, too. She's sturdy. Dad's had her in the family for a while."

"The crossbow? Is that the elusive woman you're referring to?" Kevin asks. Lucas flashes his TV-anchor-white teeth. "Yeah, Bessie."

Ronnie huffs but relents. She can never stay upset with him. He's got his Crest Whitestrips spell on her. Magic or not, though, she's insistent on one thing, "You can bring it, but I don't want to see it in my mom's face. Got it? At your hip only." Her eyes dart to the notification on her phone. "Wil, your dad is desperate. He's messaging me now."

"Later. Ignore it."

In an effort to actually be useful for once, I turn toward the TV stand behind me and riffle through one of its junk drawers in hopes of a pen and paper. After some deep rummaging, I salvage an old takeout menu from Iron Mountain and a half-dried-out Bic. The edges of the paper are creased, and it's been stained yellow from God knows what, but the back is clear, and that's good enough for me.

I smooth it out as best I can, and once it's primarily wrinkle-free, I begin to sketch. Some hazy pen strokes later and I push the paper forward with a sheepish flick of my wrist.

It's crudely hand-drawn but a map nonetheless. Trees circle the town on all sides and I've made inkblot imitations of the family motel, the police station, and every little nook and cranny in Pine Point.

"The church is my best guess." I shrug, letting the pen roll out of my hand onto the linoleum floor. I've scribbled in a large splotch to represent it. Imposing and dark and nearly stolen by the woods. "Though he could be in Clarke's basement for all I know."

Kevin squints at my doodle. "Would it be that easy? They know we were at the church already. I've seen enough horror movies to know it might be a trap."

"I doubt they're having the sacrifice at Earl's," I quip, if only because I don't want to outwardly admit I didn't think things through. I'm more of a "plunge ahead, consequences be damned" sort of girl.

Of course, saying that gives me a horrific new visual. One where the monthly meat raffle at Earl's takes a much darker turn. The roulette wheel won't be staring down a table's worth of steaks and pork chops but Elwood tied to a spit and everyone vying for a piece of him.

"Well." I cough. "Where do you think he'd be?"

"Aren't you the one who stalked them twenty-four seven? You should know their haunts."

I'm this close to snapping back on impulse, but he isn't wrong. I could've set my postal address for the bushes outside of the Clarke family house. Mom always thought something was up with the Clarkes and was always looking into their business, so I'm just carrying on family tradition.

I pull my phone from my back pocket and I force the group to crowd around my dismally small screen. With senior year halfway over, my photos should be a gallery of my youth: friends with matching grins, well-posed selfies where I actually attempt to not look like a troll, loitering with Ronnie in Marquette and freezing our asses off in Lake Superior.

Instead, my phone boasts a different sort of collection. Photo after photo of Ezekiel leaving his house, monotonous day-to-day scenes that I didn't bother showing Vrees but couldn't bring myself to delete, stills of Ezekiel bloodied in the Morguewood with a rabbit . . .

I didn't think my sleep-addled brain was capable of a light-bulb moment.

But I linger on the image and then zoom in on the towering tree behind him. It's a beast with a massive trunk and a gaping hollow. "I ran into Elwood here that first night. There'd been a rabbit skewered through one of the branches."

I shudder, and it isn't the hare I'm seeing in my mind but the distorted face of my mother. Mouth unhinged in a scream that will never fully end. Blood dripping off her skin and soaking into the roots.

Ronnie scrunches her nose. "I've seen that tree, too. It's a mural in the church. The thing's huge."

"So," Kevin asks, scratching a red path along his cheek. "The plan is to scour the woods looking for a spooky old tree?" He's chuckling, but his nerves are more obvious than before. He can barely complete a full sentence without a telling hitch in his throat.

"Guess so," I answer. I've already moved on to cataloging what we have: a crossbow (fine), a flashlight, a marker, a good knife to cut through rope, a doorbell . . .

Wait.

I stiffen at the chime, and the others are already frozen around me. Ezekiel and his merry band of murderers wouldn't seriously ring the doorbell, would they? Do serial killers do that? Knock politely and ask, "Please, may I come in and stab you once?"

Kevin would know for sure, but I'm not going to ask him. He'd whisper an entire cataloged list at me. We could have our heads on a chopping block and if I asked, "Hey, how many sightings of Mothman were there again?" his last words would be "At least a hundred."

I lock eyes with Lucas and an unspoken agreement hangs over us. *Bring the crossbow and be quiet about it.*

I never anticipated doing anything in tandem with Lucas, but I have to admit, we work well together. I follow his unspoken cues to the door and motion for him to get back and hand me the crossbow. He might hesitate, but I'm angry enough to know that I won't. He clutches the hilt of a knife instead and goes flat against the wall.

One.

I lift a finger with my other hand resting on the knob.

Two.

Have I always been this sweaty? My body's slick with fear and adrenaline.

Three.

The door swings open and I've got the crossbow in the intruder's face. I will gladly pull the trigger—"*Dad?*"

Shit. Pointing a lethal weapon at a loved one might not be the best way to greet them at the door. It's also going to be a tricky one to explain, seeing as how he's gone sheet white and all. His eyes bulge at the razor-sharp arrow, and it's only at that instant that I remember to lower it to my hip.

"Uh, hi," I say blankly.

Dad shifts, his shoulders slumping now that he's no longer in imminent danger.

"What are you doing here?"

He looks vaguely sheepish. I guess I would be too after staring down a crossbow. "I tracked your phone." He waves his own phone to clarify and there's the little GPS dot flashing. "After I saw what happened to half the motel, I was so worried something happened to you. I called Cherry. Texted your friends. And called you, as a matter of fact, more than fifty times. You nearly gave me a heart attack!"

"You what?" I don't know how tracking me is more offensive than what I just did, but I'm still shocked. Dad's never done anything like that. This town is embarrassingly small. He knows my typical haunts . . . or he thinks he does. And I haven't been a blip on Dad's radar in over a year. Grief made a stranger of him.

When did he become a father again?

He breaks the distance and envelopes me in a crushing hug. I don't meet it. Can't meet it. "She told me what you're up to," he says, his voice curdled and thick. He chokes, tears making a mess of his face. Dad hasn't cried in front of me since Mom disappeared. Rather than feeling sadness, he opted to feel nothing. Nothing at all. But now all of the emotions he repressed are uncorked. They burst to the surface, returning with a vengeance.

"She was hysterical, Wil. Said you were going to go take on the Clarkes on your own." His voice shakes. "And she told me the truth. About Elwood."

Everything goes quiet. For one heavy moment, nothing else exists. All that's real is my father's grief-stricken face, his fingers clutching tight onto my skin, and the dark implication of his words.

"If you've come to stop me, you're too late," I tell him. I don't care if each word plants a bullet in his chest. I'm not going back with him. I can't. The wind picks up and that earlier confidence drains right out of him.

"Please." His voice has grown weaker, less demanding and more pleading. His lips quiver and I see my grief manifested back in him ten-fold. I force myself to look away. "Please don't do this. We can move out of this horrible town. I'll take any job and we'll find a place—"

"No." I'm calmer now, but I'm not backing down. "I don't have a choice. I can't lose him."

"I can't lose you," he counters, and those four words squeeze at my resolve. I force myself to be firm. "I'm going. You can't stop me."

He pales even further at that, and I can see him running the idea over in his mind. His eyes are penetrating; they chip me down to my core. "Then I'm coming with you."

"You don't have to do that." But I'm not the only stubborn one in the family. I can tell there's no arguing with him by the sharp set of his jaw alone.

"I'm coming," he repeats, with no room for argument. I gotta say, I'm shocked to see him standing strong on this. And dare I say . . . proud?

"You're in luck, Mr. Greene, my car holds five," Lucas chimes in, effectively breaking us out of our emotional side huddle. "And the sooner we get out there, the better."

He doesn't have to explain why. All the missed time weighs on me already, but I force myself to drown out the what-ifs.

I'll find you, Elwood. I promise.

CHAPTER TWENTY-SEVEN

ELWOOD

Nature is violent.

Some wasps stalk their prey in flower beds, chopping them into tiny pieces with their mandibles. Others live in burrows beneath the earth, dragging prey underground for their children to feast upon.

And then there's my father.

He's come to watch me squirm one last time before devouring me. In his eyes, I'm nothing but an unfortunate moth, one that flew too close. They're the natural prey for praying mantises, moths. I never made the connection before, but now it's all I can think of. It's nature's explanation for me dying by his hand. And even God doesn't interfere with the natural world. He's the one who designed it.

"So where is my mother?" I ask. "I thought she would enjoy this sort of thing."

He scowls in response. "She didn't care to watch."

"She's never had a problem with it before."

My mother, the spicebush swallowtail. Butterflies are violent, too. Caterpillars have been known to cannibalize one another from time to time. They do away with the competition, killing their kin in an effort to stay alive.

Father strikes a match and lights one of the mounted torches along the wall. It's grown impossibly dark down here, cold enough for my breath to hang in a permanent stubborn cloud. He straightens himself up, wiping the dust off the sides of his robes. He blinks slowly, peering at me from bulging, sadistic eyes.

"So it's time for me to die?" I taste every syllable as I ask it, the rotten curve of letters in my mouth. The dark shell of the seed shines through, accompanied by a pathway of green roots snaking through my ribs. It's no longer hidden within me, my skin growing more transparent by the second.

"I've come to plant you," my father answers, and his calloused palm smooths back my hair. I shudder beneath his touch, especially as he cradles my face. His thumbs hover close to my eyes. He could gouge them out easily. "You're a seed, after all."

I flex my fingers into fists. "Then let's get on with it."

With a nod, my father unshackles me. When one restraint is removed, another one is put in its place. My hands are bound tightly behind my back.

We carry forward under the dark earth. All this time, the rot has been spilling upward from these tunnels. It's noxiously potent down here. So many bones encased in the frozen dirt, bodies worn away to nothing. There must be hundreds, if not more.

"Fertilizer," he whispers as if it's amusing. "It's a funny thing in Pine Point. The cemeteries are empty and they don't have the slightest idea. Their bodies are wasted on them. They're better served down here."

I fight the bile slithering up my throat. Maybe it's vomit; maybe it's the tickling stem of a weed shooting upward.

"How far do these tunnels go?" I ask, and my voice sounds strange. It's got a scratchy quality. Less like a voice, more like the scrape of a branch.

"As above, so below," my father answers cryptically, but he isn't looking at me. He's just staring ahead. "We're the roots of this forest."

It's a weird thing, being so deep below the earth. The top of the tunnel grazes against my head. If I were any taller, I'd have to duck. It's a shallow fit for the two of us, especially walking side by side. Father tramples over the dead like they're pebbles in a path. I do my best to weave around them out of respect.

And not all of them are strangers. I lock eyes with a corpse and my father's candlelight illuminates the familiar hollows of her face. Even with my father's support, I fall to my knees.

"Wil's mother."

I feel the cold in my blood as my father stills beside me. His laughter is hideous. "You recognize her?" Preserved in the frigid earth, her mother has yet to skeletonize, but time has taken much from her.

Once-full hair has grown sparse and soft, pink flesh withered to a tight gray. She looks so heartbreakingly close to Wil that every piece in me shatters at once.

Her world was much too full to end. Because of me, her corpse is imprisoned below the soil, hidden in a cavern so deep, Wil will never find her. It's selfish, but I hope she never does. I don't want Wil down here. I don't want her to see what's become of the woman she loved so dearly.

The woman who died because of me.

"She meddled too much," my father tuts. "Like mother, like daughter."

A stone slices through my jeans, and the blood trickling from the cut reminds me I'm alive. In a place occupied by the dead, my heart continues to beat. But not for long.

My father hoists me back to my feet, and his grip is the only thing keeping me tethered to the ground.

Without him, I think I might float.

Dad's cold, too. I feel the goose bumps along his arm as he holds me.

We walk farther. Seconds turn to minutes; discomfort turns to pain. My body is frozen over, my skin so freezing, I almost feel warm. We walk and walk, and then my father comes to an abrupt halt.

We stand before a crudely constructed ladder. It's held by thinning bundles of twine. Without my hands, it's nearly impossible to keep steady on my own. My dad keeps one arm pressed in the small of my back.

In a cave full of horrors, I brace myself for what awaits me.

CHAPTER TWENTY-EIGHT

WIL

Marking our path with a Sharpie feels very Hansel and Gretel.

Kevin says as much.

Ronnie squints at him. "Didn't those two almost get eaten alive? I think that's the last thing I want to hear right now."

The flashlight clicks on in my hand, but it's only a soft glow in comparison to the car's headlights. It illuminates the steps before me, but beyond that the world is lost. Winter transformed the Morguewood into a labyrinth of white, and night has taken care of the rest. This is the type of forest you don't come out of. It lures you in and takes its time with you. Animal carcasses lie buried in the snow, rib cages partially exposed through the ice. It's sickening how much they look like human bones.

Kevin pops the cap off the marker and brands another tree with a large *X*. We've made dozens of them at this point.

"The witch is the one that died in the end, anyway," Kevin mumbles to himself, but Ronnie is far past listening. "They put her in an oven."

A particularly nasty chill has me replying, "An oven sounds lovely at the moment, actually."

Dad is silent beside me, save for the crunch of his soles against the snow. They leave a trail behind him that will be obscured in minutes. Footprints and bread crumbs don't work out here, not in a town that's got to put visibility markers on their fire hydrants. I wonder absently how long it would take for me to sit out here before the snow would eclipse me fully.

Dad's prints are disappearing already, but the Xs have yet to fade.

It's hard to say how long we spend drifting through the trees. The hazy plan we set was to drive midway through the woods and trek the remaining mile on foot so as to not draw suspicion. In theory, it seemed like a good, well-thought-out plan. Now it seems like a horrible mistake. The forest stretches out forever in the distance. Ronnie rubs her arms across her chest like it's kindling for a fire.

We continue along the path, a nervous energy brewing between us. It burns in my chest and spreads through my veins, chasing away some of the cold still.

The silence breaks at the sound of snow crunching in the distance and the rustle of gloves brushing across bark. We freeze collectively at the noise, holding our breath. Lucas twitches with the crossbow and I click the flashlight off.

He raises his other arm and gestures for us to keep behind him. I don't move just yet, but I hope he knows if someone comes out to attack, I'll leap on them like I'm feral.

Another leaf crunches and a silhouette breaks from the shadows. Patricia Clearwater.

I'm used to seeing her with slicked-back hair and a PTO-mom-Barbie ensemble, but not today. I only recognize it's her after she sheds the skull from her face like a second skin. Her eyes hold no warmth; they're as uninviting as the blizzard around me.

"Veronica," she says, and her voice is soft and sharp all at once. A delicate rage. "Get away from them." Ronnie holds her ground and I'm proud to see the slight lift of her chin, defiance outweighing her fear.

She's grown so much in this last year, no longer skittish or easily cowed. Her eyes dart to Lucas. More specifically to the weapon in his hand. Strangely, she doesn't tell him to lower it. Not yet. "Where is he, Mom?"

Patricia's eyes flicker from her daughter's to the rest of us. They linger first on me before rolling over to my father. "Ben," she addresses him, and it's bizarre to hear his name come from her lips. "You lost a wife already; now you're willing to risk a daughter? Foolish. Now is the time to leave while you can."

Dad's eyes are bloodshot and wet, but his lips are pulled back to expose clenched teeth. His fists waver at his sides. "Are you threatening me?"

She swallows at his anger but holds her resolve. "I'm telling you to leave. The ceremony can't be interrupted. There are police forces all around the forest. This has to happen."

"Tough luck," I snap, and, God, now I'm almost crying, too. I take a step forward and I might have actually decked the woman in the face if Ronnie's arm hadn't come up.

Tears are already streaming down her wind-whipped cheeks. *"How could you? After all this time, how could you do any of this? Teach me love and repentance and all that shit and then be so unbelievably evil in the next breath. You monster!"* Her voice has gotten higher with every word.

"Veronica." Mrs. Clearwater hiccups, and I can see that there's some ounce of humanity in her because she's looking at her daughter with such broken hope. It would be heartbreaking on anyone else's face. "You don't understand. I didn't want to involve you in this. I used to think it would've been such an honor to be chosen, but then when I wasn't chosen . . . when your father died years after . . . I was relieved I wasn't deemed worthy enough for the Calling. I would be able to watch you grow and get old. And when I thought about you having kids of your own one day, I knew I couldn't involve you. I'd let you rebel and leave and never know the heartbreak of your child's name being chosen.

"But that boy—he's not what any of you think. He was chosen for this and there's no going back on it now. You haven't seen what he can become." She turns toward me, frantic as we close in. "He's dangerous. Something like that needs to be contained. He'd raise hell on this town if we freed him. He'd kill us all."

"And you'd deserve it," I snarl, meaning every word. I'd free him, even if it spelled out my own death. "You forget he's still a boy. Who cares what happens to this wretched town? If this whole forest disappears, so be it. Find another town, another job. Do anything but this. You'd kill a boy to save the Morguewood?"

"We don't have a choice. We have to. Eden commands it." Her face is torn between pity and hatred and some strange combination of the two. "If it isn't done soon, it will all be too late, Wil. You and your mother failed to understand that. You have no idea what's about to come. Are you prepared to love a monster?"

Am I?

"There's five of us and one of you, Mom. You can't stop us." Ronnie nods to Lucas as she says it, and we split like the Red Sea around Mrs. Clearwater. "Now move aside."

Patricia's expression holds for a second longer before her resolve splinters apart. She falls to her knees at Veronica's feet and her hands cling desperately to her ankles.

"Please don't go." She hiccups. "That girl will get you killed. I'm begging you not to go. As your mother, please."

Ronnie freezes for a moment and I worry this is it. Her mom's pleading eyes and digging fingers will undo it all. Her chest rises and falls in rapid succession and she sucks in her lips for a moment of painful deliberation. "You're no one to me now," she says finally, and with each word she shakes her mother off.

Mrs. Clearwater doesn't rise from the snow. We may find out after all how long it would take the snow to bury someone alive in this storm. It's hard to do much of anything with your heart wrenched out of your chest like that.

I hate her; I truly do. I despise her and the rest of this cult for what they did to my mother. What they're planning for Elwood and would've gladly done to me. Still, a strange pity burns in my chest.

But not enough to pull her to her feet. Her question lingers in my head as we continue forward.

Are you prepared to love a monster? I think I am.

CHAPTER TWENTY-NINE

ELWOOD

The world above is as dark as the one below. The moon has yet to break from the clouds. She hides in a thick, foggy veil of white. I know it won't be long before she makes her appearance.

The tree they've brought me to is the tallest in the whole forest. The trunk alone is massive, nearly as wide as four or five others combined. Among the swaying pine, it stands like a forgotten god. But it is not forgotten. It is still worshiped. This is where they brought me as a screaming child, and this is where I'll die now.

"You're changing too fast," my father admonishes between clenched teeth. "This human vessel of yours won't last much longer before you sprout."

Prudence is splayed out on the ground on a heavy fur pelt. She's alone in her agony, her husband not bothering with any amount of coddling. Like me, we are both means to an end. Her eyes lock on mine when the water breaks, her breath exploding into a frozen plume of white. "The baby is coming. Quick!"

He throws my back against the rippled bark. Then come the ropes, the sensation of hands all over, the noisy fastening of a knot. They bite hard into my ribs, trapping me here.

Winter drags its teeth along my flesh and robs the air from my lungs.

The cold is making me delirious. I squirm against the bark, waiting for my father's face to change. For him to laugh—a noise like the fall of a tree, deep and booming from his chest. *Never disrespect me again*, he'd tell me, digging his nails into my shoulder. I'd nod and he'd finally relax and release me. His gnarled fingers would reach around and untie my knots. He'd rip open my constraints and bring me home. He'd bring me home and not leave me here to die, freezing and bound to the forest. This was all a lesson.

Ba-dump. Ba-dump. Ba-dump. The ground rumbles with the echo of the forest's heart. I feel it stronger than ever before. And above it still, I hear the patter of wings in my core. Moths swarm from every direction, scurrying out of the treetops and landing on my skin. They break up the night in a prism of blood red and dusky brown.

My father unsheathes a knife from a leather case. The blade is tinged black with centuries of dried blood. Despite its age, the tip looks so very sharp. I understand that the last time it was used was on my uncle; it's the closest connection I'll ever forge with him. My dad's voice is a whisper above the wind as he leans in, his breath spilling in a smoke cloud against my cheek. "From the earth you were forged, and to the dirt you shall return."

And then he plunges the blade right into my chest.

CHAPTER THIRTY

WIL

A boy sways up ahead, his bloody body strapped tight to a tree. I recognize the slump of his posture and the mess of his hair. He's wearing the same raggedy sun-bleached jeans and faded plaid as the day he left. Only the plaid is soaked through with a telling, taunting red.

"Elwood!"

But it's too late. The clouds break and his skin is illuminated by the milky spill of the moon. That's when the screaming starts.

CHAPTER THIRTY-ONE

ELWOOD

It's a quiet pain.

I expected to feel more. The blade carves through my skin like the brush of a finger. I see it wedged deep, blood gushing from the cut and splattering on my father's face. I see it all, but I don't feel a thing. If the knife is trying to get more from me, it will be disappointed. I am only a hollow ringing. I won't fight this. I will give myself over willingly to the trees.

The moon breaks on my back, washing over my skin and drowning the rest of the world in a sharp, lethal blue. It pours over me like an acid. Every whisper of silver is a searing heat against my skin. It engulfs me in a pain so deep, so full, that all I know how to do is howl. The noise scrapes my lungs and breaks from my lips all at once. It starts and it doesn't stop.

My skin peels back, too human to belong to me now. Moth wings erupt from my spine, a splash of burnt autumn against the dark woods, and feathery antennae tear through either temple.

"Elwood!" Wil's voice cuts through the trees, and with my fading vision, I see her standing there like a mirage in the darkness. She's my own angel of death. I soak in every part of her as the pain mounts. I let her be the last image etched in my vision.

The demon in me tears through.

Wil's features turn muddy in my mind, disappearing into a blur. One second she's there in perfect detail; the next she's gone. All of her. Gone.

I close my eyes to the world I know.

I open them to hunger. Consuming, crushing, everywhere.

The earth calls for me. Every corner of the forest flashes in my eyes at once. Gray wolves with their heads moon-bound; hares among mounds of fresh ice; snowy owls in high trees, their saucer eyes wide and watching. They know better than to get close to me.

But not all creatures shy away.

Humans flank me on all sides. There are swaying figures ahead, their bodies an ultraviolet mosaic, bright light against a black canvas. I follow the stars and the constellations pull me closer. I home in on them and block the incessant buzz of the world out. There is only their stammering pulse and the slick of their sweat cropping like fresh dew.

"Ezekiel! What have you done?" Heat twists and spirals in the air. I hear words, but they don't process. They're garbled, familiar once but lost now. The only thing I've kept close is my hatred. My feeling for the men in front of me is a buried thorn. The man opens his mouth, speaks to me again in his incoherent, babbling tongue.

There's a whirr of something man-made, an unnatural piercing static. "We need reinforcements stat. Hurry up, he's already—" The noise dies.

His fear tastes nectar-sweet. I lick it off my lips and it drips, drips, drips. I lap it up and I think it's blood.

Have I killed him so easily? There and gone in the blink of an eye.

But the thorn is still there. I turn to the last man and breathe him in.

"Oh God . . . Lord in heaven, hear my prayer . . . Elwood, son. I take it back, all of it. I didn't mean—" The sound ends with a crunch.

There's a body beneath me now. A heart still faintly beating. I scoop it up and dig my teeth in. Gobble it down until there's nothing left. The human's body is no different than a fallen log or clump of snow.

Useless. Quiet.

I'm hungry. Starving. Empty and hollow and aching and I need more.

A shrill cry pierces the air. Beyond the men I've devoured, there is a woman. A child, but not just any child. I smell the woods on him. Another vessel for me, another skin to slip into and be trapped in.

No. It ends now. I'll open my mouth wide and end his screams, I'll be free forever, I— Something hits me. Ice-cold.

I thrash toward the assailant and listen to the air, count the bodies, fresh and writhing and afraid. One, two, three, four. Five hearts going wild. *Ba-dump, ba-dump, ba-dump, ba-dump, ba-dump.*

"*Will!*"

Another pelt slams against my skin. The child is forgotten, but my hunger isn't. They're running.

But I am faster. Wings slapping the sky, thunderous in the night. The moon beacons my path and they are helpless as I descend, my talons scraping ribbons against the frozen soil. I catch a man, sink my teeth in, and hit bone. A scream drags out from the human's chest, and I lap up the sound. I want to hear more of it.

"*Hurry, Lucas! He's got Dad! Throw him a knife. Something!*"

I'm about to go farther when I hear a rush of motion and feel a sharp stab in my side. I roar with the flash of pain, swatting the source, sending it flying in the distance. There's a scream and the thunk of a skull hitting a tree.

"*Dad!*"

Another stinging scrape of snow hits my side. The assault doesn't end until I am staring down a girl in the distance. There is a resounding click and a light and suddenly the moon is flashing between the trees, smaller than before yet oh so bright.

"*Over here, Mothman!*"

I turn, charging toward the new moon. The girl carries it with her, taking it farther and farther away.

She won't escape me. I am the wind weaving through the branches and the crackle of ice as frozen streams break open. I am every thrashing thorn and this human cannot outrun me.

She twists through the clearing, ducking beneath tree limbs and leaping over logs. Anything to evade me. A memory breaks from the fog as I chase her, something beyond hunger:

The same girl is staring at me with honey eyes. She's much younger, but she's got an identical grin and a smattering of freckles. Her hair is wild all around her and she hurls a snowball right at my head.

"Ow!" I whine, trying in vain to dry my winter-slicked hair. I shiver with the cold and she laughs. "Why did you do that?"

She's pretty. Probably prettier than any girl I've ever seen. Prettier than the moon and the flowers in June and even prettier than the butterfly that lands some days on my windowsill.

"My name is Wil-ah-mean-a!" she sings.

"'Mean' is right."

"You can call me Wil! My dad calls me Minnie."

"Wil," I try it. I like it. "I'll be your friend if you promise not to throw snowballs at me anymore."

"Deal."

I keep charging and shake away the strange intrusion. Fear rippled so strongly off the others, but I barely smell it on this one. Mouth salivating, blood sloshing in my gut, I reach out for her but miss by a hair. She's fast. The hunger burns and rolls in me, pushing me forward.

"Oh my God, you didn't," Wil says, but she's not upset. She's laughing. I've got two matching dandelion-spun bracelets in my hands. They're linked together at the

stems. I slip one on her wrist, holding my hand on hers for a moment longer. I pretend I'm linking our fingers. She makes a small noise and I yank my hand back, slipping on my own bracelet in a hurry.

"Do you like them?" I ask, and she chuckles. "They're friendship bracelets."

"I give them a day before they fall apart. These things never stay put."

I shake my head. I like the way the sun glistens in her hair. "These ones will."

"You promise?" She snorts.

"Promise."

She brings out her pinkie and I shake it with mine. I want to keep them curled together forever.

There it is again. This bizarre emotion rearing its head. I look at the girl and I do not feel sympathy, but I feel . . . something.

I decide then that I hate feeling. The wind whips wildly against me, branches hitting hard. I know what I'll do when I reach her. I'll dig my claws in and roar to the heavens. I'll break her down and swallow her up. Maybe then the hunger will end and the memories will fade. One more body to sate my gut and the moon.

Winter steals her scent. I lower myself to the earth and breathe her back into my veins. Her heart is spiced like cloves and cinnamon.

The slope of her nose, the curl of her lashes, the beating in my chest with each pencil stroke. There's a softer sort of beauty when she lets her guard down. Her hair runs wild down her back, so many little braids woven by my hand.

I lean against the metal bleachers. With another flick of my pencil, I introduce butterflies to her hair. A dozen monarchs perched throughout like gems. I'll color them in later, a brilliant burst of orange.

My sketchbook is filled to the brim. I've gone through several already. Sketching wings and antennae, thoraxes and mandibles, but also Wil and Wil and Wil and Wil.

Stop. I curse the daydream for clouding my focus. I can't stop now.

I'm gaining on her. Fear blooms off her for the first time. I fill my lungs with it, savor the taste on my tongue.

Not as pleasant as I thought it would be. I want to spit it back out. "Elwood!" There's that sound again. She screeches it above the wind.

She's nothing more than a flash of heat. A blurry imprint of red among the surrounding black. One strike and she dodges me yet again. I might have missed her, but the forest doesn't. I summon a root and she trips over it. She lies beneath me, back pressed into the bark, the rest of her body eclipsed in the snow.

Her blood pools in the frost. There it is. It smells heavenly.

I didn't find all of my collection myself. I have to ship in some of them from faraway places, places where the sun shines harder and the woods aren't so brutal.

The woods are dense, but they are also quiet. I walk through the trees and search for the dead. I want to make them new again. Occasionally I will find some—crumpled bodies, curled wings—but more often than not, I don't find any.

I'm already prying into today's crate. Everything is so carefully preserved, wrapped and double-wrapped, nestled underneath a mound of protective cloth. My death's-head hawk moth lies wings closed, tucked inside a protective piece of wax.

I rip the package open, unable to hold back my explosive grin. She's perfect.

Butterflies and moths come stubborn and rigid. It takes care to get them to open up. I place my new specimen gently inside a pool of water. With time, she will be ready. I'm fine waiting.

"You've got to listen to me, Elwood! Whatever the fuck this is, it isn't you." Her voice clears out my mind somewhat. I hear her for the first time, but everything is fuzzy. It stirs in and out of focus. Meaning one second; meaningless the next.

Her heart is a rampant thing in her chest.

And the moon demands I steal it. *Ba-dump. Ba-dump. Ba-dump.*

I swipe back, gnashing teeth and swiping claws and a desire so potent, so raw, I can't fight it. I'm helpless to the pull, and . . .

"I love you!"

And . . . I blink. The fog peels back, if only for a second or two. I stir, staring down at honey eyes and a set jaw.

My lips fumble uselessly with a word, my captive human spirit stirring for the first time inside me. *W . . . W . . . Wi—*

"Wil?"

CHAPTER THIRTY-TWO

WIL

There he is. The boy I know. The one I never stopped knowing.

He lets out an unearthly howl, a sound that sends the dead plants around us rippling to life. They tug on their roots, trying to push forward.

If I played my cards right, the others are safe by now. I've led Elwood far enough away from them that there's a chance for them to get away. A mile away, Cherry can get the car rumbling to life and hightail it to the hospital. Prudence's baby can be born as a child and not as an *offering*. We can break the cycle. We have to.

Dad shouts my name in the distance, but I refuse to turn. He will be lucky if he walks away with a concussion after that fall. I still can't believe he's here. My heart pangs at that. I've already lost Mom. If I lose Dad, it will be the final nail in my coffin.

As soon as the transformation stole Elwood, the bloodshed began. His dad and Sheriff Vrees are dead. Slaughtered limb from limb. I saw it all. Chests torn through, dripping out onto the snow.

I taste the salt of my sweat trickling down my face. He could kill me just as easily. Maybe he still will.

But he's in there, somewhere.

Elwood is more butterfly than man. A strange body held together by twisting vines and clumps of moss. Ribs with a dozen oozing hearts trapped inside—none of which look like they belong to it, all of which look stolen. Human.

And magnificent, unearthly wings.

He lowers his face to me, stares at me with milky-white eyes.

I feel the plume of his breath spilling across my throat. Hot and sticky. Those massive wings of his unfurl, crafted from a thousand tiny green leaves.

I conjure my remaining courage. One deep, bone-rattling breath. My lungs wheeze in the cold. What's left of Elwood is being pulled from the surface. Soon there will be nothing left.

I've got to yank him out or he'll drown.

I squeeze my eyes shut. I won't look at what he's become. I'll keep his memory alive in my mind. No more wings and bones, no more hearts and antennae. All I see in my mind is the soft and shy Elwood Clarke I've always known. Elwood and his butterflies, the way he prattled on so intensely about them. Elwood and the little portraits he'd shove in my locker, the ones he was too embarrassed to show me face-to-face. Elwood's eyes lighting up when we talked about running away one day.

So I tell him. All of it. Every little thing I've kept locked within my chest. All the quirks of his I love so dearly. The letters I wrote him but never sent (*Dear Elwood: First of all, how dare you?*). The aching I felt in his absence. Like he ripped off the most important piece of me and stole it away. I tell him maybe that's what Dad meant after all, when he said coping without my mother was damn near impossible.

Elwood has always been a part of me. The most important part.

"And I'll be damned if that monster takes you from me," I finish, my lips trembling and my nails digging into the ground. "I love you."

The world is very still after my confession. It feels a lot like the two of us are suspended in time, floating, even. But then the monstrous elements of him shift and ripple and change.

Bit by bit they peel off, and he ripples like a caterpillar emerging from a cocoon. He's human again but not fully. The forest has come alive within him. His eyes are so much crisper and greener than I remember. A veil has been lifted off them. He's alive with power. It radiates off him in a pulsating cloud—the wind rushes through his hair, his fingers grapple with the wind at his sides. It shifts directions with his fingertips.

I don't care about any of that. I bury myself in his arms.

CHAPTER THIRTY-THREE

ELWOOD

For the first time, I taste the iron tang of their blood on my lips. It stains my mouth, coating each tooth like a layer of grime. I hack and spit, but the taste lingers, gripping onto my tongue. My nails have become black talons, curving off each finger, my palms stained a hideous, telling red as I break away from Wil.

"Did I hurt you?" I breathe. I feel like I've woken from a hideous, horrible dream. I whip around myself, staring at her. Her knee is sliced through, the fabric of her jeans torn to smithereens. "Please tell me I didn't do that."

The truth tears through me just as I had torn through my father. Memories sprout all around me, bitter weeds that I cannot pluck. Reminding me what I did. What I am.

There was no chance to fight me off, no chance to stop what had already begun. I chased their pulse. My father cried and cried, but I didn't hear him. I didn't see him. A fog had drifted over my mind, blurring away the screams. Blurring away the monster inside me.

"That wasn't you," she tells me, and I feel her thumbs dart around my cheeks. She catches the tears before they fall. "It isn't you."

She holds me, and I bury myself in her arms. I want to hide away forever. The world is changing around me. She's the only constant.

"I'm changing, Wil." Even now, I'm not sure what the future holds. My breath ghosts across the side of her face. I taste pine and soil on my tongue. Wil has brought me back into my body, but I don't know for how long. I might've escaped the monster, but I can't outrun the seed within me. It's already blossomed, and soon I will become something else altogether.

A transformation, that's what Cherry said. Maybe she was right and Death isn't death after all. Maybe death is my old life burning so that my new life can be born from the ashes. The beast inside me was never really a beast. It was only a boy tainted by centuries of bloodshed and darkness. "Know I love you. Whatever happens."

"Nothing is going to happen," she whispers through tears, but we both know that isn't true. Something is coming.

I press my lips to hers and hold them there as long as I can. In my last seconds, I lift my mouth to her ear and whisper my promise. I savor the widening of her eyes as the world changes. As I transform.

My heart is replaced by a new sort of flutter, like the gentle slide of wings. A hummingbird taking off.

My vision is steady, even as my being is consumed by a thousand tiny little moths.

It hits me as the woods beckon and the saplings call my name. This is how it is meant to be. How it was always meant to be. With a twitch of my feet, the ground rumbles and breaks. My fingers curl and the breeze shifts, changing to match my whim. One long, rattling sigh is enough to shake the snow off from the treetops.

After all these years, I know who I am.

I am Elwood, born to the soil and frost, destined to give my heart to these trees. I am home.

CHAPTER THIRTY-FOUR

WIL

Elwood's voice echoes in my mind, his final words chanted over like a prayer. *Come find me in the trees. I'll wait for you.*

The words are the last he leaves me with as he splinters apart at the seams. It happens so fast, I barely have time to register it. One second he's there, smiling a heart-wrenching smile, and the next he's gone. His silhouette lingers in the air, a frozen blue imprint of him etched against the world. The wind carries him away, and I break, shattering into the snow.

This wasn't supposed to happen. I was supposed to rescue him from the beast, return him in my arms. We'd have a normal life. Hell, maybe I'd return to school in time for a senior prom with him. Things would go back to the way they were. Back before the blizzard. Before Mom. Things would be good again.

But now everything has changed.

I sob into the ice, my tears freezing down my cheeks as they pour out. I'll scour the whole forest to search for him again. What will I find, though? My fingertips burn, but I hardly even feel it. An indescribable rush of grief sweeps over me, claiming me as it did a year ago. It starts in my throat, fingers squeezing over me, blocking off my breath. I heave and fight for air that won't come—every second plays out for minutes. The fingers release, and I suck in a painful, tight breath. It tears out into a strangled sort of cry, ripping from my lungs to my tongue.

I force myself to move. I walk through the thick of the forest, barely feeling the cold as it scrapes against my bare skin. There's a false sense of peace: The snow shines blue in the moonlight; the wind has died down to nothing. If Elwood's father is still here, he's been swallowed whole by the blizzard.

And the rest of the group hasn't left.

Dad's sprawled out on the ground, whimpering to himself at the agony. His eyes flutter like someone who can't tell whether to sleep or stay awake. Blood is dried onto his scalp; it starts at his hairline and ends beneath his chin. He's always been a fighter. I just never noticed.

"Where is he? What happened?" Lucas scrambles to make sense of what he witnessed. He looks to me to fill him in, but I can't. I'm still reeling. His body is battered, a particularly nasty scrape down his cheek. His hair is matted and thick with blood.

Next to Lucas, Kevin and Ronnie look worse for wear as well. Kevin is sporting a black eye and Ronnie's lip is split open, both of them with gnarly deep purple bruises along their bodies. Cherry's parked the car and clambered out to tend to Prudence in the corner. The baby is red and screaming and *alive*, bundled tight in a heavy swath of blankets.

It comes pouring out in a sob. "He's gone."

I turn to look toward Pine Point in the distance. I want to tear us right off the map.

Not a minute later, the forest ripples. Alive with a sudden current, an unmistakable energy. Vines slither out across the ground. Branches shoot out like hands. The whole forest seems to become sentient. It grabs what's left of the church several yards away, digging its fingers into the foundations and dragging it back toward the open and waiting mouth of the woods. We watch as it all disappears. It is devoured in its entirety. From the shadows, we hear the crunch of brick broken down and the shattering of glass.

Everything is returned back to the soil. Every nightmare is dissolved, broken down piece by piece. I can't see him, but somehow, some way, I know Elwood is responsible.

A couple seconds of unleashed power and Elwood turned a room to dust. One minute passes and he does the same to the church and his own home beyond that. The woods devour what never should have existed in the first place.

CHAPTER THIRTY-FIVE

WIL

I've always hated hospitals.

Sterile white walls, the rusty roll of gurneys down linoleum tile. The bored, vacant stare of the receptionist. I shift in my seat, rocking my heels back and forth against the floor. The lobby is primarily empty. There's an old man in the corner groaning about a slipped disc and a mom on the other end, smoothing back her toddler's hair. The kid sniffles, his nose a snotty red.

And then there's me, sitting as far away as I can, nursing an obscenely large energy drink. I'm exhausted, but too wired to even think about sleep. It's a horrible combination. My eyes still sting from tears I haven't yet cried. I've shifted from agonizing grief to an all-over numbness. I'm not sure which is worse.

There's no way any of this should have happened.

A middle-aged nurse comes paddling in through the door. Her hair is in a worn, frayed ponytail. She looks as tired as I feel. "Wilhelmina Greene? Come with me."

I follow her down a labyrinth of hallways, but I'm sure she could pace through them in her sleep. With her glossy stare and half-lidded eyes, I have to wonder if she already is. She leads me down the hall to a room and ushers me inside.

He's sporting a partial neck brace and his left foot is elevated from the rest of him, clearly shattered.

He's got a row of stitches running from his ear to his hairline. I take my seat at the edge of the bed and the nurse fusses with something on his chart.

He slips effortlessly into dad mode, an MO I'd long assumed was terminated. "I'm glad you're okay. You could've been seriously hurt."

"Are you really going to start lecturing me?" I deflect, and my flippant response clearly doesn't sit well with him. I think of how easily he could have broken. Dead like Mom. My voice breaks as I snap, "None of that was your business. You shouldn't have come."

The nurse quietly dismisses herself in the background, retreating into the hall like it's some sort of nuclear-fallout bunker. I don't blame her. I'd hide too.

"Your well-being has always been my business."

I'm about to ask him "Since when?" but I don't get the chance to ask anything at all. He wraps me in a crushing half hug from his bed.

"D-Dad, lie back, you're beat up. You need to take it easy."

"I thought you were dead earlier," he whispers into my ear, his voice curdled and thick. He chokes and the tears make a mess of his face. "Your mom's old room was gone in the blink of an eye. I searched everywhere and couldn't find you. I thought I'd lost you."

His tears have some of my own prickling to the surface. I have to swat at my eyes to keep them from raining down my cheeks.

"Why couldn't you care this much when I needed you?" I ask, and the words hurt. They impale us both, leaving me gutted and him speechless. Mom never had a funeral, so I buried her in "Missing" flyers. Dad buried himself away in his room. "I lost both of you at the same time."

I spent days and weeks and months chasing answers, all in an attempt to run from grief. It was hot on my tail always, waiting for a quiet moment to pounce. I ran even when my legs heaved and my chest ached, but Dad gave up from the very start.

I juggled the bills in his stead, bouncing job to job while he lay comatose in his own bed. Not dead but determined to waste away anyway. I'd cried and screamed and begged, but the father I knew was lost to me, and no amount of "Missing" posters would bring him back, either.

"You weren't there," I repeat, and now the tears are streaming and there's no chance of stopping them. "You weren't there when I needed you to be. You left me alone. So don't act like you care now."

"I never stopped caring, I just—" He knots his fingers in his hair, and I watch as he scrambles to piece together the rest of his thoughts. "I cared too much. That was the problem. I cared so much that I couldn't breathe or move or eat. Do you understand, Minnie? Your mother was the best part of me. The most important part. When she disappeared, everything ended. She left when you were young, said this life was too stifling for her. I was broken then, and when she left again? I assumed she was gone forever. *And now I'll never—*" He bites back a sob, his knuckles grazing against his teeth. "I couldn't look at you without seeing the life I made with her. Without thinking I was the one that should've disappeared. Let's face it, your mother would have been so much better at this. With you. I didn't feel like I was good enough."

"Mom? The lady who cried at other people's funerals?" I ask him, and it hits me after the words are out that she would be ten times worse at this. I've known it forever, but this is the first time hearing the truth out loud. The first time I've ever admitted it to myself. "No, Mom was too gentle for grief like that. It would have destroyed her."

He struggles to pull himself together, but after so many times breaking down, it's a hard thing to do.

Returning to "normal" is impossible. At least, the normal we had before all this.

"It destroyed me too," he whispers, his voice so soft, it crushes something within me.

I bury my head in his chest. When I was a child, he was a giant. But after all these years, I'm the one who's grown, and all he's done is stay the same.

He startles, and I worry he might shut down again, but then his weathered hand finds its way to my hair. I can't see him, but I feel his body shake with tears.

"I'm sorry," he whispers into my scalp. "You don't have to forgive me. I'm not asking you to. But please know that I'm sorry for leaving you on your own all this time. I was so caught up in my own grief that I ended up making yours twice as difficult. I'm so, so sorry, Minnie. Er, I'm sorry. I know you prefer Wil now."

I bite hard on my cheek to fight the tears. I've had enough crying today to last a lifetime. "No," I say into his shirt before pulling away. "Minnie is fine."

"Your mother would be incredibly proud of you." He eclipses my hands with his, making sure the words hit home. "Truly."

Tears well in my eyes and trickle paths down my cheeks. "She'd be proud of you too, Dad." That's all I can get out. Everything else burns in my chest.

"Doctor said it'll be a week before I can go home again. Sounds like I'll be eating a lot of hospital food." He nods toward the leftovers on his tray. It looks exactly like what the school dishes out. "When I get out . . . I . . . I've been thinking of cooking again."

"Really?" I whisper, laying my head on his chest again, listening to the soft murmur of his heart. "Yeah, it's about time to get back to it, don't you think?" His smile lifts one corner of his mouth.

"Chocolate-stuffed pancakes?" I ask, hopeful.

"With extra whipped cream," he promises. It's difficult to smile, but I try my best.

CHAPTER THIRTY-SIX

WIL
SMALL TOWN OF HORRORS

Nothing's weirder than seeing your childhood home plastered on CNN. A news reporter reads our town's fate off a teleprompter, her face trained into a solemn, unblinking stare.

"On December twenty-sixth, an 8.1 earthquake hit the small town of Pine Point, Michigan. The massive devastation resulted in two known fatalities, with one young man still missing and presumed dead." Elwood's photo flashes on the screen—a cropped version of him out in the garden, his skin soft in the sun. It lingers for a moment before dissolving into crime scene footage. "But what started as an unfortunate act of God has quickly spiraled into a nightmare for this local community. The aftermath of the quake revealed a series of underground tunnels filled with hundreds of bodies—all beneath the now-destroyed Garden of Adam church. The FBI is calling this cult incredibly dangerous."

The wreckage of the church flashes on the TV. Boards shattered and bent in odd angles, the steeple caved in completely. The rubble transitions to the steps outside of a courtroom, Mrs. Clearwater glaring at the cameras and clinging tight to her lawyer's side. Another flash and the scene turns to her with her hand held high to take the oath.

"Now, five months later, the next round of trials for the Garden of Adam's members are set to begin. We expect to dig deeper into the sinister underbelly of the case and uncover the church's roots. More from our very own reporter Chett Adams, who is here on the scene interviewing local boy Brian Schmidt."

The cameras pan from a lumber truck barreling down a country road to a stream of coffee hitting a (surprisingly) clean cup at Earl's. They've got Brian on TV, his hair extra saturated under the fluorescents.

"Brian, how are you coping with the aftermath of all this?" Chett says, and, my God, does the man look out of place with a taxidermy bear behind him.

"Oh, it's a struggle every day, Chett. I can't even sleep at night. To think, I was *this* close to the center of everything—"

I flip the station off. Brian's annoying voice dissipates with the crinkle of static.

"They just put anyone in the spotlight, don't they?" Cherry mutters from the kitchen table. Her roots are as bright as the party streamers twirling around her head. "That kid's been on the news several times now. Swears up and down that he was part of your little posse and helped solve everything. The news is lapping it up."

"He acts like he didn't pick on Elwood and me all the time," Kevin gripes. With the way the birthday boy's leaning back, he's lucky he's got the only one of our chairs with four working legs. Otherwise he'd fall back into all of our trash. "That guy gave me a *wedgie* in eighth grade and suddenly we're buddy-buddy now?"

"You know what? Let him pretend," Lucas says, speaking over the fizz of a popped can. It's hard to take him seriously in his Mothman birthday hat, but seeing as how we're all wearing *something* cryptid-themed, I'm not able to talk. "I'm sick of interviews. Can't step a foot out of my house without some reporter shoving a camera in my face. If Brian wants to take them all, more power to him."

"Oh, you think you have it bad?" Ronnie jests. Her own party hat is lopsided on her head. The Loch Ness Monster in crude black Sharpie. Not a lot of party supplies ship out here, so we had to settle for plain hats and our own imagination. "Try being the daughter of the only Garden of Adam member willing to talk . . . I know I should be happy she's willing to finally try and make amends, but I can't catch a break. I just want to be left alone."

"I'm sorry, babe." Lucas's expression softens, and he rubs lovesick circles against her skin. He presses a kiss to her cheek and she leans into it and—

"There goes my appetite," I say because I am allergic to seeing other people's affection. Not only is it awkward as hell, but now when I see them all gross and in love, all I can think of is Elwood.

"You're not allowed to lose your appetite," my father chimes in. Between his beardless baby face and the high-pitched gasp in his voice, you'd think my dad was a child all over again. He's certainly treating the oven like it's an Easy Bake. Took him seven thousand attempts to learn to cook again without making a charred mess. "I worked really hard on this cake, and you all better eat it."

"A box cake would've worked just fine," I joke. It's weird, joking with him. Things are still stilted between us. He might've extended an olive branch, but it's still flimsy. There's a long way to go before we're normal again, if something like that is even possible. But it's a start.

"Nonsense," he quips, dropping the fondant monstrosity onto the table. "Could a store-bought cake look like *this*?"

This being a gray blob with red UFO lights and two Twinkie aliens perched at the top. It read *HAVE AN OUT-OF-THIS-WORLD BIRTH-DAY, KEVIN.*

"No, I guess it really couldn't." I snort.

It doesn't matter if I'm not thoroughly amazed. Kevin's eyes are solar-system bright. He grins with all of his teeth. "It's perfect, Mr. G. Can I have the Twinkie—er, alien—at the top?" Dad nods, and Kevin bites off the green monster's head. "Thanks, guys. I really don't know what to say. I'm just glad everyone was able to make it."

My fork's been twirling idly in my hands until this point, but I white-knuckle it now as it stabs into the wood. "Almost everyone," I whisper, and I despise the crack in my voice. *It's Kevin's birthday. Don't cry. Don't cry, don't cry, don't even think about crying.*

But it's too late. A tear goes streaking down my cheek. And when one tear breaks, all the rest follow. Ronnie's at my side in an instant. She squeezes me tight. "Don't cry, Wil," she whispers. "You can still go see him today after . . ."

That might be the worst part. As much as I want to drop in and see him—I'm scared to talk to him about the future. This whole time I've been so focused on finding Mom's killer and keeping Elwood safe that I never stopped to think about what I want. The world waiting for me just out of reach. How I long to map the universe out like the stars glued to my bedroom ceiling. How I want to leave Pine Point. "I don't know how he'll react to my news. I don't want to hurt him."

It's Lucas who surprises me. He's silent as he sits up and cuts out a square of Dad's cake. It's a sloppy piece on a paper plate, topped off with the one remaining Twinkie. "Here," he says. "Something sweet to soften the blow. I wanted to save him a slice."

A smile actually breaks out on my face. I smear the tears away and look at the buttercream offering and it gives me more strength than I've felt in months. "Thanks, Lucas."

He flashes his signature smirk, and for the very first time, I don't completely hate it. "What are friends for?"

The trees part as I clear the Morguewood—branches snap, brambles clear from underfoot. The forest is exceedingly gentle with me, softening all its wild edges, transforming into a clear picture of Elwood's heart. It is no longer dense and dark and dangerous but a flower-dotted playground teeming with life.

Summer has bloomed from the ice; spun-cotton-candy-pink petals, sweet pea and butterfly weed, and all the other workings of the sun beating hard against the soil. The silence breaks into an orchestra of crickets and summer cicadas. Butterflies stroll lazy paths through flowerbeds.

I pluck a few stray flowers as I walk the route to Elwood's tree. It towers heaven-bound, the tips twisting toward the clouds. It used to be menacing, but in the sun, it's different.

The forest is alive with noise around me. Birds sing to themselves, calling out across the dense woods; chipmunks scuttle through high branches.

"Elwood?" I clear my throat and speak louder, shouting through the treetops. "I have cake."

"I've been waiting for you," a familiar voice replies behind me. I jolt, twisting around. Elwood walks into the clearing. This version of him has antlers scraping the heavens, his eyes wide and pupils less like unearthed gems. Ivy swarms his body like flesh. He approaches me slowly, and I steel myself as to not jump or flinch at his appearance. It's taken time to get used to. I thought he'd grown into himself before, but I was wrong. This is who he is, truly, on the inside. His wings are a brilliant summer shade.

With each step, he transforms, becoming more and more like the boy I knew. The ivy washes away. Skin clings to bone. His eyes become a magnificent woodland green. He's as close to human as he can be. He looks at me and I see the whole forest.

I don't care what he is—I run to him, burying myself in his arms and accidentally smashing the cake in the process. "You dork," I breathe, digging my nails into his back before realizing what I've done. "Oh God, I'm sorry, I ruined your cake."

He swipes a streak of frosting off his cheek. "Buttercream?"

"Dad's recipe."

"Compliments to the chef."

It's so unbelievably *normal* that I have to laugh. All this time I was nervous, and here we are talking about something as insignificant as frosting.

"Shouldn't you still be at the party?" he asks, a tiny smile spreading across his face. He looks more like a boy who dropped off a bouquet to his prom date than a forest spirit. I can't tell whether it's goofy or endearing.

The happiness drains from my face. Guilt takes its place. "I left early. I wanted to talk to you, actually."

He clutches my hand, and his touch is so very warm. Human. The ground smooths under his feet, a winding path emerging before us. We take it, arriving at an empty clearing.

The air grows warmer with each step forward, so warm that I unzip my spring coat and tuck it under my arm. We sprawl out in the grass, eyes tipped to the dusty-peach sky. The sun dies on the horizon, bleeding out the very last of its color.

I should tell him my plans, but I hold on to the words a beat longer. Instead I ask: "What is it like in this new form?"

"I can't describe it," he tells me, turning over on his side, extending his hand out to play with a strand of my hair. "It all makes sense. I never felt complete before. If you asked me who I was back then, I couldn't tell you. But now . . ." His smile returns, broader than before. "Now I know. I am the forest. Every tree, every blade of grass. All of this is me and it always has been. I never knew. This is my home. The forest has accepted me because I was the first sacrifice to offer myself willingly."

I lean into the ground, nuzzling against the soft sway of grass beneath me.

When the very last of the light is gone, the fireflies emerge, shooting out in every direction like bursting fireworks. They're beautiful, made even more beautiful lit against the darkness. They dance above us, not a single one of them straying outside the invisible enclosure. The place where winter ends and spring begins.

I want to return his smile, but a bitter question still gnaws inside of me. "Can you leave these woods if you ever wanted to?"

That wipes the smile clean off his face. He opens his mouth, but then swallows back his words. "It's complicated, Wil." I make a face and he tries again. "I no longer have a human vessel, for starters, and—"

"You're trapped here, then?"

He shakes his head. "It isn't like that. Like I said, I can't quite explain it. I don't want to leave. This is my home. It's more than my home."

We both settle into silence. He looks at me—really looks. Realization flashes in his eyes. "You want to leave. Is that what you were scared to tell me?"

"Yes." Before all this, I would have shouted it from the rooftops. No hesitation. Always looking to the stars in my room and dreaming of the day when I'd find out what lies beyond this town. Now just admitting the truth feels brutal. My stomach turns from guilt. "There's so much of the world I haven't seen. I always told my mother that I'd . . ."

His thumb traces soothing circles against my cheek. "Do it, Wil. See the world."

I shake my head—he might think his feelings are complicated, but so are mine. "I can't take off. The business . . . you . . ."

"Your dad is stronger than you know." His smile is genuine. "As for me, I can wait forever for you to come home."

"You mean it?" I don't realize I'm crying until he brushes away a tear.

"I mean it," he echoes. "See the world, and then, when you come back, tell me all the stories. Tell me about every wonder of the world." His laughter is warm, and it rolls over me like a summer breeze. He flashes me a wink. "And if you've got souvenirs, that's better yet."

That drags a laugh out of me. "What would you do with knick-knacks? Fridge magnets and snow globes and T-shirts?"

Elwood shrugs. "I'll have a whole garden of souvenirs. It will be beautiful."

I can't fight the giddy rush in my chest. I twitch my fingers on the grass, inching them forward to interlock with his. "I love you."

"Let me hear it again." He smells like the woods. Pine needles and mulch and rain-slicked tree trunks. A spiced, earthy scent that's only found in colognes. I accused him of drenching himself in the scent before class, but now I've got to wonder whether I was wrong. Perhaps the smell of it runs through his veins. That's why his eyes are so green—a whole forest is sprouting in his irises.

"Don't press your luck." But even I am not immune to his puppy-dog face. "I love you. There. Happy?"

"The happiest," he whispers. "I think our story is only just beginning, Wil."

We watch as the stars come out.

ACKNOWLEDGMENTS

Getting to write an acknowledgment section is *surreal*. I feel like I've been called on stage to give a speech, and here I am fumbling with my note cards. There are so many people to thank that I hardly know where to begin.

Firstly, I'd love to thank the Pitch Wars program and my two amazingly talented mentors, Allison Saft and Ava Reid (please check out their books if you haven't already), for seeing potential in this weird little story and helping me transform it. Without them, I don't think this story would be here today. I love you both!

To my rockstar agent, Claire Friedman—you are *incredible*, and you've helped make my biggest dream come true. Thank you to Maggie Rosenthal, the magical editor who saw something special in *Together We Rot* and bonded with me over bug facts. And to the rest of the Viking team who spent so much time and care editing my story! I owe you all so much. Marinda Valenti, Abigail Powers, and Nicole Wayland.

Thank you to my husband, Derek, who dealt with me lurching out of bed each morning at four a.m. to write and prattling incessantly about my bug book. I love you. Same to my mom and stepdad, my grandparents and great-grandparents, and my little sister, Celeste. My family's been cheering me on since I was typing up stories as a child. You fostered my love of writing early on.

Thank you to my alpha readers: Kalla Harris and Phoebe Rowen. You've read every single draft of this story (and seen every version of Elwood) and are always there to keep me grounded through it all. I appreciate you more than I can say. You guys mean the world to me.

Thank you to Rachel Moore and Maria Pawlak! We all swapped stories in 2019, and it's been so wonderful to watch you grow since then. Without the two of you, my story wouldn't be where it is today, and neither would our writing group! I am endlessly proud of you two, and I can't wait to see what the future holds. Love you!

Thank you to all of my Pitch Wars buddies! Juliet Hollihan, Courtney Kae, Olivia Liu, Kyla Zhao, and the rest of PW 2020. You guys are the best.

Thank you to Hex Quills. You're way more than a writing group to me. You're all such close friends, and I'm thankful for all of you, including: Brittany Amalfi, Holly Blanchard, Alex Brown, Shay Chandler, Livy Hart, Helena Hoayun, Kara Kennedy, Shay Knell, Kat Korpi, Samantha LaVallie, Wajudah Maheeb, Marina Massino, Alex Meese, Darcy Pope, Mackenzie Reed, Lindsey Skipworth, Morgan Spraker, and Abby Welch.

To all my writing friends on Team Claire (special shout-out to Courtney, who let me scream before the Call). To Jennifer Elrod (who has let me scream more times than I can count). To Codie Crowley for hyping me up!

Big thank-you to my best friend, Cassie Bridenhagen, for being there for me since high school.

And lastly, I want to thank you, the reader, for picking up this strange little book and seeing it through to the very end. This story is yours now. 🦋